Sweet Poison

Georgia Carre

Some Books Ltd

For Sandra Hayes,
You wanted a Mafia book, so... here you go!

Author's Note

As you already probably know the town of Bison Ridge doesn't exist, but I am now certain, it should!

Prologue
Cole

"Shall we practice one more time, honey?"

My daughter chewed her bottom lip and nodded solemnly. "Okay."

"What is your name?"

She folded her little arms in front of her. "Anya Swift."

"Good. And your father's name?"

"Cole. Cole Swift."

"Very good," I encouraged, with a smile. "And if anybody asks you where you come from?"

"Manhattan," she said clearly.

"Did you live in a big house with a housekeeper and maids or a small apartment?"

"A small apartment."

"What floor was the apartment?"

She looked upwards. "Mmm... Fifth floor."

"Have you ever had a chauffeur?" I threw at her suddenly.

"Nope."

"What about a gardener or a nanny?"

She shook her head decisively. "Never."

"Excellent. Why have you and your father moved to Bison Ridge?"

"Because he wanted me to attend the brilliant Shadow Wolf Academy."

I grinned at the creative addition of brilliant in her answer. "Well done. Where did you go to school in Manhattan?"

"The Avenue Sc-," she began to say.

But I shook my head slightly, and she immediately covered her mouth with both hands and said, "Oops. Sorry, Daddy."

"It's okay," I reassured gently. "You have enough time to get this right. Try again."

"I was home-schooled."

I nodded. "That's better. What does your father do for a living?"

"He's an accountant. He files other people's taxes for them."

I nodded approvingly. "Next question, where is your mother?"

Her expression remained unchanged, but her voice felt robotic. "My mother abandoned my father and me."

"And if anybody asks for more information about her, what will you say?"

"It's hard for me to talk about my mom. Can we talk about something else, please."

I touched her little nose with my finger. "Good answer. What about your grandparents? Where are they?"

She looked sideways at me. "They live in Miami?"

"Exactly. But don't look as if you're unsure. Try again.

Say it naturally. You don't want to make anyone suspicious, do you?"

She shook her head vigorously. "No."

"Where do your grandparents live?" I repeated.

"They live in Miami."

"That's much better." I was smiling at her, but inside I was dying. A part of me was floating above us and watching what I was doing in disbelief. I was purposely and deliberately ruining my own daughter, teaching her to lie with a straight face... but there was no other choice. It was this and survival or death.

I couldn't look her in the eye another second longer. I glanced at my watch. "I think that's enough for tonight. Looks like it's your bedtime anyway."

"Will Mommy ever come back to see us?"

My heart broke for her. "I don't know, honey. She's busy with her new life. Maybe one day, when you're older you can go visit her, huh?"

"Daddy?"

"Yeah."

She looked down at a blue button on her dress. "I know Mommy is busy with her new life and she doesn't have time for us anymore, but will you check up on her sometimes and make sure she's alright."

At that moment I felt so angry with Arianna. How easily she had abandoned her own daughter. I nodded. "I will. Now, bed."

"Daddy?"

"Yeah."

She took a deep breath. "When we go to the new place,

to Bison Ridge, to start our new life, you won't leave me like Mommy did, will you?"

Fierce love filled my heart. I looked deeply into her big sad eyes. "Never. I will never ever leave you, Anya. Do you understand me?"

She nodded gravely. "Yes."

I smiled at her. "I'm afraid you're stuck with me for the rest of your life. And when you get married, I'm moving in with you and your husband."

And just like that she switched from being sad and started giggling softly. "Where will you sleep?"

"Under your bed," I said, and grabbing her began to tickle her belly while she wriggled and laughed uncontrollably. I stopped when she began gasping for breath. Gently, I stroked her soft hair. "Bedtime, Princess."

"Um… one last thing, Daddy."

"What?"

"Can I take my butterfly shoes with us? They're my favorite and I don't think I can bear to leave them behind."

"Darling, we can't take anything from this life with us. Nothing that will remind us, or trip us up. Remember we're not supposed to be rich. You never went to an expensive preschool, and never owned any designer gear."

"What about if I scuff them so that no one can see that they're expensive?"

Looking at her hopeful face made me feel incredibly sad for her. It was wrong and it was dangerous to make concessions, but I couldn't say no to her. It was such a tiny thing she was asking.

"All right. You can bring the shoes with you, and you don't have to scuff them. If anybody asks, just tell them they're fakes from Hong Kong, okay? We bought them at a flea market."

"Yay! I'll tell everybody they're fakes from Hong Kong," she repeated, beaming with innocent joy.

"And now, it really is bedtime. Go brush your teeth and get into your PJs and I'll come to read you a story and kiss you goodnight."

"Okay." She scrambled off the sofa and ran towards the stairs. I heard her running on them, her butterfly shoes clacking on the specially imported Italian marble slabs.

I didn't know if she could pull it off. But if she couldn't, I was ready. I was ready for the river of blood that would flow.

Chapter 1

Montana

https://www.youtube.com/watch?v=-KG2O5PSCSs

I'd only come into the office to change into riding boots when the phone rang. Diane was off sick and Dad was in the storeroom stock-taking. I looked at the ringing phone but hesitated. Generally speaking, I was too impatient and blunt to deal with the public, but I could hardly ignore the shrill sound. My dad would probably break a leg trying to get back for it. I picked it up on the third ring.

"Shadow Wolf Academy, can I help you?"

"Gwen Garrison here," a woman announced crisply. "I was going through your prospectus, and I have a few questions. Would you be able to answer them for me?"

"Shoot."

"Right. It says here that children are taught outdoors

regardless of the weather conditions. Does that mean rain as well?"

"Yup. Rain or shine we're out there."

"But Basil gets sick even if a drop of rain falls on his head," she lamented.

Oh God! She named her son Basil. I was glad she couldn't see my expression. "What's the next question?"

I heard the rustling of paper. "It states here on page two that children as young as eight will be allowed to use hammers, nails, Swiss army knives, and saws. Surely that can't be right?"

"Yes, that's right. This is a survivalist school. We teach children life skills and how to effectively fend for themselves. Hammers, nails and knives come in very handy in the wild."

"I see," she muttered, her voice filled with doubt. "But they will be supervised at all times while they're using these dangerous objects though, won't they?"

"No," I denied cheerfully. "They won't. We believe in our methods."

"My goodness," she gasped with shock. "What a cavalier approach, not to mention how terribly unsafe. What if they hurt themselves or the other kids? I don't think I could trust a bunch of armed little brats around my Basil. He's a very sensitive child."

I glanced at my watch. I knew I shouldn't have picked up the phone. Here was the point where I should explain that children who were not terminally bored or taught how to correctly use these utensils hardly ever hurt themselves or other children, but quite frankly, it sounded as if she'd already irreparably ruined Basil, and the poor child would probably remain a traumatized snowflake for the rest of his life.

"Perhaps this is not the school for your son," I suggested.

"Oh! Are you denying my son a place in your school?" she blustered, suddenly furious and indignant.

I sighed. "Look, Ma'am. Call back tomorrow and ask to speak to Diane. I'm sure she'll be able to explain how everything works, and if you're still minded to enroll your son you could go on the waitlist for next year's intake. Right then, bye."

Before she could reply, I quickly cut the connection and took my sorry ass towards the stables where Lola was waiting in all her gleaming white glory. No matter how many times I saw her it struck me anew how beautiful and graceful she was. She tossed her head and her mane danced like a Chinese dragon in the dim light of the stables.

I held out a strawberry on the flat of my palm and she chomped it up voraciously, the edges of her teeth strong and hard against my skin. She could, for sure, be unpredictable and wild, and no one else dared ride her, but she'd been my horse for so long I didn't mind in the slightest. After saddling her, I led her out into the bright sunshine and mounted her.

Turning away from the academy, I rode out of Shadow Wolf Ranch westwards. Once we were in the open fields, I leaned forward and let Lola fly, and fly, she did. It was a wonderful feeling. We travelled for miles, the hot wind rushing into us. Afterwards, I led her into the woods where there was a stream.

While she drank from it, I sat on a sun-warmed rock and watched the evening draw in. I didn't know why, but that day memories of my mother came flooding back. She used to brush my hair every night until it shone, but now she was only a song in my heart. A song of peace, unbridled joy and laughter.

I heard a rustling sound behind me and turned my head.

A sweet little deer had stepped into the clearing. I knew him.

"Hello, Henry," I said softly, as I hunted around in my pockets for a few pieces of dried apple. He came closer and ate them off my hand. His tongue rasped on my skin.

"That's it. No more," I said.

But he carried on begging with his marvelous liquid eyes.

Gently, I scratched the top of his head. "Sorry, but it's really all gone, Henry. Finished. No more."

He must have understood because he reluctantly wandered off. I turned back to look at Lola and suddenly a voice in my head said, 'It's time for a change, Montana.'

I frowned.

Change?

Was change coming?

For some weird reason, it made me think of excitement, accidents... and death. I froze. Whatever it was, I for sure wasn't looking forward to it. My scowl grew deeper. I didn't want change. I liked my life as it was. As a matter of fact, I loved my life and didn't want it to change at all.

Then I laughed aloud at my runaway thoughts. I was just being silly. Change was not coming. Change never happened in this small town. I'd lived here for twenty-four years and nothing exciting had *ever* happened.

Sweet Poison

I got back on Lola and rode to the Watering Hole.

It was Friday night and that was where I met my three best friends for a drink once a week. There was Pearl, who taught money management and history; Natalie, who schooled the kids in science and geography; and Kelly, who gave them biology lessons.

Chapter 2
Montana

"Ugh," Natalie groaned, flicking her flaming red hair back over her shoulder. "I wish we'd go to another bar. I really don't like this place."

"Why?" Pearl asked.

"It's obnoxiously loud, and it smells like feet and sweat."

"It's a majority male bar. Of course, it smells like sweat and feet." Kelly laughed, already a bit giddy and excited.

"Maybe we should go to the Lake club next time? It's quite sophisticated," Pearl suggested.

"No, no. Absolutely not. I'm avoiding Jack," Natalie said fiercely. "He's working in the kitchen tonight."

"Why are you avoiding him?" I asked.

But before Natalie could answer there was a sudden roar.

"Just our luck." Pearl groaned. "There's a game on."

"Better chances to meet more men," Kelly answered gleefully as she led the way towards a corner booth. She threw her purse on one of the seats, pushed her tiny miniskirt down her hips and smiled at the rest of us.

"What do you guys want to drink? I'll get it because I have my eye on the bartender."

We looked over and indeed found him to be very cute. He reminded me of a younger version of Justin Timberlake, but I was very much not into that.

"I'm having orange vodka," Kelly announced.

"French Martini, please," Natalie said.

Pearl nodded at Natalie. "You have the most excellent taste in cocktails. Same here."

Kelly looked at me. "What about you, Miss Hermit?"

"Get her a Sex On The Beach. That's the only sex she'll be getting."

"Cranberry vodka," I said dryly and pulled out my phone to check if my father had sent a message.

"No!" Pearl snatched the device out of my hands. Before I could even begin to protest, it was already locked away in her purse.

Really?" I complained, but she didn't give a damn.

"Yes, really," she replied authoritatively. "I successfully drag you out once a week and you're not going to cheat on me with your phone."

Kelly sashayed away and we focused our attention on Natalie. "Go on," Pearl said, "tell us why you're avoiding Jack."

"I ... I think he's planning on proposing."

Pearl screamed and almost exploded with excitement. Nothing about marriage thrilled me that much so I couldn't work up the same enthusiasm, but I was quietly happy for her.

"Pearl looks more excited than you," I noted. "It's about time, isn't it?"

"I guess so, but ..." Natalie sucked her breath through her teeth.

"Uh oh, are you having doubts?" Pearl asked, wide-eyed.

"I still love him, of course, but-"

"But what?" Pearl pushed.

"I thought he'd be more by now, you know. We had big dreams, dreams of getting the fuck out of here. He said he was only getting a job at the Lake club to learn from their top-class Chef, but now ... he seems ... so content. Sometimes I think he would be perfectly happy to rot in this small, nothing-to-do town forever, but me, I'm restless and bored. The way I see it, it's only downhill from here. Sedimentary and dull."

Kelly returned, accompanied by Jeff, the bartender of her wet dreams.

"French Martini for Natalie and Pearl," she directed, "and cranberry vodka for Montana."

"Thank you," we all chorused.

Jeff winked and went on his way.

I took a sip of my divinely refreshing drink and looked at Kelly. She was standing by the table without a drink in her hand. "What of you?" I asked.

"Oh, uh, I'll go back. Jeff says I should come back so I can watch him make mine. There's a special technique and a new rum he wants to try. So, a taste test."

"We already know who's going to be having the most fun tonight," Pearl teased.

Kelly stuck her tongue out cheekily before whirling around and returning to the bar. We watched Jeff and Kelly flirt with each other for a few seconds before returning our attention back to Natalie.

"See?" she said. "That's what I mean. That fire is what I want."

"That fire is called new lust. It'll fizzle out in a couple of weeks," Pearl dismissed.

"I'm sorry, but I disagree. That spark is important to me. I believe it's kept alive when couples grow and improve together, not just settling like dirt at the bottom of a well."

I looked at her curiously. "If he does propose, and you say 'I'm not sure, let me think about it,' it'll be curtains on your relationship, won't it?"

"Montana's right. Jack's a proud man," Pearl chimed in. "You have to bring your concerns up now and work on it together, or else it will be too late and you'll have to break up."

Natalie took a long sip of her drink as she processed this. "You're both right. It's partly my fault. I need to talk to him. Tell him I'm not happy with the way things are currently."

"Do it tonight," Pearl urged. "Before you overthink it and chicken out again. Do it while the intensity of this pep talk is still fresh and you're motivated."

"Okay," Natalie promised breathlessly.

"Good. Now that Natalie is settled ..." Pearl turned to me. "What about you, Miss Hermit? When are we going to discuss your problem, which, as I remember, is getting urgent?"

"What urgent problem? I'm fine," I said, confused by the direction the conversation had suddenly taken.

They both gave me a look.

"You're bored," Pearl said decisively. "And you need to have your cherry popped."

"To be clear, I'm not bored, but why not shout the other part louder?" I asked sarcastically. "There might be someone at the other end of the bar who didn't hear you!"

"Honey," Natalie said in a matter-of-fact voice, "the whole town already knows. You do realize that you're the last virgin left in town, don't you?"

I could clearly see now that the alcohol was doing its work on all of them except me.

"For heaven's sake. I'm happy as I am, okay. I'm not interested in men or in being in a relationship at the moment."

"So ... let me see if I understand this correctly," Natalie mocked, "your big plan is to remain a virgin for the rest of your life?"

I fidgeted uncomfortably. "Obviously not. I just haven't found the right man yet."

Natalie snorted. "Fiddlesticks! You've had twenty-four years and you haven't come across one off your own steam. I think you need some help. It's time we ride out to Stormy City and see if we can find a man to unclog your pipes. Someone tall, dark, and fiery."

Hoping to change the subject, I turned to look at Kelly. The scene had changed from the bartender mixing her an experimental cocktail to both of them leaning forward to drink from the same glass while staring deeply into each other's eyes. It was surprising they hadn't fallen over altogether.

"Jesus, those two," Pearl exclaimed.

"That," Natalie said decisively, "is exactly what you need, Montana."

"Eww ... a toy boy?" Pearl made a face.

"No," Natalie said, "a man toy. Older, more rugged. Someone who'll bone our Montana so hard she sees stars and be unable to walk properly for days."

My jaw dropped. "Hello. I'm sitting right here."

"Yes, I see that, but it needs to be said," she said, totally unrepentant.

"Who knew you were sexually deviant beneath all that good girl next door exterior?" I muttered.

"I've always known," Pearl said. "You should have seen the stuff she was reading in high school. Only God knows what she's reading now."

"I'm serious," Natalie insisted. "Is tomorrow a date?"

Pearl nodded. "Yes, it is." She looked at me sternly. "It is, isn't it?"

I didn't want a relationship. I had no interest in marriage. And yet ... suddenly, I was back in the woods. I could feel the rasp of the deer's tongue on the palm of my hand and the voice in my head whispering, 'It's time for a change, Montana.' Maybe, change was not accidents and death, maybe change was just a man's body, strong and sure, moving on top of me.

"Okay!" I agreed and hit my palms on the table causing the empty glasses on the table to clatter.

"Excellent!" Pearl shouted triumphantly.

"You'll have to lose the cowboy hat and dress up, though," Natalie warned. "No flannels or boots. You need to look real fancy. Fancy enough to catch the eye of the best-looking guy in the joint."

I gave it some thought, but I didn't want to be a spoil sport, so I nodded. "Alright, I will, but for the effort I have to put in I better meet someone worthy, or I'm never doing it again."

"You will," Pearl replied confidently. She threw her arm around me. "I guarantee it."

Kelly suddenly plopped down next to us. Her lips were well swollen.

"Wow!" Pearl exclaimed. "Really?"

"Yes really. I'm calling this night a win," Kelly sang blissfully. "Now, do you guys want more drinks?"

"Do you even need us here?" Natalie asked with a laugh.

"Of course," Kelly replied. "At least, until he closes the bar. Come on, you promised we would be staying late for once."

"Don't sulk," Natalie scolded. "We've made new plans. We're going to the trendiest bar in Stormy City tomorrow."

"Oh," Kelly exclaimed, intrigued. "What brought this about?"

"We're going to find a gorgeous hunk to pop Montana's cherry," Pearl said.

I smacked Pearl's arm, and Kelly hooted with uncontrollable laughter.

"Whoa! This I can't miss," she spluttered.

Chapter 3

Montana

https://www.youtube.com/watch?v=ZJL4UGSbeFg

The loud impatient rapping on my door was quite unnecessary because I was ready and waiting to be picked up. I flung open the door expecting to see Pearl but found Kelly standing next to her as well.

"I brought wine," she announced, holding up a bottle.

I cocked my head at her. "I thought we were heading out ..."

"We are, but we're going to need an extra hour fixing you up - ugh. What the hell are you wearing?"

I looked down at my perfectly good outfit, then folded my arms. "I look cute and I dressed up, what's the problem?"

"Wasn't that your prom dress?" Pearl asked unhelpfully.

I glared at her. I was hoping she wouldn't notice, but no such luck. "Couldn't find anything else suitable, and it was too late to buy one," I muttered.

"God!" Kelly exclaimed dramatically. "They warned me it was going to be bad, but I had no idea it would be this dire. Thankfully, I brought reinforcements."

"Reinforcements?" I asked warily.

"Where's your dad?" Pearl asked.

"Gone fishing."

"That's good," Kelly said with a wicked laugh. "He won't approve of what we've got planned." She pulled out a scrap of red fabric from her overnight bag.

I looked at it like the threat it was. It didn't take me long to realize what it was: her very famous, highly provocative dress, the one that Natalie had dubbed 'the sex dress'.

"No, I'm not wearing that," I immediately refused, shaking my head vehemently, but they flat-out ignored me.

"Natalie is waiting for us at the club by 8 pm," Pearl said, pulling out a pair of five-inch high-heel sandals from Kelly's bag of tricks.

I started to back away from them. "No way, I'm definitely not wearing those. The last time I wore high heels was prom night and I almost died."

"Stop being a drama queen. You're not in high school anymore and you *are* wearing these. They suit the outfit perfectly. Now, please take that Bridgerton dress off. It makes you look like a nun's idea of a slut."

"My dress is not that bad," I objected, trying one last time to convince them.

"Actually, it's completely unacceptable," Pearl stated.

"Okay, maybe it's a bit too long, but I didn't want to shave," I began to explain, but the mood in the room soured even more.

Kelly put her hands on her hips. "Now you're going to

have to, aren't you? And just in case, please shave everywhere so you don't give yourself an excuse to say no when you actually run into someone cute."

To be honest I started having second thoughts. Especially, when I thought of squeezing myself into Kelly's giant red condom of a dress. Even worse was the idea of trying to walk in those ridiculously high heels. It seemed like too much trouble for a one-night stand. I'd rather have curled up in my bedroom window seat with a good book and a box of chocolates.

I gave Kelly a disgruntled look and considered putting my foot down, but the earnest plea in Pearl's eyes made me draw in my claws. They were only trying to help. With a long-suffering sigh, I hurried into the bathroom to get ready all over again while both girls merrily sipped on wine.

About fifteen minutes later, fully shaven, glazed like a turkey, and tightly gripped inside Kelly's scrap of red lycra, I stood before them for assessment. To my relief, I passed the vibe check with flying colors.

"Oh Wow!" both girls burst out in unison.

"You look really, really amazing," Pearl gushed.

"Yup, good enough to eat," Kelly agreed.

I was quite salty about the way they had taken over my appearance and still very tempted to kick them out, but when I walked over to the mirror and saw my reflection my eyebrows shot up.

"Exactly," Pearl said. "That's what you've been hiding under those baggy men's shirts and dusty jeans."

I had to admit I looked ... pretty unrecognizable.

"My dad would have a heart attack if he saw me like this," I whispered in an awed voice.

"Don't worry, he won't see you. We'll have you back in your bed before he comes back at sunrise. Now, put on the shoes," Kelly ordered.

I regarded the dangerous things warily, the same way they were staring back at me. I didn't want to argue, but I didn't want to be ungrateful either, so I took a deep breath and succumbed. I was the same size as Pearl. It's one of the things we'd decided as kids was the sign we were supposed to be best friends forever.

I slipped the weapons on, and they fit well enough until I stood up and tried to walk. It was hell. I tottered unsteadily around the room, almost breaking my neck twice while both my supposed friends laughed until their sides hurt.

It was all incredibly amusing until Natalie's call came asking us if we were ready. It lit a fire under Kelly's backside. She jumped up.

"Okay, hair."

I looked at her with dismay. "No! I like it like this."

"Absolutely not, you're not leaving it in a ponytail. That's just lazy, Montana."

"It's neat and out of the way," I argued, knowing I was going to lose this round too.

"We didn't come all the way here to go for 'neat and out of the way'. We want 'striking' and 'in the way'. We're letting it all down in sumptuous, glorious curls."

I groaned. "Curls? No time for that, surely." But she was already pushing me back into the room and sitting me in front of my vanity.

"Curls will take me five minutes. Pearl, get on with her

makeup. Load on the mascara and give the girl smoky eyes ... and deep red lips."

"Got it," Pearl said, and ignoring all further protests, she got to work.

Ten minutes later, which I should say, was a remarkable speed, I looked like a completely different person. They seemed to have done so little and so quickly, but I looked so different.

"You're freaking gorgeous!" Kelly said, looking quite surprised.

I stared at myself speechlessly. When they noticed my dazed expression, both girls burst out laughing. "Now do you see what we mean about you making the best of yourself?" Kelly asked.

I was too dazed to reply so I nodded.

"Okay, now for the final touch," Pearl said and hurried out to the living room. She returned a minute later and thrust a purse so small it was practically useless into my hands.

"Stand," Kelly commanded.

I obeyed. Then I was hurried out of the door, thrown into Kelly's car and off we went.

I opened the purse to put my phone into it and a whole bunch of condoms fell out.

"Holy Mother of God!" I screeched.

"She found the condoms," Pearl guessed, peering at me through the rearview mirror.

"What am I supposed to do with all these?"

Kelly burst out laughing. "Hey, that's just about enough for one good night of fucking."

"I'm keeping two and throwing the rest out," I mumbled.

"Why, are you planning to let him go in raw?"

I cringed. "Oh God! Please stop."

Kelly hooted with laughter. "Stop being such a goody two shoes."

I looked out the window. "I urgently need a change of friends."

Natalie was out on the front drive of her family's farm. She was smoking and pacing nervously. She threw the butt away and hurried over.

"Finally! Where have you all been?" she demanded impatiently.

"What's wrong?" Pearl asked.

"I'm gonna break his heart," she said, slamming the door shut.

I was confused. "Break his heart? I thought you were going to talk to him."

"I did talk to him. Yesterday. And he fucking pissed me off telling me we're perfect the way we are now. Honestly, I'm better off getting out now rather than years later when he gets bored with the relationship, and because he has no self-discipline whatsoever, he'll go out and cheat on me and expect me to forgive him. Absolutely fucking not!"

Stunned and speechless we stared at her while she ranted.

Suddenly she smiled, a crazy smile, into the stunned silence in the car. "That's it. Enough about me. Let's go have fun. We need to find a splendid hunk for Montana to fornicate with and a big bowl of tomato soup for me. I'm famished."

I blinked. "Oh boy. Tonight was definitely going to be something to remember."

Chapter 4
Cole

https://www.youtube.com/watch?v=vdj6lG1aAh4

-gunslinging outlaws-

"Great! Just fucking great," I muttered, ending my call with AAA.

I kicked the tire of the rented car that had suddenly and inexplicably died on me. So, I was stuck in the middle of nowhere and, since it was Saturday night, it would be hours before I could expect any roadside assistance.

There was no way I was standing by the side of the road waiting for them. I was not all that far away from Stormy City so my best bet would be to walk into town and either find some accommodation for the night, or even better find a cab that would get me back to New York.

But first, I called Mrs. Frost and explained my situation

to her and asked her if she would be able to keep Bianca for the whole night.

"It would be a pleasure," she said.

"Thanks. I really appreciate it. May I speak to my daughter?"

"Of course. She is right here."

"Hiya, Daddy."

"Hey, honey."

"Mrs. Frost had you on speaker. You've got car troubles, huh?"

I smiled. Sometimes my daughter was so adult and mature I felt a pang of nostalgia for the little girl who used to walk around chewing at her pink blanket. "Yes, I'm afraid so. I'll pick you up in the morning, okay?"

"Okay. I'll be here waiting for you."

"That's my girl."

"Daddy?" she whispered.

"Yeah."

"Can I come with you next time? I like Mrs. Frost and everything, but I really want to go with you."

"Yes, you can come with me next time because... guess what? Until now our house looked like a building site, but it's now almost ready for us to move into."

"Really?"

"Hmmm."

"Daddy?"

"Yeah?"

"I know we're meant to be poor in our new life, but will I still have my own room?"

I frowned. "We're not meant to be poor, honey. We'll

just be middle-class, like all your other friends, so of course, you'll have your own room."

"Can I choose the color?"

I smiled. "Sure, you can decorate it in any way you like. Maybe we can get someone to paint the same Snow White and the Seven Dwarfs painting that you have on your bedroom wall now."

"Oh goodie, yes."

"Right, you be a good girl now and I'll see you tomorrow."

"I will. I love you, Daddy."

"Love you too."

"Nite, nite, Daddy."

"Nite, nite, sweet pea."

I blew her a kiss, ended the call, and put my phone away, just as an approaching car slowed down. Maybe I could hitch a lift. There were three women in it. A redhead wound down the passenger window, hung her head out, and laughingly shouted, "Hey, Sexy! Sorry we're not allowed to stop for strangers, but the town's only a mile away. We'll be waiting for you at the Dead Or Alive Saloon."

She was young and full of life, and it felt like another lifetime since I'd indulged in such clean, easy fun. Obviously, I had no intention of going to meet her, but I found myself smiling back at her. Then as the car slowly moved on my eyes alighted on the face in the back of the car.

Our gazes collided.

And I froze with shock.

The girl with the tumbling corkscrew gold curls was not smiling. She was staring at me with wide eyes. Then her lips parted with surprise and I saw her suck in a breath. It was barely seconds before the car passed on by, but I felt as if I'd been sucker punched. That girl had sucked the air from my lungs. Fucking hell!

Stunned, I watched the car pick up speed and disappear down the road.

What the fuck just happened?

My mind was blank.

Then, as if guided by pure animal instinct, I began to walk towards the town. I wasn't looking for a way to get back to New York, I was looking for a bar called Dead Or Alive.

Chapter 5
Montana

https://www.youtube.com/watch?v=yyV_eb3p3Zw

-for a few dollars more-

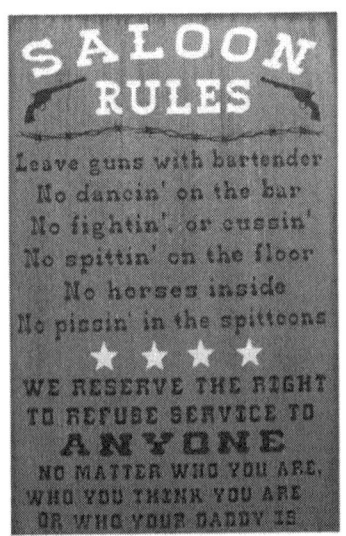

. . .

"Holy cow!" Kelly whispered, her mouth hanging open with amazement.

"What is it?" Pearl asked.

"Oh my God, Oh my God. I can't believe it."

"Can't believe what?" Natalie asked impatiently.

"Don't everybody turn around at the same time to look, but you'll never guess who just swaggered in looking all hunky and sexy," Kelly squealed excitedly.

"I'll look first," Natalie said and casually turned her head. When she turned back, she was grinning from ear to ear.

"It's the guy with the broken-down car from earlier," she announced, looking directly at me. "We've found your man for tonight, Montana."

"Hang on a minute," Kelly protested immediately. "He's only here because I invited him. He came for me."

"If Montana switches off the light there'll be no difference between you and her," Natalie answered tartly.

"Hello! I'm sitting right here," I reminded but no one took any notice of me.

Kelly looked sulkily at Natalie. "He wouldn't be here if not for me."

"Come on, Kelly. Let Montana have him. You know you can have any guy you want," Pearl persuaded in her gentle way.

"But I've never had anyone as special as him. I mean, look at him. He's one in a billion."

"It won't matter in the morning, will it?" Natalie asked. "He'll just be another guy you slept with, but you'll feel bad because you cheated Montana out of an experience she will cherish for the rest of her life."

Kelly sighed, then looked at me mournfully. "All right. You can have him."

"Actually, you can keep him. I don't want him. Especially, not if it's you he wants," I said.

Kelly brightened. "Really?"

I shrugged and grinned at her. "Yeah, go for it."

"No," Natalie argued. "This night is supposed to be for you. We went to all this trouble because we wanted this night to be special for you."

I looked at Natalie. "Thanks, Natalie. I know you mean well, but honestly, I don't want to sleep with anyone who's not totally into me too. No matter how gorgeous he is. Look, the night is young. I'm sure I'll find someone else equally hunky if not better." I knew that was a lie. Kelly was not lying when she said he was one in a billion.

"Are you sure?" Kelly asked, her eyes shining with hope and excitement.

"Totally," I confirmed, but the word stuck in my throat like a hard rock.

"Guys, he's walking towards our table," Pearl hissed suddenly.

Kelly tossed her head, and her red hair bounced like fire on her shoulders, but really there was no time to do anything. Suddenly, he was standing next to our table. My eyes travelled slowly up from his black jeans to his leather belt up to his denim shirt, along the strong brown column of his throat, up to his hard jaw, sensuous lips, narrow nostrils and up towards his eyes. Oh God! Those eyes! They were amazing and they were looking directly at me. I was so shocked I couldn't speak. I couldn't do anything except stare back at him.

"Ladies, can I get you a drink?" he asked, never taking his gaze off me.

"I'll have a glass of white wine," Kelly breathed sexily.

"Same for me," Pearl said.

"A bowl of tomato soup for me."

It was my turn to talk, but I was dumbstruck by the intensity of his stare. I'd never been in such a bewildering situation before. This man made my skin tingle. I could feel hot color rushing into my face.

"Montana will have a Dirty Martini," Natalie said into the awkward moment.

"I'll get a waiter to bring your order over," he said and began to turn away.

"Why don't you join us?" Kelly invited.

"Thanks, but I'll be at the bar if you need me," he replied, making eye contact with me again.

"My God! That guy is a sex god," Pearl breathed, her voice, low and awed.

Kelly moved, but Natalie caught her wrist. "Where do you think you're going, young lady?"

"Just to the bar."

"No, you're not. That man is not interested in you, Kelly. He barely glanced at you. He wants Montana."

Kelly frowned.

"What do you say, Pearl? Am I right?" Natalie asked.

"Sorry, Kelly, but Natalie is right," Pearl agreed softly. "He had eyes only for Montana."

"Eyes for Montana," Natalie scoffed. "He was eating her alive."

Kelly leaned back in defeat. "Fine. Montana can have him."

Natalie turned to me. "Time for you to go to the Ladies, Missy. Make sure you stop by the bar on your merry way."

"No, I can't just go and throw myself at him," I protested, but my heart was racing with excitement.

"No need to do any such thing. Just casually say hello and thank him for buying us drinks, and if he starts a conversation, stay and talk to him for a bit. We'll be right here until the bar closes, and because I was so sure you'd get lucky, I've booked a room for us upstairs. We'll wait there for you until you're ready to leave."

"You never said you booked a room," I said surprised.

Natalie smiled smugly. "I'm not known as a meticulous planner for nothing."

"I can't believe you ordered a tomato soup," Pearl said.

"Why wouldn't I? They do a good tomato soup here and I always drink copious amounts of it when I'm raging inside. It calms me down. But enough chit-chat about me. Get going, Montana, before he gets the impression you're not interested."

She shuffled out of the banquet booth and looked at me expectantly.

I hesitated. "Won't I be so obvious?"

"Yes, but he made himself obvious when he marched up here and stripped you naked with his eyes."

"He didn't do that."

"Yes, he did," Pearl said. "And anyway, isn't that what we came here for?"

"Exactly. Off you go," Natalie urged. "We live in a tiny

backwater town so it's not every day that a guy like that comes into our reach so grab him with both hands."

I glanced at Kelly and Pearl. Kelly looked openly envious and Pearl gazed back encouragingly. "Go on, Montana," she mouthed.

I took a deep breath and scooted out of the seat.

"Give him a smile," Kelly said suddenly.

I looked at her and she smiled at me wryly. "Not the hyena one, the sexy one where you lift only one side of your mouth."

"Thanks for the tip, Kelly," I said softly. I knew it had taken a lot for her to say that. It was clear she wanted the man for herself.

"Now go. Go get him, girl," Natalie whispered, giving my ass a stinging smack.

I squared my shoulders and turned away from the safe and the familiar.

Chapter 6
Montana

https://www.youtube.com/watch?v=enuOArEfqGo

-the good the bad and the ugly-

I t was clearly a grave mistake to allow Pearl and Kelly to talk me into wearing these shoes. It felt like I was walking on stilts, and I was sure I looked clumsy and graceless. As if navigating through an obstacle course, I cautiously wove my way around busy waitresses and groups of customers towards the bar where I could see him standing with his back to me.

As if he had felt my gaze, he abruptly turned and our eyes met.

And Holy Freaking Cow! The force coming from the inscrutable jaw, hard muscles, and the sheer animal magnetism was shocking. The universe fell away, the bar became like a blurred impressionist painting. The noise, the hustle and bustle around me became oddly muted as if I was underwater. The air itself became as thick as syrup. Time slowed down.

In this strange world there was only him and me ... and the feral urge to mate with him. This kind of pure lust had never shown itself before, but now it was undeniable. Full of fierce hunger, it uncoiled inside my body. God, I wanted him. How I wanted him.

In those hushed seconds, I couldn't move.

I didn't dare move.

Paralyzed, I just stared at him in amazement. The virility of the man was impossible to describe. It seemed as if sparks of electricity were jumping out of him, flying through the air and landing on my body. The sparks ran through my veins making my heart race, my skin bristle, and my stomach feel as if it had been invaded by a swarm of madly fluttering butterflies.

I felt alive in a way I'd never experienced before. Gosh, I'd never even dreamed I could feel this way by just looking at a man. I'd lived my whole life as innocent as a lark, and my self-imposed celibacy was no hardship at all as I had no interest in the boys around me, or exploring the pleasures of the flesh. Even watching porn just bored me.

Until now ...

Now my whole being throbbed for him.

As if he knew I was unable to move, he started walking towards me. His walk was unhurried but purposeful. Like a lion walking towards its stunned prey. As he got closer, I saw that he was even more wildly handsome than I'd originally thought.

His eyes were especially mesmerizing.

Translucent gray and so intensely beautiful you

couldn't look away. In general, I preferred the look of clean-shaven men, but his five o'clock stubble was masculine, rugged, and so, so sexy, I had absolutely no problems with it. What would the rough skin feel like between my thighs? The thought was involuntary and so uncharacteristic for me, that I felt my knees wobble. Then my ankle turned, and to my dismay, I started to go down.

Pure horror flashed through me. Oh, God no! I was going to end up on my butt and disgrace myself in front of this god-like man.

But lightning quick, his hand shot out and captured my elbow in an iron grip.

I leaned into the solid support. "Thanks," I whispered.

"My pleasure," he drawled. His voice was rich and warm, his accent was polished, the way newscasters on TV were.

"These are not my shoes," I babbled. "I can't do high heels. I must look a total fool."

"Not in that dress you don't," he murmured, his luminous eyes looking right into my very soul.

"The dress is not mine either," I prattled unnecessarily. My mouth had become a runaway train I had no control over. More pointless explanations tumbled out. "Borrowed for the night from my friend, Kelly."

His eyes widened with surprise, but of course, I couldn't stop myself from adding to my humiliation by exclaiming, "Wow! I thought only cats and archangels have eyes like yours."

He looked genuinely curious. "Do you generally blurt out everything that comes into your head?"

"Kinda," I confessed ruefully.

He grinned, a wolfish grin. "In that case, you and I are going to get along just fine."

His presence bathed me in a glow of desire. I could feel the heat from his hand warm the skin on my elbow. That simple touch was a delicious pleasure. When he released me, I missed the sensation and hungered for more.

"You're not from around here, are you?" I asked softly.

"Was it the rented car that gave it away?"

"That and the fact that everything about you screams city slicker."

He looked amused. "Ouch."

"It wasn't meant to be an insult. We're all wholesome simple people living off the land here. You're deeply mysterious and sophisticated."

He raised one eyebrow. "Simple and wholesome? You're wearing a dress that would drive a man to the brink of insanity and shoes that a lap dancer would consider risqué."

I decided to be blunt as I'd already made up my mind. Either he was the one I was hooking up with tonight or I was going home early.

"I *am* simple and wholesome," I insisted, "but I came out tonight with the intention of finding a no-strings-attached, one-night-only fling with a complete stranger. What I'm trying to say is I'm not looking for anything serious. Not tonight, anyway."

For a few moments, he stared at me, a strange expression on his face. Then he smiled, a gorgeous smile, "And have you found your ... fling for the night?"

I nodded slowly. "I'm looking at him." My voice was hoarse with a strange anticipation.

His eyes never left mine. "If nothing else you are direct."

"Do you have a hotel room?" I asked boldly.

His pupils grew so large his irises looked like silver rings. "Yeah, I've got a room booked upstairs."

I gazed into his amazing eyes and couldn't help but feel curious about who he was. But that was a dangerous thought. "Good."

A thought occurred to me. This was all too good to be true. I come out dressed like a bimbo and find the most beautiful man on earth who already has a room booked upstairs. Life was great, but not that great, surely.

"You're not married, are you?" I asked, my gaze sliding down to his ring finger.

"I'm separated."

I felt my heart sink a little. If I was on a separation with someone because we were still working something out I'd hate it if some woman thought my man was fair game and slept with him. "Separated as in-"

"Separated as in never ever getting back together again." His voice was dry and decisive.

The relief I felt was enormous. Like a bright sunshine, it filled my entire being and made me smile with happiness. "What's your name?"

"Cole."

The hesitation before he answered was almost imperceptible, but I saw it.

"There you go. That's what I mean by mysterious," I pounced. "You almost didn't even want to give out your name."

He laughed and it truly had to be the most mesmerizing

sound I'd ever heard. Deep, quiet, and as rich as one of Mrs. Dearborn's famous fruitcakes. I loved it. It showed his gorgeous teeth and lit up his face.

"It was the one-night-only thing that threw me," he mocked. "Some one-night-only encounters are conducted without names and I wasn't sure if this was to be one of them."

I stared at him. "I suppose you'd know all about them."

He shrugged. "Sure, I've had a few. Is this your first?"

I crossed my fingers and, tossing the curls that Kelly had skillfully put into my hair, proceeded to lie with a straight face. "Of course not. I've had loads and loads of experience at this kind of thing."

Chapter 7
Cole

I stared hypnotized into those beautiful eyes and didn't quite know what to make of her. One thing was for sure, she was lying through her teeth. *Loads and loads*! Hell, I wouldn't be surprised if this was her first one-night stand.

To be honest, I'd never expected to come to a town in the middle of nowhere and find a raving beauty offering me a one-night stand. Everything about her awakened a primal instinct in me to take and possess, a reflex I'd long ago set aside to provide and care for my daughter; but without even trying she made it all come roaring back. The iron restraint I had was gone.

I was like a fucking caveman.

I wanted to throw her over my shoulder and carry her off to my bed.

My cock throbbed with need as my eyes roved the firm, full breasts that were nearly popping out of her dress. I let my eyes travel to her flat stomach, her flaring hips, and down those long, long silky legs before I came back to her plump lips. I had all kinds of things planned for that sexy mouth. My gaze moved up to her eyes. They looked like circles of wet moss strewn with flecks of pure gold underneath transparent epoxy.

My situation was complicated, dangerous even, but she was only offering one night. What's the harm in that? Surely, I could allow myself to bite into this sweet fruit for just one night. It wouldn't be selfish or careless to indulge in just one bite.

Just this once. I would lose myself in her sweetness.

Tomorrow I would go back to reality where my only focus would be protecting my daughter. For once, since the day I knew I would soon be a father, I would take the night off. My child was safe with Mrs. Frost.

Montana was an unexpected gift from Fate. And I wasn't about to say no. It was yes, yes, yes. A thousand times over.

I smiled at her. "I think your drink has gone directly to your table. Can I get you another?"

She nodded. "Okay."

I took her hand, and to my surprise, the skin on her palm was not soft, but raised and rough with calluses. I couldn't help but stroke the warm coarse skin. She was an enigma. This was the hand of a woman who worked hard at honest labor. I think I liked her even more at that moment.

I turned around and she let me lead her to the bar.

The bartender came over to me.

"A Dirty Martini and a Whiskey Sour, please," I ordered.

Chapter 8
Montana

Even though the bar was air-conditioned, I felt flushed and overheated. Probably because I was more than slightly embarrassed by my callused hands. The skin on his palm was smooth and his nails were clean and nicely manicured.

I turned to face the bar, towards the vast assortment of bottles that lined the old-fashioned wooden shelves. The muted LED lights shone on them casting the rows of alcohol in a warm, luxurious glow. It was sort of soothing to stare at them.

In actuality, I was very nervous, but I tried to convince myself that I was being silly. Women did this sort of thing all the time, and it wasn't as if I didn't know how everything worked. Obviously, I did. I just hadn't actually done it before. At the end of the day, I couldn't carry on being a virgin all my life. Having my cherry popped was long overdue.

And I was ready to get it done and over with.

Pearl and Kelly had taken extra time with me to make

sure I looked great, and Natalie had even gone so far as to book a room for them to hang around in, so I wasn't about to turn into a little coward and let them down.

My only real worry should be tripping and falling while wearing Pearl's ridiculously high heels, but I told myself that if I was really careful and took it slow, I should be able to manage myself long enough to make my way up to his room. Once there I could instantly kick them off.

No matter what, I was determined that tonight, I wasn't going to be Montana, the little tomboy who turned her back on boys. Tonight, I was going to be Montana, a woman who went out and took what she wanted. Cole's attention, whether real or imagined, made me feel like I could do just that.

I felt his hand touch mine. There wasn't anything overtly sexual about the action, but a frisson of longing and awareness ran up my spine. Taking a deep breath, I curved a smile on my face and turned towards him.

He stared at me and I stared right back.

In the background, the bartender prepared our drinks, and people laughed and went about their ordinary business. To the casual onlooker, I was just another person standing at the bar waiting for my drink, but inside me, an absolute explosion of foreign sensations was taking place. I didn't know what to do or say, what to think even.

But he seemed calm and in no hurry to break the erotic silence.

Eventually, the drinks were delivered, and I raised the glass and drained it. The alcohol ran like a fiery spirit down my throat and into my belly.

"Want another?" he asked.

I shook my head. "I have to go to church early tomorrow."

He watched me with intense curiosity. "You believe in God?"

"Don't you?"

"No."

Wow! It was my turn to stare at him curiously. I'd never met anyone who was not God-fearing. "Why not?"

A strange look crossed his face, and his voice was bitter. "If God existed this world wouldn't be the hell it is."

The hurt in his voice pierced my heart. I reached out and touched the warm skin of his hand.

"Look again, Cole. It's a beautiful world. So very beautiful I say a prayer of gratitude every time I wake up because every day that I open my eyes is a precious gift."

He looked at me almost with disbelief. "You're serious. You actually believe this world is an earthly paradise."

"Yes," I said simply.

His eyelashes swept down, hiding his expression. "And you've never known suffering?"

I thought of the way Mama smiled as she lay dying. I thought of my wet pillow and the terrible, terrible loneliness and sadness I felt. I thought of my dad howling like a wounded animal into the night.

"Yes," I admitted. "I've suffered pain, but the suffering passed, and the world became even more beautiful afterwards."

"I'm not a nice guy, Montana," he warned suddenly. His eyes were cold and his voice steely.

I ran my finger along his skin. My skin looked pale against his deep tan. I tilted my head up and looked into his eyes. In the depths secrets swam. There was also hurt, terrible betrayal, fear, and disappointment. And yet, despite it all, they were the eyes of a man clinging by his fingernails to hope, hope that there was something better out there.

"It's okay. I'm not looking for a nice guy to put a ring on my finger." I smiled softly at him. "Just the one-night stand will do."

He blinked, then his mouth curved downwards as if he was mocking himself. "Of course."

Just then I was startled by a touch on my shoulder. I swung my head around and my gaze met Natalie's slightly amused blue eyes.

"Hey," she said.

"Hey," I croaked.

"Everything alright?" she asked, an eyebrow raised.

"Yeah. Everything's alright."

She glanced at Cole, then smiled at him. "Thanks for the tomato soup. It was delicious."

He nodded. "No worries."

"Do you mind if I borrow Montana for a quick trip to the Ladies?" she asked.

"Nope." His eyes slid to me. "I'll be waiting here."

I stood, and with careful steps followed Natalie. She didn't say a word until we got the Ladies, then she whirled around like a snake, her eyes shining. "Damn, but that man's cuter than a speckled pup. He was staring at you like he couldn't wait another second to climb on top of you. What's he like?"

"He's ... mysterious and ... deep."

She looked surprised. "What do you mean?"

"I'm not sure exactly, but on the outside, I get the

impression of someone powerful and urbane, perhaps even wealthy, but inside he seems sad and broken."

She frowned. "Hey, don't you go getting all soppy on him. You're supposed to have fun. You know? For just once in your life, can you be like Kelly? Let your body be the boss."

"I'm not going all soppy on him at all," I denied. "I understand we're ships passing in the night. You'll be happy to know he's booked a room upstairs."

She nodded approvingly. "Good work!"

"I can't take credit for that. His car broke down, remember?"

She shook her head. "I wasn't born yesterday, Missy. That outlaw booked the room because of you. One of us is going to be sweating like a sinner in Church later tonight and it's not going to be me."

I flushed but tried to play it cool by walking towards the mirrors. Heck, I sure looked excited. My eyes were sparkling and there were twin spots of color on my cheeks.

Natalie followed me and pulled a tube of lip gloss from her purse. I watched her slide it over her lips with practised ease. Then she met my gaze in the mirror.

"Not much talent here so Kelly wants us to bar hop for a bit, but we'll be back in an hour. Whatever you do, don't leave this bar, okay?"

"Okay. Um ... is Kelly okay?"

She grinned. "She's still madder than a wet hen that the man she wanted chose you instead of her, but that's not your fault. Don't give it another thought. She'll get over it, especially if she finds someone she likes in one of the other bars. If we're late and you want to go up to his room, then just text me when you're done and we'll bring the car around to the front. Okay?"

I nodded.

"Right." She dropped her lip gloss into her purse and snapped it shut. "Let's go."

"Don't you need to use the toilet?" I asked.

"Nah. Do you?"

"Nope."

She grinned. "Time to return you to your hunk."

"Natalie?"

"Yeah ..."

"Thank you. I really appreciate what you've done for me."

"No need for thanks, but I do expect details."

I laughed.

We left the Ladies and went back to the bar. As soon as Cole's tall figure came into view, I felt my heart start to beat a little faster.

"Give him one for me," Natalie said with a wink.

I watched her walk away before I began my journey towards Cole.

Chapter 9
Montana

Natalie was right.

My approach was all wrong. This was not supposed to be the beginning of a great romance. All I had was tonight. He was a stranger in town and tomorrow he would be gone from my life forever. There was no need to get to know each other better. The less I knew about him the better.

He should be nothing more than a magnificent body with no last name, history, or personality. Talking to him about God or feeling I was making a connection on a deeper level was just madness.

As I reached him, he turned to look at me. When his gaze unashamedly lingered on my cleavage it made my teeth ache with lust.

"I, uh … we should get going to your room," I said.

He cocked his head in surprise, and to be honest, I couldn't believe such bold, nonchalant words had come out of my mouth either. I could feel hot color rising up my neck and rushing into my face.

He smiled ... slowly, languorously. And the effect was magical, like the doors of a cage opening, or warm sunshine pouring in through the open windows on the first day of spring. It spread into every part of me. At that moment it felt as if all the damage in the world had been healed. Beautiful heat simmered and pooled in the pit of my belly.

'Surely, this is not what one-night stands are about,' a little voice in my head said, but here we were.

I was so mesmerized by him that when he offered his hand to me, I intertwined my fingers intimately with his. So weird, but all I could think about was kissing him. He pulled me towards him until I was flush with his hard body. It was overly sexual to be this way with a man in a bar, but it felt right.

He led me towards the side door that led to the foyer of the hotel.

Soon, we were standing side by side in front of a highly polished wooden staircase. I didn't know what he was thinking, but I was thinking, these freaking slippery steps, these murderous shoes. I'd just decided to take my shoes off and walk up on my bare feet when ...

"Oh," I exclaimed, shocked. He had suddenly swept me off my feet and nestled me inside his strong arms.

"Can't have you breaking your neck," he murmured close to my ear.

"You're not planning to carry me up the stairs, are you?" I protested, still stunned, although my hands were already curled around his neck.

"Got a better idea?"

"I could take my shoes off and walk barefoot up the stairs."

He shook his head. "I don't think so. Your feet might be going in my mouth soon."

I gasped at the idea, but he looked down at me with a teasing smile.

And so it happened that Cole carried me up the stairs. I felt as if I'd been transported to another time; when men were big and strong and women were fragile and had to be protected. I could feel the hardness of his body and my heart raced in my chest. I was Scarlett O'Hara being carried off by Rhett Butler. A little voice warned, '*Gone with the Wind* didn't end well for Scarlett. She didn't get her man'.

He transported me down a corridor and set me down in front of a door marked 23. Turning a clunky metal key in the door, he pushed it open and stood aside.

I took my shoes off and carrying them my hand walked into the room.

It was decorated in the French bordello style; massive King-size bed, dark furniture, and blood-red drapes. My eyes returned to the bed and I was suddenly so hot I felt as if I had a fever. I didn't dare look at him.

I unceremoniously dropped Pearl's poor shoes and tried to think what I should say or do to appear experienced and sophisticated, but my brain had turned to mush, and my mouth started to spit out the most stupid stuff. Even though I knew I was babbling nonsense I couldn't stop myself.

"Did you know the bar downstairs and these rooms are meant to be a recreation of the saloon bars of the Old West? Dancing girls used to bring their customers; gamblers, gunfighters, and pickpockets, up here. A hot bath would cost 50 cents and a cold bath 35 cents. Soap was ten cents and a clean towel was-"

His hand had shot out, grasped my wrist, and yanked me so hard, that my body slammed into his. His mouth swooped down on mine, eating up the nonsense flowing from my mouth. He tasted of whiskey and his lips were warm, soft and sweet. I held his stubble-roughened cheeks between my palms and completely melted.

His arms slid around my waist and tightened as his tongue darted over my lips. I groaned as he explored my mouth. He sucked my bottom lip into his mouth and bit it. I gasped, and suddenly the kiss changed. It was no longer exploring, but taking.

My mouth was crushed possessively.

I was stunned. Letting go of his face, my hands roamed over his powerful shoulders and the steely muscles of his arms, my brain exploding with pleasure and awe.

I'd never been kissed like this.

My breath came out in a hiss, and he thrust his tongue into my mouth. Something inside me snapped, and I lost control. I sucked his tongue mindlessly. This, this was what I'd wanted all along, all night long, from the first moment our gazes touched. He ran his hands over my back, my butt.

I moaned, thrusting my tongue into his mouth. Asking for him to suck it. He didn't disappoint.

The lust was simply incredible. It was a thing that had a mind of its own. It made my head sing and my blood roar in my ears. We were both panting, grunting... desperate. The ache between my thighs had become urgent. I moaned, throwing my head back, ready to lose myself in him, but he stopped suddenly.

My heart clenched. "No. Don't stop," I moaned restlessly.

He separated from me, but he didn't take his hand off my skin, and that made me more aware of him than I could describe. It was as though that smoldering heat and connection between us were searing my skin. It was both wonderful and fearsome at the same time.

"You have done this before, right?" he asked, his forehead creased in a frown.

Chapter 10
Cole

"Um ... Why are you asking that?" she said nervously, almost guiltily, and did that biting down on her lower lip thing that nearly scrambled my brain. I wanted to lean forward and kiss her again, but something was not right. She smelled like heaven, kissed like an angel, and was like a magical erotic being that had been created especially to push all my lust buttons, but her behavior and movements were ones of innocence. Even her eyes were pure and devoid of sexual knowledge.

I could have sworn I was dealing with a virgin.

I stared at her. The floor lamp in the corner was the only light source and it cast a warm intimate glow over the room and her face. "Just curious. Are you going to answer the question?"

"The answer is ... kinda," she whispered.

"You've never had sex before, have you?" I muttered in awe. It was unbelievable that in this day and age, such a beauty would remain untouched for this long.

She shook her head slowly, ruefully. "But I've been

49

horse riding all my life so I don't think I'll bleed and make a mess."

My eyebrows rose with surprise. She was almost too good to be true.

"Is that a deal breaker for you?" she asked uncertainly.

I shook my head. "Nothing about you is a deal breaker, Montana."

Holding her hand, I twirled her so I could view her ass. It looked wonderful in that tight dress. Round and full ... When she was facing me again, I grabbed her by the ass. My fingers sunk wonderfully into the pillowy softness.

"How much time do we have?" I demanded thickly.

"What do you mean?"

"I'm assuming your friends are waiting for you downstairs," I murmured.

She licked her lips. "Don't worry about them. They'll be fine."

A gasp escaped her lips at the force with which I slammed her against my body and ground her against the hardness of my cock. I was harder than I could recall being. There was so much stress, urgency, and nervous energy that I had to get rid of. I wanted to fuck, ram mindlessly into her, and wear us both out, but that was clearly out of the question.

I slid my tongue into her mouth. The kiss was dirty, wet, and lush and all the while I maneuvered her backwards until the backs of her knees hit the edge of the bed. I gave a slight push and she fell, her purse hitting the floor with a dull thud. She bounced onto the white bedding like a fucking dream.

She was so damn gorgeous it was hard to believe. I

couldn't stop staring at her as I unbuttoned my shirt and unbuckled my belt.

"Shy?" I teased, still astonished at what I had found for myself.

"Maybe," she replied and blushed.

Gazing into my eyes, she slightly parted her legs. It was a shy and timid movement, but it hit like the most erotic invitation I'd ever experienced. When my eyes returned to her, she had the most beautiful smile on her face.

I got onto my knees on the bed and catching her ankles, spread her legs wide open. Her freshly shaven sex, barely covered by a skimpy black lace thong was adorable. My mouth watered at the mere sight of it.

I needed to taste her. Needed her to be dripping her sweet nectar into my mouth. I didn't hesitate for a moment further. I leaned forward and inhaled deeply at the scent of her arousal. Why, she smelled exactly as I'd imagined she would. A sun-ripened fruit. I buried myself in her honeyed scent, my tongue moving slowly between her glistening lips. Her taste was sweet and intoxicating.

She gazed at me with dazed eyes as my thumb found the swelling bud in her center. I rolled it and slowly massaged the soft wet flesh around it, and her eyes fluttered closed. Her head fell back against the bed. An incredible and bizarre thought occurred to me: I was never going to get enough of this beauty.

'I could suck your wet pussy all night long,' I whispered.

She gasped with a mixture of shock and excitement.

Through the lace, I covered her soft mound with my mouth and felt her hand claw into my hair. I stroked and teased her through the fabric until I could no longer contain my anticipation. Hooking my hands into the strings of the thong, I pulled the scrap of material down her silky legs. Then I wrapped my hand around her leg and draped it over my shoulder.

She was exposed before me, her wide-open sex was flushed, swollen, and dripping.

As I feasted hungrily on her pink sweetness, she grasped my head, pressed me closer still, and moaned restlessly underneath me. She wanted more.

Cupping her ass, I took the hood of her clit between my teeth, and bit down. She hissed and swore at me, but her body shuddered with intolerable pleasure.

How strange, but I felt it in my heart, her whimpers, her restlessness, her moans. I sucked on her clit till she was close to a climax. Her body was impossibly arched when I narrowed my tongue and began to repeatedly and violently spear it into her opening.

She screamed.

It was beautiful to watch how responsive she was to my touch. I realized it would be insanely easy to get obsessed with her. She was all woman in the sweetest, warmest, most sensual way possible. It even made me wonder if 'tonight only' could be enough. How effortlessly I could grow a compulsion to eat her out on a daily basis just so I could feel the desperation in her body and hear her cries when my tongue applied just the right amount of pressure on her sensitive spots.

"Oh, Cole," she called, and the sound she made afterwards was so soft and harmless it tugged at my heart. I was enthralled by her. For a hardened city man like me, she felt almost unreal.

Collecting her slick juices on my finger I nudged it gently into her opening. She was snug, very snug, but so wet that it pushed right in. I gave her a few seconds to acclimatize, then pushed in a second finger.

"Cole," she breathed, her teeth sinking down into her bottom lip. Her eyes were glazed with desire.

"I know," I said soothingly and slid my fingers in and out of her, keeping it slow and deliberate while my thumb gently circled her clit until her muscles began to contract and tense.

When my pace became more frantic, I leaned down and distracted her by kissing her. My fingers thrust so rapidly into her that the hard, illicit slamming noises filled the room, and a cry ripped out of her and pierced right through me. Shaking, she grabbed my wrist with both her hands. Instantly, I stopped, but barely a second passed and she was moving her hips, fucking herself with my fingers just as violently if not more.

"Keep going, don't stop, please," she pleaded.

I finger-fucked her until she climaxed, so hard her eyes rolled into the back of her head, her body seized up, and she gushed her juices all over my hands. I covered her sex with my mouth and drank greedily.

"No," she cried because she was still sensitive and sore, but with gentle suctions, I extended the indescribable bliss of her climax.

Afterwards, her eyes opened and she leaned forward, grabbed my head and pulled me toward her. Her lips connected with mine and it was wild.

This woman was a goddess.

Chapter 11
Montana

Lord have mercy, but Cole had just fucked me with his tongue as though he were starving, as though my pussy was all he could think of and want. His greed was filthy, obscene and wonderful, but now my brain was buzzing. If his fingers and mouth could make me explode like that, I was craving what his cock could do for me.

But I couldn't break away from kissing him. There was something so carnally exciting about tasting myself mixed with his taste on his tongue ... I couldn't get enough. My pussy was clenched tight when he broke off the kiss, got up and pulled his boxers down.

My eyes widened and my breathing stopped.

"Holy hell," I mouthed. I almost couldn't believe what I was seeing. His cock had to be the most perfect, gorgeous cock ever created. But what made me nearly choke and cry was the size. Good God, he was massive. Was that thing really going to fit inside me? It looked like it could stretch me to the point of ripping.

"Oh wow!" I whispered. Fascinated, I leaned forward to touch the pulsing flesh, but he captured my mouth in a deep, heart-melting kiss instead. By the time we parted, I looked up into his eyes and realized I'd completely lost my train of thought.

I could no longer stand to be clothed around him, so I pulled my dress off and flung it away. I hadn't worn a bra; impossible with such a skimpy dress, so my breasts immediately bounced out.

"Fuck," he swore. For a few seconds, there was silence as he stared greedily at my body. Then he met my gaze. "Montana, Montana, Montana," he crooned. "You're determined to drive me crazy, aren't you?"

Just as I had reached to touch his cock his hand reached out and brushed my hardened nipples. "So pink. So fucking beautiful," he exclaimed in an awe-stricken voice.

"Not as beautiful as your cock. I want to suck it," I said boldly. I couldn't wait to give him the kind of pleasure he'd given me with his mouth.

He grabbed his gorgeous shaft by the root and brought it to my mouth.

"Have you ever had a man's cock in your mouth?" he asked, brushing the hot, satiny soft head against my lips. I loved the sensation so much I couldn't breathe. Everything about his body was so faultlessly sensual.

"No," I whispered. "But I've sucked a lot of lollipops in my time." I didn't tell him Kelly had shared in great detail her best blowjob tips with all of us. This was my secret, my little surprise for him.

"Lollipops?" he repeated, holding his cock just out of

reach, teasing me, driving me crazy. His scent was so intoxicating I almost couldn't hold myself together.

"Cock. Now," I demanded with shameless urgency, and he laughed.

"Alright," he said and led the glistening head of his cock to my lips.

My tongue slipped out then, and as per Kelly's technique, I fisted the thick, jerking shaft of hard meat and then in one smooth movement sucked the entire broad head into my mouth. His big beautiful cock was in my mouth.

If he thought I was going to take any more of him like some newbie, he was in for a surprise. I just wanted the head. This was Kelly's winning technique. No man could resist, she said. Now that I knew how good he smelled and how much I liked his taste, I sucked him so hard, more of his release raced through the slit and into my mouth.

"Fuck," he snarled, astonished.

I sucked him harder still, taking as much of him as I could, then pulling back out with such suction that my cheeks hollowed in. With my gaze locked onto him, I slipped my tongue out and licked the aggressive veins bulging under the satiny shaft. Just like an ice-lolly. A tease. A little break after the intense sucking, I traced the bluish ridges with the tip of my tongue, loving how masculine and dangerous they made his cock look. Without warning I swallowed his cock, taking it deep into my mouth. Hot damn, I wanted to remain here, sucking him off till every drop of his cum was sliding down my throat.

"Hang on a minute," he growled suddenly, his hands holding my head still. "You're much better at this than I gave you credit for. If I don't get inside you real soon, you're going to be disappointed with how long your first fuck lasts."

I smiled with satisfaction. Kelly's method had come through with flying colors. Confidently, I shoved him hard so he fell back on the bed. Quickly, I climbed on top of him and sat astride his hips.

"I've got condoms," I announced.

He nodded. "Okay."

Clinging to him like a monkey, I fished a condom sachet out of my purse that was lying on the floor by the bed and handed it to him to deal with. No need to show my inexperience by fumbling the next steps.

"Glow in the fucking dark?" he asked, looking up from the package.

"What can I say? I have friends with a strange sense of humor," I explained sheepishly.

"They sound like a bag of fun," he said with a grin as he bent to the ground and retrieved a packet from the pocket of his jeans. Expertly, he routed the plastic with his teeth and sheathed himself.

"Let's get you super wet first," he said, and positioning that gorgeous length of him between my damp folds, he began to move me like a rail car over his thick shaft.

My attention-starved clit came back to life with the new attention. It was throbbing so hard it was almost excruciating. As soon as he got a good hard rhythm going, I let all pretense of modesty go and abandoned myself to pure pleasure.

"Oh," I writhed, as my hips moved without my control. I loved the way we moved together. He wasn't even fucking me yet, and I was completely gone, overtaken by the heat and intimacy. Without warning he lifted me off his body, and rolled me onto my back.

"Keep your knees up," he instructed and positioned himself between my legs.

I knew he was going to stretch me like I couldn't believe, but I also knew he was going to be perfect. I loved our bodies being entwined and joined, his chest crushing down on my breasts, his hard naked body pressing down on mine, and those strong powerful thighs spreading me wide open.

My fingers gripped his gorgeous arm muscles. I could feel them flex when he raised himself slightly and, pointing the enormous head of his cock over the entrance into my body, pushed in.

I inhaled sharply, my eyes widening with surprise.

Good God. He was only partially inside me, but it felt like a thick, deep intrusion. Painful and not pleasurable at all. My thighs were spread wide, but my body was distressed. How would all of him fit? Suddenly, I felt tiny and helpless under his big powerful body.

I must have whimpered because he paused.

Dipping his head down, he murmured, 'It's OK. Just relax. It won't hurt in a while.'

He looked down at me almost intently, while his hands stroked my body, soothing and calming me. Then his tongue entered my mouth and my fear faded almost instantly. The kiss was hard, demanding and fiery and I became lost in it. I sensed my body supplicating to his, my legs spreading even further apart. His mouth was locked on mine. I was vaguely aware of the turgid shaft slowly working deeper and deeper into me with each gentle thrust. Slowly but surely, he was travelling into the depths of my body.

I sucked his tongue blindly. Nothing else existed but us and what he was doing to my body. When he tried to pull away I moaned into his dominating mouth. My walls gripped him and sucked him in like a glove.

"Ahhh," I moaned.

"Damn ... You're so fucking tight," he growled.

I couldn't think or speak. All I did was tremble and writhe helplessly as he moved inch by inch into me. I loved that he went so slow and gave me time to accommodate his length and fullness, but I could hardly wait for the time when he would go hard and fast. My body pulsed around him. When he reached the hilt, he stopped. We stayed that way for a while, basking in each other, holding each other tight. I cherished every moment of it.

Truly, this man could not be any more perfect, and as I leaned up to take his dark, hardened nipple into my mouth, it saddened me once again that our time together would be so brief.

Now, I wished I had taken the time to get to know him better in the bar. Taken the time to, at the very least, ask where he had come from so that I could know if there was even the ghost of a chance I could get to have another night with him.

It was all I could think about as I kissed his body.

"Oh!" I trembled when his hips began to move. My veins felt as if they had been turned into electric wires with currents of exquisite pleasure running through them. I'd never dreamed one could feel like this, more so with a complete stranger. I knew now without a shadow of a doubt that my attraction to him from the get-go had not been a fluke. We had connected in a way that was rare, and as he

59

thrust into me with a steady rhythm, I knew that I was having an experience that I would remember for the rest of my life.

He leaned forward to suck on my nipples. It heightened my pleasure, and pretty soon I was lost to the exquisite pleasure of it all. His rhythm and angle changed again. The head of his cock rammed into one spot over and over again. I was sure I was going to lose my mind. I lost control of my breathing first. It came in sporadic bursts. Then all I could do was chase. Something was waiting. Just out of reach. I chased it with greater and greater intensity, more and more until I was crying out. I reminded myself to keep quiet, to control my reaction, but I couldn't. It began from the place where we were joined, then it was spilling down to the sheets. I was unraveling into red-hot bursts of nothingness.

All I could hear were the parched cries coming from my throat as he went even faster into me, my nails dug into his skin, refusing to let go. As his cock milked me of every ounce of pleasure inside of me, he lost control too. Deep inside me, I could feel the vibrations from his roar. His twisted, straining face was something to watch, his eyes appeared like chips of ice in clear water, and that made him even more beautiful. I could feel his chest heaving beneath my hands and his almost brutal grip against my sides.

"Noooo ..." I cried and clutching his body, choked on sobs when the wonderful sensations started to lessen and ebb away.

"Shh ... it's okay," he soothed, and licked into my mouth as though our bodies were one, and at that moment, I was convinced I was so connected to him I didn't know where he started and I ended.

I threw my arms around his neck. If only this moment could last forever. I could die in this moment, and I'd have no regrets. To think this was what I had been avoiding for so long?

"Oh, Cole," I whispered huskily. "That was so indescribably beautiful."

Chapter 12
Montana

I didn't mean to, but I was so spent, so utterly exhausted I must have fallen asleep.

When I woke up I was in darkness, but I didn't need time to acclimatize. I knew exactly where I was and who I was lying next to. Slowly, I turned my head and I saw that he was lying on his side facing me.

My God! He was heartbreakingly beautiful when he slept. With that strange tension and hidden brokenness gone, he looked like an angel. A sleeping angel.

I wanted to touch his skin, I wanted to take a picture, but I didn't want to wake him up.

Instead, I took a mental photograph. Forever, I would remember him like this. Without cares, without sadness. Just an angelic being sleeping next to me.

I knew I had to go. My friends were waiting for me.

Very carefully, without disturbing him, I slipped out of bed. I found my phone. Wow! It was already 3.00 in the morning. Quickly, I sent a text to Natalie to tell her I was done. After I got dressed, I found the hotel notepaper, wrote my number on it, drew a little love heart next to it, and left the note on the bedside table.

The truth was I didn't want to leave.

I wanted to text Natalie and tell her to leave without me, I'd find my own way back home, but I knew Natalie would die first before she left without me. Anyway, I had a Church date with my dad.

I took one last look at him before I picked up my shoes and crept out of the room. There was no one about in the corridor. I hurried down the stairs. There was a middle-aged man sitting at the reception desk and I should have felt shame, but I felt none. No one and nothing could ever make me regret what I did last night. It was beautiful. Totally, absolutely, and wonderfully so.

He nodded at me and I waved at him. Then I pushed open the front door and walked out into the street just as Pearl's car turned out of the car park and came towards me.

Natalie was driving. "Jesus, girl. Did a hurricane hit you?" she asked with a big grin.

"Yeah, tore me right up," I replied, grinning back.

Both Pearl and Kelly laughed.

They would be looking for details, and I would give them enough to keep them happy, but what happened between me and Cole was too private to share.

It was almost sacred.

Chapter 13
Cole

https://www.youtube.com/watch?v=4JVaRloezno
-bella ciao-

I stood hidden behind the drapes and watched the car pull up. I saw her walk towards it, holding her shoes in her hands. Her feet were very pale on the dark asphalt. I spied her open the car door and slip inside. I opened the window a crack and the sound of feminine laughter wafted up in the silence of the night. The door shut, and the car began to move.

My hands were clenched so tight, that the veins in my forearms popped. The need to call out to her was spectacular. But I did nothing. I just stood there and watched the car drive away into the night.

I ran my hand through my hair agitatedly. My mind felt blown.

Restlessly, I pulled back the drapes and opened the

window wide. The stars seemed very bright and I was struck by the blanket of stillness and silence that had fallen over the town. At no time could one ever find this quality of quiet in New York.

A racoon crossed the empty street.

Thoughts of Montana filled my head. Her smile, her body, her smell, her laughter. In my mind's eye, I could still see her: so fucking sexy. Naked as the day she was born and sprawled out on her back, her skin flushed and misted with sweat despite how cool the room had been. Until tonight I'd never met anyone who thought earth was paradise or said a prayer of gratitude when they opened their eyes in the morning.

I'd always thought earth was some sort of hell. I'd never known true happiness. The only time I felt something close to it was when my daughter was born and even that moment was tinged with fear:

They could hurt me now.

My daughter had made me vulnerable.

My real name is Luca Rossi. Son of Enzo Rossi, the cold, detached second in command of the *Occhi Morti* (*Dead Eyes*) Mafia syndicate. My mother, Hanna, is a tiny, painfully thin Hungarian woman. I never understood how she came to be with my father. They were as different as night and day and had nothing in common except for me, their only son. Even as a small child, I knew instinctively they should never be together.

I'd never once seen my father be violent to my mother or even mildly admonish her, but my mother was terrified of him. Whatever had happened to frighten her must have happened early in their relationship, but her terror of him was all-encompassing. It dictated her every move. She became a shade paler as soon as his car pulled up onto the driveway.

Once, she wet herself while sitting at the dining table. Urine dripped and trickled down the chair and formed a puddle on the floor, but she sat there and slipped fork after fork of food until my father decided the meal was over and left the table.

When I was young, many a time, I would watch her fill an olive-green suitcase with her clothes and mine, her movements vigorous and hurried, but as soon as she snapped the locks shut, she suddenly would lose courage. Then she would sit on the bed, with me wrapped tightly in her arms, and sob pitifully. Once her tears were spent, she would beg me not to tell anyone about what she had done and I would promise not to.

"My good, good boy," she would croon sadly, and stroke my head.

With great grief, she would unpack the suitcase and put it away with meticulous exactness in the same position it had been in. Then she would return to her life of capitulation, dread, and unrelieved unhappiness.

She was a wretched figure and as a child, I knew I was the reason she was trapped. Without me, she would have been more nimble and more courageous. So I was fiercely protective of her, even if there was not much I could do to help her. From early on she had insisted that I should learn to protect myself so she sent me to self-defense classes. By the time I was fourteen, I was already the owner of the black belt, but it was of no benefit to her. The harm that was being done to her was not physical or even visible to the casual observer.

To all intents and purposes, my father was a model husband and father. By anybody's estimation, my mother's fear of him would be classed as irrational or a construct of her own imagination.

Once, I'd come home from school and found her slumped at the kitchen table with her head in her hands, and I said to her. "Let's go, Mama. Let's go where no one can find us."

"He'll find us," she said sadly. As long as I lived, I would never forget the look of utter defeat in her eyes.

Her distress and panic were such that it even changed her physical body. She once told me that at the age of twenty, shortly after giving birth to me, she stopped having periods. When she turned forty-two the unrelenting fear started to affect her mind. At first, it was nothing serious. She would forget to add potatoes or onions to her shopping list, but in a few months her decline became obvious, then rapid and aggressive.

The drugs didn't help.

Eventually, came the day she called me from the super-market because she couldn't remember where she lived. After that incident, she withdrew completely into herself. She wouldn't look anyone in the eye, not even me. Her dementia became so severe she could no longer take care of herself. I told my father I wanted to care for her. I had just finished university and started working so I could afford a private nurse for her at home, but he refused point blank. I had my life to live and she needed the proper care that only a specialized care home could provide. It was almost surreal to pack her clothes and some of her personal items into her olive-green suitcase.

My father checked her into a reputable mental asylum.

I visited her every month, but she hardly responded to my presence. Although, sometimes, just for an instant, I would see the old her again in her eyes. I would see her love for me shining in her eyes and I would eagerly call out to her with hope, but almost instantly her gaze would become blank again.

Five years almost to the day after he checked mother into her care home, my father was found guilty of racketeering and money laundering and sentenced to ten years in Sing Sing Correctional Facility, a maximum-security prison. His lawyers told him good behavior could reduce his punishment to seven years, but in fact, with the enemies my father had made, he was looking at the very real possibility he would come out much earlier in a body bag.

As I walked down the courthouse steps a limousine stopped in front of me. A man in a suit jumped out of the front passenger seat, came around and held the back door closest to me open. I knew without being told who was in the car.

I stepped in and the door closed.

Chapter 14
Cole

https://www.youtube.com/watch?v=fmY7kH-KB48&list=
PLLhu_aWzuRciPpJIZLYZ7-UsUHojohWoH&index=7

T he interior of the car was perfumed and *O Fortuna* from Carmina Burana was playing softly in the background. I turned my head and met the soulless, glassy, obsidian eyes of the Capo, the Don, the Godfather of *Occhi Morti*.

Tommaso Paganini was the perfect embodiment of evil incarnate. A demon. Evil poured out of him like oil when he spoke. His nickname was Nice Guy. He earned it a long time ago when he was still doing his own wet work. Always, before he cut his victim's throats, he told them with believable sincerity not to fear or worry, he was not going to hurt them because he was a nice guy.

Even though he worked closely with my father, I consciously kept out of his way and had only met him on a handful of occasions. He made my skin crawl. I could still vividly remember that hot summer's day by the pool. I was sixteen and lying on the grass with my eyes closed when I felt a shadow fall on me. I opened my eyes and he was standing over me with his hands in the pockets of his trousers. The sun was in my eyes and, at first, I couldn't properly make out his expression, but when I shaded my eyes with my hands, I saw it. As clear as day ...

He wanted to fuck me!

So badly his eyes burned with hunger as they roved over my almost naked body.

That inexhaustible supply of beautiful women that he dated and discarded was a lie. He was a raging homosexual!

Neither of us spoke as I vaulted to my feet and walked away. From a distance, I heard my father calling to him from the back door. Years passed with no interaction between us and now he was sitting next to me and in the depths of those cold, dead eyes the lust I had seen all those years ago glimmered. He still wanted me.

His thin lips curved into a sly smile.

"I can protect your father," he said softly. "I can keep him safe and comfortable. I will arrange for him to get his own room, quality steak three times a week, access to alcohol and cigarettes, the services of hookers whenever he has the urge, and I have a small army of men to protect him and run menial chores for him."

I kept my voice respectful. "Forgive me, Don Paganini, but he's your second in command. He's given his whole life to you. Shouldn't you be doing that, anyway?"

He narrowed his ghoul's eyes, and the air in the car throbbed with his irritation.

"Is it possible that your father has not informed you of even the smallest detail of how our *familia* works?"

I said nothing. I knew I was not expected to say anything.

"When a man is careless enough to end up in prison, he becomes a risk to the whole organization. If not now then at some point in the future he may be incentivized to talk. It is in the best interest of the organization to silence that man. Your father understands that." He paused. "But because of the high regard I have for him and your considerable skills in financial matters, I am willing to consider the option of keeping him so sweet he doesn't talk."

I frowned. "What is it you want me to do?"

His voice was smooth, his smile oily. "Nothing too difficult for someone like you. Move some of my money for me. Invest it. Make it clean."

From a very early age, I'd been something of a savant genius at math. At school, I was called the human calculator. I could remember long strings of numbers effortlessly and using a mental abacus inside my head I added, subtracted and multiplied those numbers with ease.

Less than a year ago I left University and went to work as an accountant. Very quickly I'd begun to make something of a name for myself. My special talent was finding little-known loopholes in the tax code and finding new ways of implementing them. And the best part, they were all completely legitimate methods of reducing taxes. I had a few corporate clients, but mostly I preferred to work for Mom-and-Pop stores or the ordinary man on the street. I got a kick out of beating the IRS at their own game. Whenever I found myself facing petty, hard-faced tyrants masquerading as IRS agents, I thoroughly enjoyed seeing their impotent frustration when they failed to squeeze the hard-earned money of my clients so the government could waste it in ever more spectacular ways.

Until now though, I'd always steadfastly avoided ever dealing with dirty money no matter how much remuneration was on the table for me. Moving money around for this monster would mean I was cleaning the dirtiest of money, money tainted with blood.

I was not responsible for my father's life choices. When he took his pledge of honor and silence he understood the consequences, both good and bad, of joining 'the family'. But I also understood refusing the Nice Guy's offer would mean signing my father's death certificate.

I hesitated.

"Wasn't he a good father, Luca?" the Don asked ingratiatingly. "Didn't he provide for you and your mother? The kind of education he gave you surely didn't come cheap. Isn't it time you manned up and showed some gratitude? Paid some of that debt down?"

I looked away from him to the scene outside the car.

My father was supposedly second in command, but for the incredible amount of danger and risk he undertook, the money he was allowed to make was paltry. My father kept my mother on a very tight budget, but he expected a lavish meal every time he sat for dinner. Often my mother would buy an expensive piece of steak for him and cheaper cuts of fatty meat for us. Even while inflation was tearing into her budget he never once raised the amount he gave her every month. By the time I was ten, I was already out doing odd jobs around the neighborhood to help my mother cope with the rising cost of everything.

As for my education, it was public schooling followed by a full scholarship program. Even my self-defense classes I paid for myself by teaching my master's daughter math for the equal amount of time he spent with me each week.

And when my mother fell ill and my father insisted on sending her away, I used my own money to upgrade my mother to a much better mental health facility than the cheap flea-ridden one he wanted to send her to.

So there was no great debt that I owed him.

To top it all, I understood that getting involved in Tommaso's business was like climbing into a snake pit. My father had shown me no love. He had never attended a school meeting, taken me on a single social outing, or shown the smallest bit of interest in me or what I was getting up to. It wouldn't be a lie to say he tolerated me as if I was a necessary evil to keep his family-man image intact. And over the years I found myself feeling remarkably detached from him.

But even more important than that. Arianna was pregnant and I had my unborn child to think of. The last thing I wanted to do was plunge myself and my family into this monster's world to save a man who cared not one bit about me.

Chapter 15
Cole

https://www.youtube.com/watch?v=KamNmbNoYHo&
list=PL1_7zfY1M9t9RcyYQczlfGt1PF8kRQJZx&
index=7
-speak softly-
(Italian version)

"I'll think about it," I said slowly. I already knew I was going to refuse, but I had to consider carefully how I did it.

"This was actually your father's idea," the Don interjected softly. He had scented victory and his eyes glittered like a rat's.

I shook my head at my own naivety. Of course, it was my father's idea. He was willing to sacrifice his own son to save himself.

He smiled cunningly. "You will be a father soon, I hear. God has blessed you with a daughter."

My blood ran cold. Very few people knew the sex of my child. I recognized his statement for what it was. A threat. In exactly the same way he advised people not to worry because he was a nice guy before he slaughtered them.

"Yes. A blessing it is," I agreed, trying not to show the fear churning inside me.

"Perhaps you might want to see this ... venture I'm offering ... as an opportunity that will pay handsomely," he said persuasively. "As an occasion to use the gains to build an education fund for your daughter if she turns out to be as smart as you."

He believed I needed his blood money to educate my daughter. He'd be very astonished to know I was already many times richer than him, and in a few years, I would be worth billions. Many years ago, while I was still in school, I secretly bought as many Bitcoins as I could.

To me, it was a no-brainer.

The coding was perfect and the scarcity factor was even more amazing. There would only ever be twenty-one million coins. I understood immediately that there had never been an asset like it, and probably never another one like it in my lifetime. I was willing to bet everything I had on it. I borrowed money from anyone who would lend it to me and bought twenty thousand coins at the price of nine cents each. I'd been buying more ever since and my secret stash was now pretty impressive.

But that money was of little use to me now. He wanted me to work for him and he was unsubtly telling me if I didn't, he was willing to hurt my unborn child. I felt trapped, furious, and impotent. I hated being in that help-less position, but there was nothing I could do.

Not at that moment, anyway.

He was a dangerous, duplicitous snake, but even a King Cobra had its enemies. In seventy-five to eighty percent of the fights between Cobras and mongooses, the venom-immune, fast-moving creature darted at the snake with Ninja-like speed, forcing the reptile to repeatedly strike at it until the snake was completely exhausted. Then the little hero crushed the cobra's head in its jaws.

By asking me to move his money he was allowing me to make many little strikes and get close to his most vulnerable parts. Once I was inside his books, I would forever have the means of destroying him, and I would be able to do it without him ever suspecting I'd done it.

"Fine. I will work for you."

He smiled victoriously. "Bravo, Luca. I always knew you were a smart kid. You've just made a wise decision."

Yes, good. Keep thinking of me as if I was still the kid by the swimming pool.

"I will work for you until my father is released, but after that, I never want to see you again." Even as I said the words, I already knew it would never be over with him. He would never let me go. I would have to find my own way out.

"Of course," he agreed slickly.

I opened the car door and stepped out.

I would be trapped for seven years, but after that no matter what I would make sure I set things up in such a way I would free myself.

And so I worked for him and I laid the groundwork. Six years passed. Then one year before my father was to be set free, Paganini, the snake that he was, changed the rules of the game. He seduced my bored wife into an affair. Poor Arianna thought she was leaving me for a very wealthy man. She didn't know the Bitcoin I bought all those years ago for nine cents each was already worth more than fifty thousand dollars each and I was a billionaire.

I knew he didn't really want her, but he thought taking my wife would drive me crazy and inspire me to do something stupid that could further consolidate his control over me.

He had miscalculated badly.

I wasn't jealous and furious at all. I knew exactly why he had done it, and I didn't blame Arianna either. How could I? She was an unhappy woman. She knew I didn't love her, never had. I only married her because she'd tricked me into it by becoming pregnant with my child.

Ours was a loveless marriage and if it had been any other man I would have been happy for her, but I knew she would quickly find out Paganini was not the charming wealthy gentleman he had obviously portrayed himself to be to her ... and then she would want to come back. And when she did, Paganini would take that as a sign of intolerable disrespect requiring harsh punishment. In his eyes, the only fitting punishment would be my daughter or me working for him for the rest of his lifetime.

I knew I had less than six months before the magic wore off and Arianna came crawling back. I immediately laid new plans to prepare myself for that day. My plan was to take my daughter and disappear without a trace. That would give me time to carry on working on my long-term plans to destroy Paganini in such a way that it would not implicate me.

That was three months ago.

As things stood right now, I was nearly ready to move my daughter and me out of harm's way, but Paganini was not to be underestimated. He was not the head of his organization by accident. For now, there could be no thoughts of a woman clouding my judgement. Not even of a beauty called Montana. I needed all my wits about me to survive the next few months. The sooner I put thoughts of her out of my mind the better.

I closed the window and went back towards the bed. She had left her scent behind on the sheets. Her tantalizing perfume swirled around me. I switched on a light and saw the slip of paper she had left behind. I picked it up and looked at it. She had hastily written her number and drawn a love heart next to it.

Ah, Montana!

I would never forget her. She was the girl who thought life was a precious gift. I'd rather die than drag her into my nightmare and give Paganini another means of hurting me. Before my brain could automatically imprint the numbers into my mental database, before I could change my mind, I tore the piece of paper into tiny fragments.

Then I dressed quickly and moved towards the door. At the door, I hesitated. The desire to fling one last look at the bed was overwhelming. I didn't give in. I turned the handle and walked out. I went downstairs, where the night porter, a middle-aged man, was minding the reception desk.

"Can I help you, Sir?" he asked politely.

"Yes. I need to return to New York. Could you call me a taxi please?"

"At this time of the morning? I'll have to get someone

out of their warm bed, it won't be easy," he warned doubtfully.

"Make some calls. I'd be willing to pay five hundred dollars for the trip. Cash."

His eyes widened. "Name is Maxwell, and I do declare I could get someone to jump out of bed for that."

"Good. Can I get a drink while I wait, Maxwell?" I pushed a hundred-dollar bill towards him.

Beaming from ear to ear, he slipped the note into his pocket. "If you follow me, Sir, I'll open the bar for you."

I waited while he found the keys and opened the double doors. My shoes were loud on the bare wooden floors. Maxwell switched on the lights in the bar area. I glanced around and the bar looked and felt like a completely different place without people in it. A sad shadow of its earlier glory. It was the way I felt.

"What'll you have?" he asked from the other side of the bar.

"Whiskey, neat."

He splashed a generous amount into a glass and pushed it towards me.

I slid another hundred-dollar bill out to him. "Leave the bottle."

Chapter 16
Montana

https://www.youtube.com/watch?v=CdqoNKCCt7A&
list=PLBuCS1pc_KoaqEXC2q1hNrEwf8WC2MZSf&
index=11

-don't you forget about me-

He never called. Every day, I waited. And every day, he did not call.

I couldn't believe it. How could he not call? After what we went through. Was he pissed that I crept like a thief out without waking him up or saying goodbye? Surely, he was not that petty.

Did I scribble the wrong number in the dark? No way. I had the light of the phone and I was stone-cold sober. Did the note fall and he didn't see it? That was impossible too. I had put the pen on top of it. My mind went around in circles.

The aches and bruises on my body assured me I had not

80

hallucinated the night we shared, but perhaps it was not as amazing for him. Otherwise, why the hell couldn't he send even one little message while I hadn't been able to stop thinking about him for even one second.

Maybe he needed a few more days.

A part of me bitterly regretted leaving that night. I had cheated myself. I should have stayed. Insisted the girls go back, called my father and cancelled our Church date. Then I should have waited for him to wake up and talked to him. Even if he rejected me then, at least, I would live in this limbo world of not knowing if he would ever call.

I had made the important decision to leave in a hurry and I had made the wrong choice. I knew that now, but there was nothing I could do to change things. All I had were beautiful memories of us entwined in bed. I felt lost and sad. When I rode out into the fields, some of the magic was gone. The colors, less bright.

But as the days passed into weeks, I became angry and disillusioned. I couldn't forget him, but all those wonderful feelings were slipping away and all I had left was a simmering resentment. A slow-bonfire of hate. Yeah, I understood that it was a one-night stand and that was how those things inevitably ended, but to completely block me off like that after what we shared. That was just callous. Unforgivably so. At some level, I knew my hatred was my way of coping with my grief. I lost something important and special that night and it was never coming back.

"You keep staring at your phone," my dad pointed. It was his turn to make breakfast and he was standing over the stove cooking sausages and eggs.

"Sorry," I said looking up from my empty inbox.

"What's going on?"

"Just Natalie. She's having problems with her boyfriend. I'm waiting for an update."

He brought the food over to the table. "There's toast if you want."

"Thanks, Dad." I buttered a slice of toast and bit into it.

"Did something happen that night you went to Stormy City?"

I stopped with the fork midway to my mouth. "What do you mean?"

His bright blue eyes stared into mine. "What happened that night, pumpkin? You've never been the same since."

I couldn't stop the tears from running down my face. That night seemed so far away, it was almost like a figment of a dream.

"Did someone hurt you?" my father demanded angrily.

I wiped the tears away. "Nothing happened that night. I'm just tired."

"I've known you since you were born," he countered calmly, "who the hell do you think you're kidding, Buttercup?"

"It's nothing, Dad. Really," I insisted. "And don't you think it's time you stopped calling me Buttercup? I'm twenty-four."

He stared at me worriedly. "Now I know for sure something's wrong. I couldn't stop calling you Buttercup if I wanted to. That's how I think of you. Bright, sunny, wild, thriving where she isn't supposed to, bringing beauty to field and forest alike, but beware, she ain't no soft touch. A severe case of the runs is in store if you try to eat her." He shook his head in wonder. "What's going on with you, love? You used to be so happy all the time."

I smiled through my sadness. "I did, didn't I?"

"Yes. Always. Your mother always said she'd never seen a happier baby in her life. You were always smiling and laughing at everything."

I nodded. I wished I could go back to being the person I was before I met him. Perhaps I would. In time. My grandfather had a saying, 'This too will pass.'

One day this awful feeling of loss would pass and I would be whole again.

Chapter 17
Cole

37 Days Later

I was meeting a client for a breakfast meeting.

Since I was early, I ordered a coffee and had just opened my client's file, when I heard someone whisper my name. It was starting. Two months earlier than I had thought. Still, I was ready. I kept my expression blank as I raised my face to Arianna.

Arianna had become a mystery to me. I thought I knew her and I did not. The way she had turned her back on her own daughter shocked me. Even if it was a condition imposed upon her by Paganini, God knows, he was capable of such cruelty, it was still unforgivable behavior. Not once had she called or come to visit Bianca since she went to live with him.

She stared at me through eyes that were red and

swollen. "I've made a terrible mistake. A terrible mistake. I miss you ... and Bianca."

Even though I was trying to remain impassive, some of the disbelief I harbored must have crossed my face because she rushed into the chair opposite me and gazed at me with a pleading, desperate expression.

"Of course, I miss her. How could you ever think otherwise?" she cried passionately. Tears streamed from her eyes. "She is *my* daughter. I carried her inside me for nine months. I need her like I need air. Without her, I've been slowly dying inside."

Arianna had always been overly dramatic. "I have never stopped you from seeing her," I said quietly.

"No, of course you haven't. You're too good for that."

I watched her dispassionately as she began sobbing in earnest.

"My Bianca. My Bianca."

I said nothing. There was nothing to say.

"She needs her mother. I want to come back. How can you be so cruel to stop me from being with my own daughter?"

I knew this moment was coming so I was well prepared for it. I thought I might be, at least, resentful or angry with her. She had after all betrayed me, but I felt nothing. Her real crime was being stupid. She didn't know she had unwittingly become a pawn on a chess game Paganini and I were playing. She definitely didn't understand the damage she had done.

But now that she turned her back on me and my daughter, she could no longer expect my protection. My sole concern now was my daughter.

"We could go back to how we were before," she cried. "I won't ask for more. I understand now how precious what we had was. You were a good husband and a fantastic father. I know you don't love me, but we were good together. Let's do it for Bianca's sake."

"So ... why didn't you come to see Bianca all these months?" I asked quietly.

She shrank back with guilt. "I'm sorry. I don't know what happened to me. I think I went a little mad. He made me choose between him and her and I did a very stupid thing. I chose him because I really thought I could bring him around to accepting her with time."

"Have you told him yet you want to leave?"

She took a deep breath. "No."

"Why not?"

She shook her head and cast her guilt-ridden gaze down to the table surface. "I don't know."

I knew why. She wanted to be sure she could go back to him if she couldn't persuade me to take her back.

I looked at my coffee cup. Time was running out. She didn't know it, but Paganini would have ordered a twenty-four-hour surveillance team for her. Perhaps even now someone across the street was telling him that she was meeting me.

I smiled at her. "I want what is best for Bianca too, so can you give me a couple of days to think over what you have said?"

Her face lit up with relief and happiness. "Yes, of course. We should put Bianca's needs before ours."

I stood. "I'll call you in a couple of days."

She jumped to her feet. "Thank you, Luca. Thank you.

I promise you won't regret taking me back. I'll be the best wife and mother you could ever hope for."

I nodded curtly and walked out. Across the street, I saw a young man loitering outside a florist. I pretended not to notice him and walked away as if I had all the time in the world, but as soon as I got back into my car, I retrieved my burner phone and called my mechanic.

"Can I pick up the car in an hour?"

"Sure, it's been waiting and ready for the last three months. I'll just start her and make sure she's good to go."

"Thanks, Mike."

I called the client who I was meeting, apologized, made up some excuse, and told him my secretary would call to arrange another appointment. Obviously, there would be no new appointment, not for many months, maybe even never, but I had to be careful to do nothing out of the ordinary. Nothing that could cause suspicion.

Then I drove to my mother's care home. Other than Bianca my mother was the only person in the world I loved and gave a damn about.

I went to her room and she was sitting by the window looking out into the enclosed garden. She didn't look around when I opened the door or walked up to her. Usually, I pulled up a chair, sat next to her and told her about my life, and what Bianca was up to, but today I knelt on the ground next to her.

I knew she most probably couldn't hear me, or if she could she wouldn't understand or remember, but nevertheless, on the off chance she could hear me and would remember, I spoke into her ear.

"Mama, I have to take Bianca away and leave the city

for a while ..." I stroked her small white hand. "While we are away, we won't be able to come and visit you, but it will only be for a few months. As soon as we are settled, I will come back to visit you."

She showed no reaction, but I carried on talking.

"Tomorrow some friends of mine will come by. You won't know them, but they are people I trust. Do not be frightened. Everything will be fine. They will move you to a new apartment where you will stay for the next year. I know you're probably used to the staff here and you're fond of them, but at the apartment, you'll have two full-time nurses who are the best in their fields to care for you. I've spoken to them and they are both kind and caring people. I think you'll like them. Oh, one of them is actually Hungarian and she says she can cook all your favorite food for you."

I smiled at her and enveloped her tiny hand inside mine.

"You know what else? Your bedroom has been painted in your favorite color, marshmallow yellow. It overlooks a beautiful park so you'll be able to sit by your window and enjoy the view. And because you love birds so much, I've ordered some bird feeders to be hung outside your window. You'll be able to watch the birds come and go. I think you'll be happy there."

Slowly, her fingers curved around my thumb. I stared down in surprise as she held onto my thumb as tightly as my newborn infant once did. It was sad and sweet.

"Mama," I called, moving back and looking into her face, but it was blank. There was no reaction at all in her eyes. She gazed far into the horizon, seemingly lost in some other world.

Even so, for a few minutes, I stubbornly clung to the illusion that in some tiny way, my mother was responding to me.

'I love you, Mama."

But she showed no reaction, her translucent eyes staring at something far away. I knew then it was only an illusion. I kissed her thin cheek. She smelled of powder, which made me feel good. They took good care of her here.

"I'm sorry, Mama, but I have to go now. I'll be back as soon as I can."

Her grip on my thumb was surprisingly strong and I had to prise her pale fingers off my thumb one by one.

In the corridor, I called my mechanic to tell him I would be there in about two hours, then I headed towards Bianca's, no, not Bianca anymore, but Anya's school. From this moment on I had to start thinking of her as Anya. On-route I called my estate agent and asked her to meet me at the house in an hour.

Chapter 18
Cole

Pulling up to Anya's elementary school in the middle of Manhattan was a strange affair for me. It was all coming to an end and this would be the last time I would be picking her up from here.

I hated running, but running was the only way ... for now.

I had plans. Anya and I would not be running for long. A year at most. Anya would not be forced to look over her shoulder for the rest of her life.

I parked my car and headed to the principal's office. I knew exactly what to say and it didn't take me time to get her out of class. There was a medical emergency with her absent mother.

My daughter walked towards me worriedly. They would not have given her any reason why she was being taken out of class, but her instinctive questions were, "What's wrong? Is it Mom? Is Mom alright?"

I smiled at her reassuringly. "Your mom is fine, but it's time."

"Oh," she said quietly.

"Can I say goodbye to Melanie?"

I shook my head.

She nodded, and I took her hand and walked her to the waiting car. As I leaned down to buckle her in, she asked, "Will I ever see Mom again?"

"Yes," I said simply. "Just not right now."

"But what if she forgets all about me?"

"She won't ever do that, honey. Moms don't ever forget their children. She told me she misses you."

"She did?"

"Hmmm..."

Her eyes were enormous. "When did she tell you that?"

"This morning."

Her mouth opened with shock. "Oh."

I shut the door and went around to the driver's seat, and soon we were on the road.

"So ... if she misses me, why didn't she come to see me?' she asked.

I debated whether to tell her, then decided the fewer lies I told the stronger we would be as a team.

"Because your mother fell in love with a new man, but he's not very nice. He doesn't really like children and he could try to hurt you."

"So she chose him instead of me?" she asked sadly.

"No. It's not as simple as that. When she chose him, she didn't know he was one of the bad guys and now it's too late. So really, she's protecting you by not contacting you. Do you understand how much your mother must love you to do that for you?"

She nodded, her pigtails bouncing against her serious face.

"Hey," I called, taking my eyes off the road.

"Yes, Daddy?"

"I know that you miss her a lot, but staying away from her is the best thing for both of us. I say this to you because I found some letters you wrote to her earlier this morning."

"I wasn't going to send them. And anyway, I wouldn't know where to send them," she muttered rebelliously.

I gave her a look. "You weren't going to send them, but by just writing them you already planted the possibility. Someday when you really miss her you might decide to send them and that will give a clue to the bad guys about where we are living. You understand that, right?"

She was silent for a while, and I gave her the time to process. Eventually, she nodded. "I'm sorry, Daddy."

"Don't be. Ultimately it's my responsibility, and I am working to make everything better. Today we're going to our new home, far away from anyone who knows us."

Her eyes widened as she turned to me. "We're going today?"

"Yes, we are. There you'll be able to ride horses, plant vegetables, and paint."

"Plant vegetables?" She made a face, and I had to laugh out loud. She was so unbearably cute.

"You never know. You might love it," I said.

She wrinkled her nose. "I don't think so."

I took a left and pulled into Mike's automobile workshop.

A man's loud whistling rang out just as I got out. "Whoa! This is it?"

"This is her," I replied, and we both turned around to look at my matt black Lamborghini. I knew this would be the last time I would see her, but felt nothing. Which was strange when I remembered how excited I had been to purchase her. I guess, no luxury or lifestyle was worth the safety of my daughter.

"How much do you expect her to fetch?" I asked as I motioned to Anya to stay put, then walked with him.

"Quarter of a million," he replied. "I've been peddling the specs for the past few weeks and I have an Arab from Bahrain and a Chinese businessman interested."

I nodded. "That's good."

"They were a bit suspicious as to why you're selling it so cheaply, but I explained that payment has to be in Bitcoin. That seemed to sit well."

"Alright," I replied. "I collect the Chevy now and leave the Lambo with you so you're free to complete the process."

"Cool," he said and we entered the workshop. He led to an old Chevy ready and waiting.

"She looks good," I nodded. "Did you polish her up?"

"Nope. You told me the rougher the better, but knowing you'd pick her up today, I ordered a wash. The scuffs are still there, but that's just the way you want it, right?"

"Yes," I replied, amused by the disbelief and wonder that was still in his tone.

"Why anyone would dispose of a brand new Lamborghini and overhaul a 2004 Chevy Impala instead to become their primary mode of transport is beyond me."

"But with the upgrades you've done, it should be on par with the Lamborghini, right?" I asked.

He gave me a dry look. "I'm going to pretend I didn't hear that."

I smiled. "Walk me through the specs again."

He popped the hood open. "Upgraded camshaft for the output and airflow. Aftermarket headers, performance air filters, exhaust system, and the increased horsepower, of course. Turbocharger kit, upgraded to an automatic transmission of course, and—" he stepped back. "Upgraded rear to handle the increased torque. Stronger axles and adjustable coilovers. Larger brakes, brake pads, roll cage, high-flow exhaust system – the whole works."

I nodded. "So how fast can it go now?"

"Hmm ... 0-60 in about 4-5 seconds. Originally, she was limited to 130 miles per hour, but with the upgrade, she can go up to 150 miles per hour."

I nodded again. "I like that. It'll do."

"All that's left now is for you to test it."

"I'll do that now."

He looked at me curiously. "You going far?"

"Hopefully," I replied, and he gave me a peculiar look. "Well, safe journey, and if there's any problem you know where to find me."

I handed over the keys to my Lambo and he gave me the keys to the plainest Jane of cars, the Chevy Impala 1967.

"Anya," I called and it felt strange calling her that, but to my surprise, she immediately turned her head and looked at me. I motioned to her to come over. She hurried over, and in no time, we were headed back to my safety deposit boxes in Manhattan. I came out carrying two holdalls with our new identity; passports, bank accounts, credit cards. I stuffed them into the truck. From there we went to a small hotel at the edge of the city.

Chapter 19
Cole

"Wow, Dad, you're unrecognizable!"

I turned around to see my daughter walking in from the bathroom, all dressed and ready.

"You look different as well, kiddo," I said, but she shook her head.

"You look way different. You're wearing a baseball hat. You never wear baseball hats."

"Well, it's a new life," I said. Back at the apartment, my walk-in closet was filled with dress shirts, slacks, ties, loafers, and blazers. But now, I was in a flannel shirt, scuffed boots, and washed jeans — I looked like a hillbilly.

Getting on my haunches I touched my daughter's hair. She was seven, but it felt as if she was growing up too fast. It seemed only a short time ago that her mother and I were picking out everything she wore. Now she was able to put herself together so immaculately.

I adjusted her pink corduroy jacket, the cute flowery tank top within, and her black jeans.

"We match," I smiled as I noted her brown boots.

"Yes, we do," she said, smiling, and my heart swelled.

"I loved her so much it hurt. And this alone was all the confidence and confirmation I needed that I was doing the right thing. I needed to protect her with my life and give her a normal childhood. Eventually, I would deal with every single threat that stood in her way. But first, we had to run from immediate danger.

"Alright, we'll be leaving soon," I said as I rose to my feet. "Go check to ensure that you didn't leave anything."

"Okay," she said and skipped off.

The phone rang just then. It was my real estate agent returning my call.

"I'm sorry I missed your call, Mr. Rossi. I was stuck in a meeting."

"No problem. Just wanted to let you know that you can proceed with the sale. Everything in it is for sale."

"Oh! That's great news! Thank you for choosing us. You'll be glad to know we have many people on our books who would line up for a property like yours."

"Sure," I replied. "Sell it as quickly as possible and as discussed payment can only be made in Bitcoin."

"Yes, I can see that in the notes. That'll be no problem."

"Are you moving far away?" she asked.

"Yes, it's time for a change," was all I gave in response.

"That's nice. I wish you the best of luck wherever you're going," she said.

"Thank you. You won't be able to contact me on this number after this, so deal directly with my solicitor."

"Yes, we have his contact details."

"I'm ready," Anya said, and I wrapped up my call and picked up our luggage.

"Let's go," I told her. "We'll get something to eat on the way. You haven't had lunch yet, have you?"

"No," she replied.

We hurried out of the building, got into the newly upgraded car, and began our journey together towards our future in Bison Ridge, a tiny town nearly five hours away with a population of less than five thousand people. It was just the perfect place for me and Anya to hide out for a while.

I hated having to uproot her, but needs must.

As I had done all morning, I constantly checked the rearview mirror to ensure we weren't followed. It was such a huge weight off my chest we finally left the city.

"Look, Daddy, look, Daddy," Anya yelled excitedly. "Is that a horse and buggy?"

"Yup."

"Oh! Wow," she said, turning her head to stare at the horse and cart. "Are we going to live in a place where everybody rides horses?"

"No, that man is Amish. The Amish don't believe in using cars or electricity. We're just going to live in a normal town."

She was instantly curious about the Amish and their customs, and for the next half an hour I was fielding questions about them. Eventually, she fell asleep and I drove in silence. As we reached the intersection that led to

Bison Ridge, I saw the signage for Stormy City and felt a strange tingle run up my spine. Ah, Montana. She was like a delicious cool breeze on a hot day. But she had blown away.

Where are you now?

At first, it had been hard to force myself not to think of her because she came into my head so much, but as the weeks went by it hurt less and less.

She was gone and that was that.

When we arrived at Bison Ridge, I woke Anya up. "We're in Bison Ridge, honey."

She came awake instantly and looked around her curiously. "Oh look, there's an ice cream place, Dad. It's pretty. We should go."

"Perhaps tomorrow. We should settle into our new home first."

We left the main street and drove towards our house. As I turned into the driveway, Anya swung around to face me, her eyes were shining with delight.

"Oh wow, Daddy. You didn't tell me our new house is called Duck's Pond."

"It's called that, but there are no ducks here."

She looked disappointed. "No?"

"Sorry."

The evening sun was slanting onto the house and it looked absolutely stunning. I was too stressed and anxious the previous times I had come and had not realized how lovely it was around here.

"Is that it? Is that our new home?" Anya asked enthusiastically, hanging her head out of the window.

"That's it. Do you like it?"

"Yeah, I like it. It looks like one of the houses in my *Fairytales For Princesses* book."

I stopped the car in front of the house and got out. We stood side by side looking around. It was greenery as far as the eye could see. We had no neighbors within viewing distance and that was exactly how I wanted it. My daughter put her little hands in mine as we stood before the two-story house. I turned to meet her gaze.

"Do you think you can be happy here, Anya?"

It took her a while to make up her mind. "I don't know yet," she said truthfully. "Does it have good WIFI?"

I laughed. "You bet. Brand new fiber optic internet."

"Then we're cooking," she said with a big grin.

She went exploring while I checked out if the expensive high-tech safety measures and alarm system, I'd purchased to be built during the extensive renovation worked the way they were supposed to.

"The house is Gucci, Dad." The use of that slang word told me Anya had genuinely given her seal of approval.

"Have you chosen your room?" I asked innocently.

"Yeah, the one next to the big bedroom," she said with immense satisfaction. "The one with Snow White and the Seven Dwarfs painted on the walls."

"That is an excellent choice. I'm glad you like it. Did you know if you sit on the bed you'll be able to see the big ancient oak tree on the field yonder," I said, relieved now that I knew she liked the house. I had entertained niggling worries that she would hate her new accommodation. After all it was a total change of everything she had ever known or been used to. But she showed genuine enthusiasm about her new living conditions.

"Thank you, Daddy," she squeezed my hand.

I knew then she was scared but trying to be brave. Clearly, the suddenness of the move had scared her, but she was such a considerate soul that she was trying to hide it.

I got on my haunches and embraced her. "I'm sorry I uprooted you from everything you know and brought you here where you know no one and everything is so unfamiliar to you."

She shook her head. "Don't be sorry, Daddy. It's going to be okay."

Her sweet innocent warmth made my chest feel like it would burst with love. "How about I show you our super-secret room?"

"We have a super-secret room?" she gasped, her eyes widening.

I nodded. "We sure do. Let's go."

I took her down to the basement through the invisible door hidden within wall panels, down a small, narrow corridor where the lights automatically came on, until we came to a thick blast-proof steel door.

She stopped and slapped her cheeks with amazement. "Oh wow! It really is a secret room!"

I had asked for steps to be built under the identification device so it was at the perfect height for her, so as soon as she stood before it, it lit up.

"I'm going to register your face," I told her. A blue light started scanning across her face.

"Now this is what we call the panic room," I explained.

She turned to me with a frown. "The panic room?"

"Whenever you feel panicked, maybe when I'm not around or you can't reach me, or you feel like someone might be trying to intrude into the house for any reason, no matter how small, you run down here. Don't grab anything because that will waste your time. You stand in front of the camera exactly here. It will recognize your face and open the door for you."

I activated it and immediately the door slid open with remarkable speed.

She looked around at what was technically a cube-like studio apartment. It was quite claustrophobic, but she seemed to find it thrilling. "Daddy, this is a great place for vibing," she gushed.

"I'm glad you like it, but there are some things I have to tell you, so come sit with me?" I pulled out the table and the two benches from the wall.

"Whoa," she cried impressed.

"There's a bed you can pull out over there too, but you have to remember that I didn't put any of this in place to be exciting or fun. This room is designed to save our lives. You know, we're in the middle of nowhere now. We have a few neighbors, but we don't completely trust them yet. There might be bears or cruel people around, so I want you to always know that if you run in here you'll be safe. Nothing can get through to this room. The walls are reinforced steel and about ten feet thick. So nobody can get in here if you don't want them to. Do you understand me?"

She looked intensely at me for a few moments before she nodded. "Okay."

"This also means then that you can never tell anybody about this room. It's our secret. Okay?"

She nodded so hard, she looked like she was in danger of giving herself whiplash.

"No one can hurt you while you are in here. So if ever you have to run in here never open the door no matter what the person outside tries to tell you through the video feeds over there." I pointed to the six screens on the wall.

"I understand, Daddy," she said. "I will never tell anyone; it's our secret."

I smiled and then leaned my forehead against hers.

"Okay, now it's time to go to the fun part," I told her.

"What?" she asked eagerly.

I laughed. "This room is full to the brim of toys, snacks, food, drinks, clothes, actually everything you could possibly need. I pointed to all the drawers lining the other side of the wall. "You actually could live in here for two weeks if the need arises and not want for a single thing. And that's why I told you that if you have to run in here, never bother to look for anything else. Just come straight in here to save time so no one has the time to follow you. The doors will automatically seal when you shut them and after that, nobody can get to you. When the danger has passed and you need to open it to go out, use your face once again. Do you understand?"

"Yes, I do," she nodded again and smoothed her hair.

Then I showed her all the food and told her all of it was for emergency purposes only and that she wasn't allowed to ever to come down here and eat them otherwise.

She nodded, and my heart for the very first time in a long while felt somewhat at peace.

"And now ... how about we go get some ice cream from the Frozen Strawberry?" I asked.

Chapter 20
Montana

https://www.youtube.com/watch?v=HQW7I62TNOw
-Islands in the Stream-

I was coming out of the bakery carrying a box full of mini cherry muffins when I ran into Jesse Craven.

"Hey, Jesse," I greeted.

"Shall I help you with that?" he asked, moving forward to take the box out of my hand.

"Thanks, but it's not heavy."

"You alright?" he asked, shifting from one booted foot to another.

"Yeah, I'm alright. Send my regards to your ma," I said and moved on.

"Montana," he called.

I turned back. "Yeah?"

He adjusted his cowboy hat uncomfortably. "Will you be my date to the Summer Festival dance?"

The sun was in my eyes and my dad was waiting in the truck for me. "Sorry, Jesse, but I don't think I'm going to the dance this year."

"That's a shame."

"Look, I got to go. Dad's waiting for me."

"Let me know if you change your mind."

"Yeah, sure."

He tipped his hat at me. "See you around."

"See ya."

I walked back to the truck and Dad looked at me funny. "Why was that kid sniffing around you?"

I carefully balanced the box on my lap. "He wasn't sniffing around me."

"Well, what did he want?" he asked grumpily.

"He asked if he could take me to the Summer dance, okay?"

"What did you say?"

"I said I didn't think I was going."

"Good," he replied heartily.

I turned to look at him curiously. "I thought you liked the Cravens and their boys. Don't you like Jesse?"

He swung the truck out into the street. "I like him well enough. He's just not good enough for you."

I wound the window down and hot wind rushed into my face. "Apparently, no one's ever going to be good enough according to you."

"One day you'll understand that being choosy isn't a bad thing." Dad switched on the radio and country music filled the air.

"Any news for the week?" I asked.

"We have a new student, a girl, coming in on Monday," he replied.

"What? Why is she coming in halfway through the term?"

"Well, her dad paid for her to be in school from about three months ago, but talk is they only arrived in town two days ago. Single dad and very easy on the eye, I hear. Word has it, yesterday's baking club meeting had to be terminated early because of spinsters and their mothers being catty to each other."

I smiled. "To be expected, I suppose, when fresh meat is thrown into a pool full of piranhas."

He glanced at me. "He's not much older than you, I believe."

I actually felt sick to my stomach at the thought of being with a man again. I just couldn't. Not after that night with Cole. I stuck my palm out towards my father. "Oh no ... don't go there. Please Dad."

Dad sighed elaborately, and on the radio, Dolly Parton started singing *Islands in the Stream.*

Chapter 21
Cole

"Why is everything made of wood?" Anya asked as we pulled up to her new survival school.

I smiled. "The kids probably made it!"

"Look, Daddy, there's a horse eating hay," she cried excitedly.

"And a cow by the barn," I added.

"Oh, wow. I see it. Dad! There's a baby donkey wandering around in the field. Can we pet it?"

"No, let's get you registered first," I said, parking the car underneath a tree.

My daughter sprinted out of the car enthusiastically. It seemed weird to be sending her to school wearing jeans and tough boots, but the catalogue I received was clear. There was no formal uniform, All children were to be dressed as if they were going on a day picnic in the woods.

As we walked to the main building, we could see a group of students gathered around a woman who was kneeling on the ground and showing them something. My eyes were drawn to the teacher as she rose to her feet. She had dark hair that half-covered her face, but there was something vaguely familiar about her. It wasn't a good start if there was someone in this town I knew from the past and I wanted to wait and catch sight of her face properly, but our appointment was ten, and we were already a little late, so I had to let it go and hurry to the Principal's office.

Noah Moore was exactly as I had pictured him.

A tough old boot of a man. He had bright blue eyes that shone with intelligence and a nonsense approach to life. His handshake was dry and firm and his smile was warm and welcoming. I felt as if he was someone I could go out and have a few drinks with. He seated Anya and me in front of him in his office and answered my questions in a way that made me sure I had chosen the right school for Anya.

A few minutes later, there was a knock on the door, and he smiled at Anya.

"Your new teacher is here," he said. "She was out in the fields teaching the kids to plant. If you wish she'll be able to give you both a little tour of the projects you and your class-mates will be working on this year."

"That would be good," I replied and waited for the teacher's entrance.

"Good morning," a woman said from behind.

And I fucking froze.

I didn't need to turn around for my ears to instantly recognize that voice. Suddenly, I knew who the dark-haired woman kneeling on the ground was. That was her friend, Natalie. Fuck! It must have seemed so rude, but I was too stunned to move. She came around, a hat on her head, perhaps to shield her face from the sun, and a pair of gloves that she had taken off and was trying to fit into her pocket. She looked completely different from the painted Jezebel from that night, but to my eyes, she was even more beautiful and alluring.

"Montana, meet Mr. Cole Swift," the Principal introduced. "Mr. Swift, this will be Anya's new teacher, Montana Moore. She is also my only daughter."

My gaze connected with a pair of very, very familiar eyes. Her ghastly white face was staring at me with disbelief which flushed bright red a few seconds later.

Her hand was frozen in the air, and I could see the surprise on her father's face.

"What's wrong?" he asked his daughter with a frown of concern. It was the catalyst I needed to recover from the shock of finding her in my daughter's new school.

I rose to my feet and smoothly accepted her offer of a handshake. I stared into her eyes and found anger simmering in the depths.

"Mr. Swift," she said formally, almost robotically. "Good to meet you."

"It's a pleasure to meet you too. This is my daughter, Anya."

My little angel immediately sprang to her feet and stuck out her hand. Instantly, Montana transferred her entire attention away from me and focused it on her new pupil. Treating me as if I were a complete stranger, she smiled brightly at my daughter.

At that point, her father stood. "I have another appointment, but as mentioned earlier my daughter will give you a tour of our facilities." He turned towards Montana, his eyebrows raised inquiringly. "Everything alright?"

"Of course," she replied grimly.

"Fine. I'll see you later. Have a nice day, Mr. Swift."

Without another word, she went to hold open the door of the office. She remained silent as we walked out of the reception area and onto the spacious hallway of the administrative block. She even pretended not to see me, and I understood that she was probably just trying to recover and regain her composure, or perhaps she was just thinking of how best to ignore me given our history.

Chapter 22
Montana

For a few seconds there I thought I was seeing things. My mind had finally snapped and I was hallucinating. I knew it couldn't be a Cole looka-like because the girls and I had unanimously agreed that he was one in a billion. There was no one else like Cole.

So it had to be him calmly sitting in my father's office.

And he had a daughter, which he didn't tell me about. Although, to be fair it was my great idea to reveal as little about ourselves as possible. Not even last names, as I remember. And when he clasped my hand, I felt so dizzy I was ready to swoon. Thank God, I didn't. I held my nerve and spoke to his daughter instead. And that worked. I felt slightly more grounded.

Even so, I couldn't think straight as I walked away from my dad's office.

Thank heavens, I'd made a list of the places and things to give the new pupil and her parent a tour of on my phone so I pulled it out and went through it.

I stared at it.

The words swam before my eyes. I saw the words Science Lab.

Good idea. It was quite secluded and not currently in use. Given the circumstances, I wanted to be far away from prying eyes so I could try to gather my thoughts.

I turned to go but slammed into an immovable wall named Cole. The impact would have sent me flying if his strong arms had not grabbed my own and kept me upright.

"With or without heels, balance is not your thing, is it?" he noted, close to my ear.

Because I wasn't crazy, I avoided looking directly into his eyes. Instead, I shifted my attention to his daughter. She was a sweet little thing.

"Are you okay, Miss Moore?" she asked, and I turned around and smiled at her.

I plastered a big, fake smile on my face. "I am. Thank you."

She held my gaze, and I held hers simply because I couldn't look at her father, but then she said something that made me even forget he was there for the moment at least.

"You're pretty," she said.

I couldn't believe her compliment because I was, at that moment, a hot, mud-stained mess from working in the field. My gaze flew towards Cole. I couldn't begin to imagine what he must be thinking. The last time he saw me I was all dolled up. Seeing the real me must be a great disappointment.

He smiled at me, and my heart nearly stopped because even though I had convinced myself I hated his guts he seemed just as beautiful as he had been that night in Stormy City.

"She's right," he said softly. "In spite of the mud and all."

I frowned. What the hell was happening to me? I hated this man.

"What are you doing here?" I demanded aggressively, but even as I spat the words out, I knew I shouldn't have uttered them in front of the girl. Instantly my gaze swung to her. She was looking at me curiously. Cole got down on his haunches next to his daughter.

"Did you see the seats outside in the hallway on our way here?"

She nodded solemnly.

"Good. Go sit there and wait for me," he instructed. "And remember, don't leave until I get there. For any reason."

She threw me another inquisitive glance, then skipped away to do as she had been asked.

He straightened and met my gaze. "I just brought my daughter to her new school," he said in response to my aggressive question.

I felt incredibly silly, but then again, he wasn't going to gaslight me into thinking that all of this was normal and that I should just take it all in my stride, without any drama.

"I ... I thought you were just passing through."

"You may have assumed that, but I never divulged that information."

My frown deepened. "Then why didn't you resp-" I started to say, but then I cut myself short. I was beginning to whine, I could hear and feel it, and I swore against that embarrassment.

"You know what it doesn't matter. I'm glad she's here; we'll take good care of her."

I turned around to leave then, but he caught my hand, and immediately my body responded, which infuriated me. I twisted my hand out of his grip and backed away.

"That's inappropriate. Please don't interact with me like that again when we're in such a public setting."

"I understand," he said, but he continued to stare at me in the most inappropriate way. "I didn't respond because-"

"No need," I stopped him with a hand in the air. "No need. It's all water under the bridge now. It will never happen again. You're just one of the parents, and I'm your daughter's teacher. Let's continue on with the tour."

"I didn't respond," he continued as if I had not spoken, "because it was the wrong time for me. Too many things were happening and I couldn't handle a new relationship. It wouldn't have been fair to you. I had to put my daughter's needs before my own."

My heart ran wild in my chest. For me, that night was unbelievable, amazing, out of control. Our chemistry was insane, and things could have got really wild between us. But for him, he simply decided to shut it down because it was inconvenient.

"So you decided to forget I existed?"

"As per our initial agreement, yes."

"Well, I'm fine with that," I lied. "We can continue to maintain the stance that we've never met each other. It will be easy. Our only connection will be your daughter, and as a parent, the interactions between us need only be few and far between."

Every word I had spoken had caused me pain, and he

watched me with a strange expression on his handsome face.

"Alright," he said finally.

I sent him a dry smile then and turned around to leave. I headed over to where he had told Anya to wait, and I was impressed to see her waiting on the bench, still and watchful. She turned as we approached, and a large smile of relief came across her face when she spotted her father. Most kids did not react like that from such a tiny separation.

It made me wonder just where her mother was. I knew absolutely nothing, and it was killing me. But given the terms of our uneasy truce, I decided that it would be best for everyone if I never found out.

Chapter 23
Cole

Once we had agreed that our relationship was to be purely one of a teacher and parent, she conducted the tour without once looking at me again. Addressing all her comments to either my daughter or an invisible being about six inches to my left.

It gave me the chance to stare uninterrupted at her. The hunger was real. In the sunlight her hair glowed, in the dim bunker where their camping equipment was stored, I thought I smelled her heady scent and nearly reached out and touched the delicious curve of her cheek.

"We'll be sleeping outdoors?" Anya asked with amazement for she had never been camping before.

"Yes, under the stars," Montana replied and smiled.

And for the moment, I felt as if I was back in the bar in Stormy City. There, she had smiled like that at me. A real smile.

An old sheepdog came to sniff at us, and Anya got to meet the baby donkey and see the horses in the stables. She petted some farmyard animals through the wooden slats of their pens and even had a fat rabbit put into her arms. To say she was thrilled and impressed would have been an understatement. She was almost jumping on the spot like a rubber ball with excitement.

The cookery room was the last stop of the tour. I was surprised to see it full of mini cookers and ovens. They were really serious about giving children all the life skills required for a good life.

This place compared to Anya's school in New York was like chalk and cheese. No one told us their pronouns and no one cared to ask us ours. The emphasis was completely different. There were no bored children pretending to be cats, dogs or frogs either. All we saw were children who seemed to be fully immersed in activities that engaged them totally.

In spite of my raging hard-on, I was so impressed that by the time we arrived back at the principal's office, I was sure moving Anya to this one was one of the best decisions I had ever made in my life. This experience would ensure that she was hands-on in every aspect of her life in a way that only men were usually expected to be. Not only would the theory be taught to them, but it was fully in conjunction with the practical, and their environs were so adequately equipped for it.

"Are you satisfied with what you saw?" the Principal asked.

"This is an astonishingly good idea, and you and your staff are doing a wonderful job," I told him sincerely.

He beamed with quiet pride. "This was once a ranch.

My father and I started this school just before Montana was born."

He glanced behind me at Montana, and I didn't know what her reaction was, but it was enough for her father to cock his head at her in amusement.

"Well, I'm impressed," I told him. "And I look forward to seeing how my daughter adapts."

"Thank you for your trust, Mr. Swift," he said. "We look forward to doing our very best with your little girl."

With that, the meeting concluded, and Montana was assigned her class.

"It's a half day, but she can join her classmates in the field now," Montana said as she stood to leave.

I watched Anya stand up to follow and a strange sensation of fear filled my chest. When she was out of my sight I couldn't protect her.

"Please take care of her." The pleading desperate words were out of my mouth before I could stop them.

Montana turned and looked at me with surprise for a few seconds, then she nodded. "Don't worry, I will."

She had no clue what I was truly asking, and how I wanted to tell her, explain the real reason I had not called her, but Anya's life was at stake. I couldn't afford to make any mistakes whatsoever. Besides I would rather die than drag her into my mess and endanger her too.

"You've just arrived in town a few days ago, haven't you?" her father asked.

I nodded.

"May I ask why you moved over here from New York? It must be a huge change."

"It is," I replied smoothly. "But I wanted the slower pace and a more practical education for Anya."

"You made the right choice," he approved. Then he took my hand in his and extended a most unusual invitation.

"Are you free tonight by any chance?" he asked.

"I guess so," I replied, surprised by the question.

"Would you like to join me and my daughter for dinner at our home?"

Behind me, I heard Montana gasp with surprise. He must have heard it too but he continued as if he had not.

"It's nothing official. We won't mention school matters whatsoever. It's just our way of welcoming you to our little town. We're a close-knit community. We watch each other's backs."

My old self would have made up an excuse and politely refused, but that part of me was gone. I took the decision to move from the bustling, never-sleeping heart of New York to a sleepy small town because I believed it was the only way for me to effectively monitor and control my surroundings. There was no better surveillance system than the human equivalent of a goldfish bowl where everybody knew everybody and intruders were instantly obvious. The sooner I embedded Anya and me into this community the sooner we would become part of it, and anyone coming from outside of it could be considered with suspicion until proven harmless.

I could feel the waves of anger emanating from Montana, as I replied, "Of course. It would be a pleasure to spend an evening at your home."

"Good," he replied energetically and shook my hand once again.

His daughter hated my guts, but there was something sincere and inviting about him and I warmed to him. He was definitely a guy I could go out and have a few drinks with.

Chapter 24

Montana

"What?" The girls' jaws all dropped open. It would have been funny if I wasn't so churned up inside. We were sitting on the picnic bench in the garden for lunch. The kids were scattered around in groups having the sandwiches they had prepared themselves.

"What-," Kelly started, sounding absolutely confused. "His daughter is here? Right now? He's a parent here? Like an actual parent?"

I nodded morosely, and I slipped a potato chip into my mouth.

"Oh my God. So he's the guy who was doing all the renovation work on Duck's Pond," Natalie deduced.

"So is he like a stalker?" Pearl asked. "I mean, you have to consider that he is giving stalker vibes if he's suddenly so close to you."

"He's not a stalker," I groaned. "He just brought his daughter here."

"Now that you mention it, is she even really his daughter?" Pearl asked. "Maybe she's a paid actor in all of this, and he really just came after you."

"I really think he came here because of you," Pearl said in a hushed voice.

"Stop it, you guys. Him being here has absolutely nothing to do with me. Dad said he'd already enrolled his daughter here last term, but he couldn't get here before that."

"I'm sorry, but I don't believe in coincidences. This is fate," Pearl declared.

I gave her a dry look.

"Going to the Chapel and we're gonna get married," Kelly sang and the others snickered.

"I'm leaving," I said exasperated by their antics, but they pulled me back down.

"Stop being so serious," Natalie scolded. "But let us get serious about this though. I mean, now that he's here and his daughter is in our school, how do you plan to navigate this potentially explosive situation? Are you going to use your Aikido technique?"

Another bout of laughter followed.

"No," I said with a long-suffering sigh, "I'm not bringing any drama into school and definitely not my classroom with his kid's welfare at stake. We're going to keep it all very professional. Strictly teacher and parent relationship."

"Look," Kelly said. "We're all adults here. Trust me, everything can be navigated easily when clear boundaries are set."

"That's what I'm saying," I said.

But she shook her head. "No, we're not saying the same thing. Your boundaries mean 'don't go there', mine is a bit more porous. 'Go there outside work hours, in your free time'. You're just behaving this way because you're pissed that he didn't call. But think about it. Life is short. Why deprive yourself of clean good fun? Why not keep it going with him? I certainly would. You say it was the best night of your life so why blow out the flame when it's still burning so bright, why not let it die out naturally when all the wax is gone? At that time, you can both mutually agree to revert back to a strictly professional relationship as teacher and parent?"

"Wow," I looked at her. "Are these kinds of sticky personal matters usually this easy for you?"

"Yeah," she replied, and I had to smile.

"I agree with Kelly," Pearl said. "For me, I say don't cross your heart when there's no reason. I mean, how many things happen the way we want them to? Maybe this could still develop into something special. You shouldn't walk away so fast because it didn't fit what you expected?"

I was so confused. "So, what are you saying I should do, go after him?"

"No," Pearl replied. "What I'm saying is that if he's coming after you, then let him and embrace that scenario until it comes to an end."

"That, I must admit, is solid advice," Natalie put in. "You're brave with everything else. Why chicken out on this matter?"

"By the way, Dad has invited him to dinner tonight," I said glumly.

"Way to go, Mr. Moore," Kelly approved with a chuckle.

"Methinks Principal Moore is trying to play matchmaker."

I could feel my whole face blaze while the girls cackled like a clan of hyenas at my discomfort.

While the rest of the day wore on, no matter how I tried, I couldn't take my mind off the impending dinner. I wondered if the girls were right. My dad had taken a shine to Cole and thought he would make a suitable suitor for his daughter.

Eventually, the end of the day came to pass, and I grew even more horribly nervous. My stomach was in knots and I actually felt queasy. I usually waited in the playground with my students until they were picked up by their parents. Thus, more often than not, I was exchanging pleasantries and meeting a lot of their parents on a daily basis.

I wanted to avoid meeting with Cole, but I was sure it would start unnecessary gossip and speculation about why I was behaving so differently since Cole showed up. So, I sucked it up and stayed in the playground. My heart was doing somersaults when he arrived.

"Treat him like all others," I chanted to myself over and over again, but I soon realized that might draw even more attention because the moment he arrived, he became an incredibly hot topic, actually, the only topic of conversation for the moms who had come to pick up their kids.

I'm not a materialistic person but when I saw him get out of his car, I felt there was something quite off to me, though. I wasn't exactly sure why, but his car simply didn't suit him. Why would a man as worldly and sophisticated as him drive a car like that? Was that his idea of what a small-town hick drove and he was trying to blend in?

But the moms, I noted very clearly, didn't raise any brows at anything other than the man himself. They all turned from where they had gathered chatting and watched him until he came over to where I was with the kids.

"Daddy!" Anya called as she hurried over to him.

He lowered himself down to her height and gave her a kiss on the cheek, and I knew then that he was legit. At least with her. No kid was that happy to see their parents if they weren't showered with all the affection and love in the world. With her hand tightly in his he straightened and looked at me.

"How was the day, Miss Moore?" he asked.

I could hardly believe this man had laid with me. Seen me naked. Eaten me out. Oh God! I pretended to brush away at a fluff on the sleeve of my top, so I didn't have to look at him and could clear my thoughts.

"Um ... it was good. Same old, same old."

"How did Anya adjust?"

I smiled at her. "Pretty well. She's incredibly active. She might still have some dirt under her nails from working in the flower bed with the other kids, so please wash her hands when she gets home. She's already done so here, but I've taught them to do it again as soon as they return home."

"Will do," he said, his gaze once again meeting mine.

At that moment one of the parents detached herself from the group and sauntered over to him.

"Hello," Marylin Davis greeted. She was a good-looking, slim, fashionable woman in her late twenties. She wore a tight-fitting pink T-shirt and a pair of low-waisted jeans that showed off the strip of flat golden skin on her midriff. Her son was in Pearl's class.

"Hello, Mrs. Davis," I greeted, but I had apparently turned invisible. Or perhaps she just hadn't heard me since she was giving her full attention to Cole, I mean, fluttering her eyelashes and all that.

"Whatever," I muttered under my breath.

I felt unreasonably jealous and irritated. I knew I should expect it though, given the specimen of a man standing before me. Mrs. Davis held out her hand, all sickly smiles, and googly doe eyes, but Cole only looked at her with cold detachment. He wasn't scowling, but there was something about his demeanor that made him instantly unapproachable. Had she paid attention she would have realized it too, but she was too taken by his physical presence and to notice such nuances.

"You're new here, right?" she cooed. I noticed she had retained his hand in a handshake. "I'm Arnold's mother. He is in third grade along with the older kids."

"Oh, right." He nodded and gently pulled his hand away. "I'm Cole, and this is Anya."

"Nice to meet you, Anya. I'm Marilyn."

Anya however, frowned at her. It was quite amusing and I was secretly happy the smart girl was not responding to Mrs. Davis' fake overtures. I turned to look at Cole to see his reaction, and to my surprise, I saw him watching me. Marilyn looked up then too, and I don't think she was particularly happy to see that Cole was watching me rather than her.

"She must be really shy," she said to Cole, "but don't

worry, it's because she's new. She'll loosen up soon and have a wonderful time with the other kids."

Cole lowered his gaze down to his daughter. "Are you shy?"

"No," she replied.

I choked down a laugh. I had to quickly cough to cover the laugh up. Marilyn turned to me, but luckily, I was saved from eye contact because a couple of the other moms had started to walk in our direction as well.

Jeesh, he was popular. I almost rolled my eyes.

"I'll go join the other kids now," I said. "See you tomorrow, Anya."

"No, later tonight. We're coming for dinner, remember?" she reminded loudly.

Ouch! She wasn't supposed to have said that out loud for the other parents to hear and speculate about. I hoped they didn't hear. The last thing I needed was to be the butt of their gossip sessions over coffee.

"Right of course," I said awkwardly.

"It's time to go home now," her father said and tugged on her hand.

"See you later, Miss Moore," she called.

Just as the other women arrived, her father gave a wave and kept going. Marilyn, however, refused to let it go and instead went after him.

Chapter 25
Cole

"Mr. Swift?" the woman Marilyn called, and even though I tried to walk away as fast as I could to deter her, she just came even faster.

"Mr. Swift."

There was no way I could avoid this, so I stopped and turned. Behind her, the other women I had hoped to avoid were trundling towards us like a snowball.

"Sorry, we're in a bit of a rush," I muttered.

"Of course, you are. A man like you must be so busy." She smiled smarmily before the other women ambushed us.

"We wanted to invite you to a little parents' welcome meeting," the leader gushed. "We have a little group here and would, of course, we're a friendly bunch and like to welcome all newcomers to our town."

I looked at them. Yeah, this group of nosy busybodies was perfect.

"That's great. Let me know when, and I will do my very best to make it."

"Oh wonderful," she cried. Excitedly, she pulled out her phone and, so I noticed, did a few of the other women. "Can I have your number then? I'll let you know when the plan has been set in place."

I charmed her with my smile. "I'm not always on my phone. Let me give you my email address instead. That way I'll definitely get your message."

"Alright," she said, but I could see the disappointment on her face.

I spelled my email address out and she put it into her phone. Afterwards, each woman introduced themselves; Nancy, Mary-Beth, Rebecca, and Megan."

"There are a few more of our group you haven't met, and not all moms. A few are dads, but we'll be sure to introduce you to them soon so you both feel more at home here."

"Thank you kindly," I said.

She beamed happily. "Not at all. It'll be a pleasure."

"Have a great day," I said and tugging my daughter's hand, walked away.

Women were always drawn to me and their attention was more often than not a nuisance. I never wanted it, but maybe now it would form a protective net around me. The issue of Paganini appearing in this town loomed over me. I had to remain as vigilant as possible, but maybe these people would act as my early warning signal.

As I got in my car, I couldn't help sneaking a look at the one woman I wanted a lot more from than just an early warning signal. I could never in a thousand years have imagined she would end up as my daughter's teacher. But now that she had been put in that role, I was even more impressed by who she was.

I turned to Anya.

"Why did you frown when Marilyn said hello to you back there?" I asked. "You didn't seem very happy to talk to her."

She bowed her head and said nothing.

"What is it, sweetheart?" I insisted.

"She's okay, but ... she reminds me of Mom."

I stared at my daughter with surprise. She was absolutely right. I couldn't put my finger on it, but I got the same vibes from her that I had got from Arianna. She didn't look like Arianna, but something about her was the same. It was probably why I had been slightly repulsed by her. Just like Arianna, she had big hair, a fit body, fake boobs, and blue eyes. Attractive, of course, but I was done with that type.

"Yeah, you're right," I said. "I almost didn't notice. So what did you think of your teacher, Miss Moore then?"

"She's pretty."

Pretty? More like drop-dead gorgeous, but there was no need to say that out loud.

"Um ... Dad. I think she saw my phone."

"What?"

Her smile was sheepish. "Sorry, Daddy. It fell out."

"We talked about this. Phones are not allowed in this school, and you can't let anyone ever know you have a phone on you. You also can't let anyone ever take it from you. If that happens, call me immediately. I need to be able to reach you at all times."

I was beginning to sound stern, and she had grown quiet and tense.

"I'm sorry, sweetheart," I apologized. "I don't want to scold you. I'm just really trying to be careful."

"I understand," she said. "I'll do better next time."

"Good girl. Now tell me what you studied today."

"We had a history class and we studied about Communism in China."

I turned towards my daughter in surprise. "What?"

"Yeah, we learned about Mao. Did you know he killed 60 million people?"

Yes, I did know that, but I had not expected her to be learning about that at the age of seven. The more I learned about Shadow Wolf Academy, the more impressed I was by it.

Chapter 26
Montana

"Dad, are you sure you don't want me to help?" I asked as I sipped on the beer on the couch.

"Nope," he replied. "I ordered most of it in. You can help with plates and cutlery, and while you're at it you might as well take the trash out too."

"I'd love to transfer the food instead while you get the plates and cutlery and take the trash out."

"Get to work!" he said without acknowledging my observation.

With a sigh, I did as I was told. Sure, I was acting all nonchalant, like I wasn't nervous, excited, and scared all at once, but the truth was that I was immensely conflicted.

I had no clue how tonight was going to go, but I did know that constantly being in his presence was not going to make my decision to maintain a professional relationship with him easy. Plus, I had been to bed with this man. How the hell was I supposed to not be terrified that my father was going to figure out that something was off between the two of us? He knew and understood me better than anyone else, but as far as Dad was concerned, I was his little girl who didn't even know what sex was. To be fair, until I met Cole in Stormy City, that was exactly what I was.

His pure virginal daughter.

"Montana?" My father's voice startled me out of my reverie. He was standing on the back porch with his hands on his hip, a slight frown across his face.

"What are you doing?" he asked.

"Nothing."

"Why are you so distracted?" he demanded.

"I'm not distracted. I was getting a bit of fresh air before your guests arrive."

"Well, they'll be here any minute," he said.

"Yeah, I'm coming," I groaned.

"Hurry up and wash your hands and maybe change?"

"Yeah, yeah," I mumbled to myself until it occurred to me what he had just said. I looked at him curiously. "Change? What does that mean?"

"Just throw something nicer on, you've been in jeans all day."

"These are my new pair of jeans. I had a shower thirty minutes ago, remember?"

"Throw on something else," he said and turning away, went back into the house.

I ran after him because a dark suspicion began to rise in my heart.

"Oh no, you don't just say that and disappear. What do you mean?"

"It's dinner." He sighed. "So maybe a dress?"

I gasped. "You traitor."

He chuckled in amusement.

"I just want what's best for you, sweetheart."

"Jesse is not good enough, but the complete stranger you know nothing about who rolls into town is."

"I like him. I'm not going to be around forever, so if I see someone I think is going to be good for you, I'm going to point you in that direction to see if anything positive happens as a result."

I was silent because it took me a few seconds to process this.

"He has a kid. You don't mind?" I asked, still surprised.

"So? She's young, and the way he takes care of her, tells me he's a fine man and a good provider. Trust me, you could do worse. Why do you think I've never suggested anyone else to you? Plus, there's something about him. He's no ordinary hick even if he's pretending he is. I sense a refinement and a sense of culture, and can you blame me that I want you to be associated with the best?"

"Dad, you're talking as if you want to get rid of me."

"But someday I won't be any here longer, and I don't want to leave without ensuring you're taken care of."

"Then don't leave, Dad," I said.

"Ever?" he asked, with a little teasing smile.

I stared at him and the back of my eyes began to sting.

"Sorry, Buttercup," he said gently. "That knock on the door is coming for me. Just like it came for your mother."

Chapter 27
Cole

I drove through the gates of the ranch and felt a strange sense of homecoming, belonging even. Strange, as I had grown up in the busy-busy-busy city with skyscrapers all around me and people packed as tightly as sardines, and all these peaceful rolling sparse lands should have been unnerving, but I found it relaxing and welcoming.

"Mr. Swift," her father greeted warmly, his hand outstretched.

"Cole. Please, call me Cole."

"Cole," he echoed, smiling broadly. "And you must call me Noah."

"I will," I said. "Say hello, Anya," I softly squeezed my daughter's shoulder, and she complied.

"Good evening, Mr. Moore," she greeted softly, and I smiled down with pride.

"Good evening, Anya," he greeted, taking her tiny hand in his. "Welcome to my home. I've got a good meal and a terrific dessert for you, and I hope you'll enjoy it."

"I'm sure I will," she said politely, then looked up at me.

"She's so well-behaved," Noah remarked.

"She knows which side of her bread is buttered," I replied indulgently.

"They all do," he said and then turned around to look at his daughter. The one I hadn't been able to stop thinking about ever since I saw her again in his office. Even now, I was so aroused I wondered how I was going to get through tonight. There was something about her pouty expression that made me want to rip her clothes off and suck her pussy. I didn't even need to close my eyes to picture her... panting, her body bathed in a sheen of sweat and her eyes rolling into the back of her head.

I couldn't remember a time when I was this crazy for a woman. There was no denying it, and if I wasn't careful her father would be throwing me out of his house soon.

I turned towards her. I couldn't take my eyes off her. "Miss Moore."

"Good evening, Mr. Swift," she said coldly.

"Good evening, Miss Moore," Anya greeted, and just like that, her expression changed. From being aggravatingly pouty and cold, she straightened, her face lighting up. Her lips curved and she beckoned Anya over. A few seconds later Anya was enveloped in her arms. I was somewhat surprised to see it. I knew that Anya liked her, but the ease in their relationship was somehow surprising to see.

"Where are all the animals?" Anya asked shyly.

"It's not a working ranch anymore," Montana replied.

"Why not?"

Montana glanced at her father and a look passed between them. "Well, because my grandfather decided he didn't want it to be a ranch anymore, and he and my father started a school instead on the west plot of the land."

"Oh, okay," Anya said thoughtfully. "Where's your Mom?"

"Anya," I cautioned. "Don't pry into other people's business."

"That's okay," Montana said, with a small smile. "My mother passed away a long time ago."

"So you live with your Dad like me?" Anya said with a huge smile.

Montana smiled. "Of course. This way I can pester him all day long."

Anya's peal of laughter was infectious. "I pester my dad a lot as well."

"As you should," Montana said firmly. "It's our duty as daughters." She held out her hand for a high five, and Anya smacked it enthusiastically.

"Come on in. The food is getting cold," her father said, and I returned my attention to him. He was not one to miss anything and I was certain he gave me a knowing smile.

Dinner was meatloaf, vegetables and roasted potatoes."

"This is incredibly thoughtful, thank you," I said, unsure of who to look at as my gaze switched between father and daughter.

"We spent all afternoon whipping these up," Montana said.

Her father turned to her and frowned, but she smiled back brightly at him, and I knew then that she was lying.

"There was no time to do all these personally," he explained. "I got the meal from Mrs. Sheridan. She makes the most wonderful dinners. However, for dessert, you'll be having brownies that were made by Montana and ice cream, made by me. We whipped them up last Sunday."

"Bought or not, I deeply appreciate the gesture," I said.

I put a forkful of meatloaf into my mouth and instantly became a fan of Mrs. Sheridan's cooking. It was easily one of the most delicious things my tongue had ever tasted.

After Montana's sweet pussy, obviously.

Chapter 28
Montana

Throughout the meal, I was aware of my father's watchful gaze and Cole's intense scrutiny. The only person without an ulterior motive who was simply enjoying herself was Anya. Oh, what a joy it was to be a child. Innocent and free of worries and scheming.

I thought of her mother and wondered if it would be appropriate to ask her about it. Probably not. I didn't want to come across as a prying, snooping busybody.

"Do you have any special requirements for Anya?" I asked. I made sure to look directly in his eye, as I did with the other parents, or else my dad was sure to make a mountain out of a molehill.

"Not really. What sort of things did you have in mind?" he replied evenly, but because he gave his whole attention to me, it was unnerving.

My God, he really was so unfairly beautiful. I took a sip of wine. I might already have drunk too much out of sheer nervousness.

"Anya was excellent today. She participated in all the

activities, but considering she is from the city, I wondered if she might have special needs. Perhaps her mother would know..."

Something flashed in his eyes, but his expression and voice remained neutral. "If at any point something comes up, I'll be sure to let you know, and of course, I'm always open to your recommendations."

"Alright," I nodded and stabbed a piece of carrot with my fork. That attempt to find out about Anya's mother sure fell flat on its face. Only recently, I'd finally managed to convince myself I could forget about him, but now that he was back in my life, I didn't know how to resist him.

"Montana, are you alright?" my father asked.

I turned to him, startled by the question. He raised his eyebrows at me and it was only then I realized I was repeatedly stabbing a piece of carrot. I instantly corrected this by putting the mangled vegetable into my mouth and chewing vigorously.

"I'm great," I replied robotically. "Just a little tired."

"That can't be right," he said with a smile. "You're never tired. Your stamina is unbelievable."

This statement he directed at Cole, and I wished he hadn't because I knew Cole would see my father's innocent compliment in a sexual light. I couldn't help but glance over at Cole, hoping he wouldn't disappoint me, but he behaved true to form.

"She does seem like the kind to be able to go all day and all night," he said.

I nearly choked on the piece of carrot I'd been chewing for the last five minutes.

I fumed at him, but he smiled and winked at me.

Quickly, I returned my attention to my father. Thank God, he was picking up his wine glass and didn't notice.

Blissfully unaware of the undercurrents between Cole and me, my father continued. "She has loved the outdoors since she was a kid, and I think that's where her great energy mainly comes from."

I smiled then and rose to my feet. "I need to go check on something in the kitchen. I'll be back soon, please excuse me."

"Of course," both men replied.

I gave Anya a much-deserved smile for stressing me out the least, then took my leave. I headed straight to my room because frankly, I needed to lie down. My head was swirling. Probably a mixture of confusion and grade-A lust.

I went out to the back porch, pulled out my phone, and face-timed Pearl. She was sitting on her bed eating ice cream directly from the carton. In the background, I could hear the faint sounds of the video game she was playing.

"My father made me wear a damn dress! And I swear this dinner is some sort of test. There's a swarm of alligators waiting underneath to devour me if I lose my footing and fall," I grumbled when she answered.

"Wow, that's unnecessarily dramatic," she said.

"It's how I feel."

She sucked her spoon. "Yeah, I got that from your attitude all morning."

"I wasn't sulky or anything like that, was I?"

"Not sulky, but you were definitely on edge," she countered, "and you have been for the past several days. In fact, ever since Stormy City. And now it's incredibly obvious why, so..."

She paused, mischievous as usual, and I rolled my eyes at her. "So what?"

"You need to make a definite decision, or else you'll keep being tormented... and unstable."

"You make me sound like a mental case."

Then she asked in a no-bullshit voice, "Are you falling in love with him, Montana?"

My immediate reaction was to deny it, but what was the point in lying to myself and further tormenting myself?

"Maybe," I replied, "so far, I mean..."

"I understand," she agreed sagely.

"You do?"

"Of course I do. You really, really, really like him and you want more, but you also know he doesn't want that. However, you don't know how to move on so you're stuck in this maze in your head, trying to figure a way out."

This, though it made me feel uncomfortable, sounded immensely accurate to me.

"Am I wrong?" she asked.

"Stop gloating," I admonished.

She laughed. "I'm so good at this I should become a psychiatrist."

"He's in the dining room right now. What should I do?"

"Observe him," she said. "What if, unbeknownst to you, he wants more as well? Have you asked? I mean, he has a daughter. Every single dad with a daughter I've ever known has always wanted someone in their lives to help guide their daughter."

I went silent.

"What's really holding you back? The fear of being rejected? But you're a woman, and you should know how to take the hint. Which means that an outright rejection is not on the cards."

I found myself nodding at her 'soft rejection theory' because this made a lot of sense, but for some reason, sounded implausible.

"Why don't you hint at what you want? What's the worst that could happen?"

"I embarrass myself beyond any hope?"

"If you're too cowardly to take him on, let Kelly have him. She is smart enough to never look a gift horse in the mouth."

The might of the black jealousy that slammed into my body at the thought of Kelly being with Cole was unbeliev-able. Until I met Cole, I really thought I was a mild person, and jealousy was not part of my nature, but since meeting Cole, I've become the quintessential green-eyed monster.

"Before Kelly goes for Cole she should prepare her grave," I snarled.

Pearl laughed uproariously and I was about to say more when the door behind me opened. I thought it was Dad, but to my surprise it was Cole. My heart jumped into my throat.

"Call you back," I croaked to Pearl and cut the connection.

Chapter 29
Cole

She tried her best to act as if we were strangers, but up close, I could almost convince myself that if I just reached out, I could kiss her, and she would respond. Her eyes were clear and alluring as she watched me, her lips plump and rosy, and her scent of vanilla and lime intoxicating.

"Is there a problem?" she asked, glancing behind me. "Where's my dad?"

"He went out to get some wine."

She nodded. "Oh, do you need help?"

I continued to stare at her. "Toilet paper, Anya went to use the guest restroom, but there's no toilet paper. She's in there right now."

Her eyes widened. "Oh shoot. Forgot, Sorry. We don't get many guests."

She darted towards the door behind me and I had no choice but to follow her. I waited in the kitchen while she grabbed a roll out of the pantry and emerged with it in hand.

"Will you take it to her, or do you want me to?" she asked.

"Let's go together," I replied.

She nodded and we walked side by side down the corridor. "Here's your toilet paper delivery," she said.

"Thank you, Miss Moore," Anya said and quickly shut the door.

Montana started to move away, but it was so private in that hallway that I couldn't stop myself from catching her hand. She yanked it away violently and while rubbing the area I had touched, faced me.

"Um... is there a problem?" she asked in a cold voice.

For a few seconds, I stared at her. I wanted her so bad it fucking hurt, but perhaps this was neither the time nor the place to be doing this.

"No," I replied and turned away, but her hand closed around my wrist. My eyes fluttered closed. My body remembered her touch. Oh, how my body remembered it. I released a deep breath and then turned to look at her. Instantly, I detected the doubts gathering in her eyes. She was full of questions and doubts. There was only one way to solve this issue.

I slid my hand around the back of her neck, pulled her towards me and kissed that bewitching mouth. I remained alert to the fact that her father was around, but she threw herself completely into the kiss. She ground her mouth against mine. A movement that was ferocious, almost angry. There was not a trace of shyness about the way she responded. It was as though kissing me was all she had been able to think about, and now that she had found this opportunity, she wasn't going to waste it.

The toilet flushed, and she jerked away abruptly. Her chest was heaving and her eyes were wide as she stared into my eyes. The door opened, and Anya appeared. She didn't seem surprised to see us both standing there.

"Were you two waiting for me?" she asked innocently.

"Kind of," Montana replied in a shaky voice. "Are you done?"

"Yes, I am."

Montana spared me one last glance before she turned her whole attention on Anya. "Alright, let's go get some brownies and ice cream."

"I snuck a brownie to eat earlier on," Anya confessed.

Montana pretended to gasp.

"I'm sorry." Anya laughed. "But it looked so good."

"Yes, they do. Make sure to tell my dad that as soon as he comes back."

I stood there, my cock still hard, and watched as they turned and disappeared around the corner.

"Will he teach me how to make them?"

"Ask him when he gets back. Make sure to look extra cute while asking so he agrees."

I could still hear their voices in the distance, but the words were indistinct. I leaned against the wall, deep in thought. This was not supposed to happen. More than at any time in my life, I was supposed to be vigilant and careful, but here I was unable to stop thinking of fucking her. It was not fair to her. I would be intentionally putting Montana in danger without her knowledge.

I sighed then and headed out to join them. They were seated next to each other at the table, exchanging mischievous looks as they chewed on the brownies. I took my seat and Anya held out the last piece she had in her hand to me.

"Have some, Dad," she said. "It's really good."

I frowned as I looked at her. "Did you wash your hands?"

She stopped, her eyes widening, and I gave her a stern look. "Oh, did you use those hands to give Miss Moore a brownie?"

"No!" She immediately protested. "She picked one up herself and broke it in half for the both of us."

"Good, but imagine if you had."

"Sorry," she said.

"It's okay. Now go in now to wash your hands."

Without a word, she hurried back to the bathroom. "You really decided to guilt-trip the baby because you wanted us—"

She caught herself, as she realized how inappropriate and presumptive she would sound, and flushed red.

"Because I wanted us alone? Is that what you were about to say?" I asked softly.

She lifted up her glass of cranberry juice, got up, and she was about to walk away when I caught her hand.

"Escaping again?" I asked.

"Not escaping, I got stuff to do."

Her tongue lightly grazed the top of her lips. I didn't even know if it was intentional or if she was just trying to drive me mad, but whatever it was, it was working. I could see my daughter through the window. She had found a white cat and was playing with it. Fortunately for her, I heard her father's heavy step returning from the wine cellar. He was heading for the dining room.

I had no option but to let her go, but before I did, I slipped my hand under her dress, grabbed her pussy, and pushing aside the crotch of her panties, I thrust my middle finger into her. She was so soaking wet that my finger made a squelching sound.

She gasped in shock and glared at me, but I was far from apologetic.

"Should I be sorry?" I growled, as I roughly rammed my finger in and out of her.

Her mouth opened and closed in shock. It was taboo, dirty, and quick, but I knew she was so turned on, that she was already close to a climax. I had no intention of giving her release, though. No, she was going to suffer as I did. I could hear her father leave the dining room and make his way in our direction. Her eyes were wild with desire. Staring at her flushed face, I pulled my finger out and smeared her own slickness on her lips, before I casually moved away from her.

She was breathing hard when her father walked in.

"Ah, there you all are," her father noted.

"Hey, Dad," she greeted thickly, but I noticed she didn't dare turn and look at him.

"Where's the little one?" he asked, and I could see that he had noticed the thick atmosphere in the room because he was looking intently at his daughter's back.

"Outside. Looks like she found your cat," I said casually.

"Montana, can you check if we have any grapes left in the fridge? It'll be nice to have some with the cheese I got from Alan."

"Alright," she said and walked over to the fridge, but her voice was still shaky as fuck.

Chapter 30
Montana

I found the grapes and washed some, but I was shaking. My fingers were trembling. I stared out of the window. Anya had pulled Tolstoy into her arms and was kissing his head. The sun was setting on the horizon and the sky was red. Everything looked so normal.

But...

Wow!

What the fuck just happened?

If it had been one second later, my father would have come and seen Cole with his hand up my skirt finger-fucking me. What a risk he took! My father's estimation of him as something special would go down the drain. He would have become nothing more than a sexual pervert.

My dad would never have understood.

My dad would never believe that I was dripping for that sexual pervert. That I wanted him to keep on finger fucking me until I climaxed.

That way he had grabbed me had instantly drained the

strength out of my legs. The shock and pleasure had sent bolts of electricity through my entire body, and now I was so worked up I needed him more than ever. As I returned to the table with the grapes I realized he had turned the tables on me.

Cole called Anya and she came running in. Everyone was seated at the table. The new bottle of wine was opened.

I wished more than anything that I could just leave. That we could both leave right now and head over to his house so we could just spend the next several hours in each other's arms. Fucking until we both forgot our names.

I watched as he drank his wine and conversed with my father, and my blood began to boil. He was so elegant, so sophisticated, so cultured, so fucking charming...

"Did you grow up in New York?" I asked suddenly.

Both men turned to me, somewhat startled to hear me speak, and it was only then I realized I had most likely interrupted them. I was immediately horrified at being so engrossed in my own world and fantasies about him that I had ignored basic human manners.

"I'm so sorry," I apologized. "Dad, I'm so sorry, did I cut you off?"

My father laughed, but he looked at me strangely. "No, sweetie, you didn't. You're so quiet I'm sometimes startled when you speak." He turned to Cole. "She's like that, you know. She gets lively, then goes mute for a period of time, thinking, contemplating, and watching. It's interesting, because..."

"Dad, there's nothing interesting about going silent after talking too much," I protested because I was embarrassed.

But Cole was having none of it. "I completely understand you, Noah. Everything Anya does is interesting to me too. I think our personalities are quite similar and I absolutely love that."

My dad went quiet. "You're a good man, Cole. I'm glad you came to our town." Then he turned and gave me a soft, kind smile that genuinely brought tears to my eyes. It's been so long since he had looked at me like that. I had to look away to collect myself.

"You grew up in New York?" my dad asked.

Cole nodded.

"What do you do for a living, Cole?"

"I'm an accountant."

"So you'll be needing new clients..."

He cut a bit of meat. "I guess so."

"Are you good at what you do?"

"The best." He said it simply the way one would state a fact.

My father must have believed him, because he said, "Our accountant is retiring next year. You can have us as your client if you want. We'll give it a year and take it from there."

Cole nodded. "Sure. Why not?"

"Good." My dad rose to his feet and tapped down on his stomach. "I think I need to take a nap, I'm a bit drowsy."

"It's the wine," I said, and he gave me a look.

"Most probably. I'll help you clean up when I get up. See you later."

"Happy sleeps, Dad," I said.

He nodded and turned to Cole. "It was a great pleasure hosting you today, Mr. Swift." He offered his hand for a shake, and Cole earnestly accepted it.

"The pleasure was all mine," Cole said.

I couldn't help but be amused as I watched the two of them. They sounded so formal and strict, and it was truly amusing. My dad left then, leaving me to my own devices, and I could almost have sworn it was on purpose.

Chapter 31
Cole

I didn't want to waste the very blatant opportunity her father had given us both to be alone. I got up, found a bowl, put a brownie, as well as a scoop of ice cream in it, and handed it to Anya.

"Go enjoy this out on the porch with Tolstoy. I'll come and get you when this mess is cleared up," I said.

She grinned happily and hurried out through the back door. The moment it was shut, I turned to look at the woman standing before me.

"Successfully gotten rid of all external parties, I see?"

I laughed and started helping her gather the dirty dishes. "One of the joys of being a parent is never having to clear up, especially when you cook dinner. Too bad I won't get to enjoy that from Anya today. All because of you."

Her mouth opened. "You're blaming me? I'm not the one who sent her out to share her dessert with the cat."

"But we need to be alone, don't we?" I asked. "Even if it's just doing the dishes."

She said nothing and silently we cleared the table and

she joined me at the sink. Soon enough, all the dishes were done, and the rubbish bag was tied and ready to be taken out to the trash can.

"What next, Montana?" I asked.

She shrugged. "You tell me."

"About time we talked, huh?"

I held her gorgeous Montana gaze. "How about we skip the talking and ... um ... have some fun one more time?"

I was surprised to hear this, but at the same time, curious as to why she would say that. She read my expression and instantly provided an answer.

"I don't know, I feel as if you're not really ready for something serious right now, and I don't want to force or trick you into anything you're not 100% into. I don't do casual relationships, but that one time with you ... apparently wasn't enough to get you out of my system, so I'm proposing maybe we hook up and fuck like rabbits until we don't want to anymore."

I grinned at her. She couldn't have said anything more perfect. Little sweetheart had no idea that I had plans for her, for us. I couldn't tell her yet, but the day would come when I would claim her for my own. She was already mine. She just didn't know it yet.

"Deal," I said.

"I didn't imagine it would be so simple to talk to you."

"I'm a pretty simple guy."

She shook her head in disagreement and disbelief. "For some reason, I find that very difficult to believe."

Chapter 32
Montana

My clit was still throbbing and I felt like an addict.

Even so, I was certain that I had survived the night until we went outside and I noticed that the windows of his car were tinted. Of course, my mind had registered it earlier on when he'd come to the school, but as I stood staring at it now, I couldn't believe the insane ideas that were rushing into my mind. I didn't want to have sex. Way too dangerous with my father just shouting distance away. I just wanted to see his gorgeous cock again.

He threw the trash bag into the bin, then stopped to look at me. "What's so interesting about my car?"

I dragged my eyes away and looked at him. "Why do you drive such a deliberately ordinary car?"

He seemed surprised by my question. "It's what I can afford, I guess."

I didn't need to see the slight amusement in his eyes to know he was playing with me. I gave him a look of disbelief.

He shrugged and turned to glance back at it. "It has all

the bells and whistles of a sports car. I guess I just wanted to see what I could do with such an old model. More interesting than a new one, isn't it?"

"Can you give me a tour of the inside?" I asked, not believing what was coming out of my mouth.

He narrowed his gaze at me then looked toward the house, and nodded. "Let's go."

I didn't dare look up. My father's room was on the side that faced the backyard, but still, I didn't want to imagine that he could see. I was probably going to piss my pants if I thought he was watching. Still, the windows were tinted.

I got into the passenger side.

"We're just talking," I said as soon as I shut the door.

He smiled and activated the locks. "Sure. We'll be using our mouths most definitely."

I stared ahead quietly for a few moments, and then he did that thing I absolutely adored. He wrapped his hand around the back of my neck and leaned in to kiss me. His lips were soft and sweet, and in seconds, I lost myself. All I could do was feel the rush of red, torrid lust filling my veins, and listen to my heart raging inside my chest.

The added danger of the thrill of the possibility of getting caught was definitely part of the equation. I tried to control my breathing, tried to control how much what he was doing affected me, but it was no use. At the back of my mind, I understood we couldn't go for long, because of Anya. I grabbed the buckle of his belt

"Keep talking, Montana," he said, and adjusted himself, inclining his seat and leaning back comfortably.

I was hyper-focused on what I wanted to the point of it being an obsession. I needed ... needed to see his gorgeous cock once again. I felt as if I was spiraling out of control and I could never have believed that this incredibly promiscuous side of me existed. The side that I couldn't even wait to find somewhere decent first to fulfil my lust.

As the flushed, pulsing head of his cock was revealed, all of my doubts vanished like smoke into thin air. I watched it, mesmerized and hungry, leaned down and took the broad head in my mouth.

"Hmm," I savored it with a deep moan, sucking and licking across it with my tongue.

I could feel his reaction in the harshness of his breathing and the way his back was now straight as a rod against the back of the seat. In that tiny space, it was impossible to miss the intensity of what I was doing to him. Sounds filled the space and echoed around.

I committed all of it to memory.

Pulling away, I gazed greedily at the glistening, clean tip. When I lifted my eyes up to him there was something akin to wonder in his eyes. I relished the moment, but I needed more of him, so I lowered once again, and this time, I tried to take him all the way to the root.

It was difficult though because he was fucking big. Perhaps even bigger than I had judged. And so, I had to adjust, taking him all the way back to my throat to see where he would end. I soon found out, but it was difficult to take, so I pulled out.

In love, I rubbed the entire rock-hard length and felt it swell even further at my touch. I urged spills of pearly precum back to the root, then I leaned forward once again with my mouth to suck him weak. He moaned softly, his hand gripping the steering wheel handle, and his head thrown back, his face to the ceiling of the car.

I watched the Adam's apple on his strong, brown throat bob convulsively. I sucked and pumped him even harder. With both my hands grasping the base of his shaft, my mouth worked in tandem to ensure that he forgot his name. Perhaps he did because for the next several moments, only mine fell from his lips, in soft pants almost as a warning to himself, in adoration, in hunger.

Each of them spurred me on as I went even faster, my singular focus to have him unravel in my hands. He always seemed a bit too composed, I realized. Too in control, impossible to be flustered. And so, I loved the fact that I could make him lose control.

Holding my head gently, he pumped softly into my mouth, and I increased the strength of my suction. Groaning, he collapsed back into the seat and tried to catch his breath.

"Fuck, you're good," he praised. "Too good. Fuck."

I was sucking a man's cock outside my father's home. I couldn't believe it, yet at the same time, it made me so incredibly excited. Shutting my eyes, I milked him of every ounce of pleasure until my jaw ached, until he grabbed me and warned me to stop because he was coming.

Ignoring him, I held on, and his release flooded my mouth. It shot down my throat and I took it all. I lapped up the strands of semen around my lips and made sure to lick up and down his still-hardened rod. I loved the sight of him oozing out, still pulsing and greedy, and so I pulled him into my mouth again.

I sucked in until I could no longer remain in the position, bent over, aching. I straightened and turned to the man beside me, who still had his eyes shut, his cock out, and his chest heaving. I leaned forward and pressed a kiss against his cheek.

"I'm going to send Anya out," I told him. "Is that alright?"

It took him a few seconds, but soon he opened his eyes and turned his iridescent irises towards me.

"Yeah, thank you," he replied, more softly than I had ever heard him speak before.

I smiled, but just before I turned to go, he grasped my hand, angled his head, and caught my lips in the slowest, sweetest, most sensual kiss.

It was as though he was trying to solidify this moment between us in my memory. As though he was trying to ensure that no matter what, I never forgot it. But how was it even possible that I would?

About a minute later, he pulled away, and there was absolutely nothing to say between us. In fact, it was almost dangerous at the moment to speak, as I had no idea what nonsense would spout. Perhaps I would get on my knees and ask him to marry me because right then, it was all I could think about.

Thankfully, I was able to compose myself albeit on shaky feet as I pushed the door open and got out of the car. I headed back into the house and, to my surprise, found the little girl on the porch. Her bowl of ice cream and brownie was finished, and she had fallen asleep on the cushions of the swing. Cuddled in her little arms was Tolstoy, which was very surprising because Tolstoy hated strangers. He hissed and avoided them as much as possible.

Anya looked so sweet and angelic against all that white fur that I couldn't help but wonder once again about her mother. Where was she? Who was she? I had been merely curious before, but now I really wanted to know in a way that was overwhelming.

But I had to wait for her father to tell me. Gently, I lifted her into my arms and took her back out to meet her father.

Chapter 33
Cole

M atthew called just as I drove out of the ranch gates. He had good news. I wasn't surprised though. For the price I was asking, it was a steal.

"I told you it would go fast," Matthew said.

"Yes, you did. Well done," I congratulated softly, as I plugged in my headphones, my gaze moving quickly to the strapped-in sleeping baby beside me.

"The sale price minus costs is already in your bitcoin wallet. I transferred it myself."

"Thanks, Matthew. Really appreciate it."

"No problem. Always a pleasure doing business with you, Luca."

I had so completely integrated myself into my role as Cole, that hearing someone call me Luca felt strange. "Take care."

I ended the call and looked over at my daughter. She was sleeping peacefully. Even she had completely morphed into Anya. Not once during the dinner had her mask slipped. Many times Noah had tried to draw her out with questions and every single time she had stayed within her script. She had played her 'pretend game' perfectly. I felt both sad that she was enveloped in so many lies and proud that she had carried her part so naturally.

My thoughts returned to Montana, the woman who had just minutes earlier turned this old banger of a car into a pleasure seat. A smile curved my lips. My mother's life had taught me silver linings were a myth, but what was happening to me now was incredibly interesting. I moved away from danger, and by a stroke of incredible luck and magic ran again into what had to be the most beautiful woman in the world.

Montana was everything a man could want in a woman. She is the dream find. I literally couldn't ask for better. She was everything! Sassy, loyal, funny, and extremely sexy. Who would believe that after living for years in the city with its millions of inhabitants I would find someone like her in a tiny town like Bison Ridge?

My telephone rang. It was Leila, I'd hired her to be the go-between, the extra layer of separation between me and my private investigator, Tom. This way even if Tom got careless and was in some way compromised, there were no trails for Paganini to follow back to me.

"Any news?" I asked.

"You sure kicked that hornet's nest. It's been going crazy here. They even paid a visit to your mother's previous care home. Paganini is incandescent with rage. The guy was so livid he threw a tantrum at the restaurant when he first heard the news. Smashed up the table and scared all the other customers. Tom says heads have rolled since."

Sweet Poison

"What about Arianna? Any news on her?"

"Tom got someone to befriend the Chef and he says her meals are brought up to her. It's clear she is now locked away in one of the rooms upstairs. Don't worry though, nothing's going to happen to her. She's the one card he's got left to play."

I couldn't feel too bad for Arianna. Her freedom was gone, but she was safe for the moment. What did she expect from a Mafia Kingpin? Sunshine, flowers, and unicorn farts forever.

"What about my father? Any change in his condition?"

"No. Your father is valuable to Paganini. He's paid for him to stay alive in luxury all this time and soon he'll be wanting his pound of flesh back. Your dad will be working for him till the day he dies."

I exhaled softly. "Good work, Leila. Contact me again if there's anything I should know."

"I know that this is a delicate time for you and your daughter," Leila said, "but I want to assure you that Tom has eyes on everyone that needs to be monitored and everything is under control."

"Right. Thanks."

"By the way, your car was sold yesterday at 2:54 p.m. to the son of a Mexican multi-millionaire, drug money. His girlfriend is Russian, but they're both harmless. Young. No connection to Paganini. Just saw it and couldn't resist the quick purchase. We'll keep our eyes on the house sale as well and ensure nothing leads back to you."

"Fantastic," I replied and ended the call.

After those two calls, I could breathe easier and try to concentrate on settling down in Bison Ridge. I looked to the side to see that Anya was stirring several times. She opened her eyes and smiled sleepily at me. "Daddy," she whispered.

"The ice cream put you down?" I asked.

She straightened in her seat. "Tolstoy was cute. Can we have a cat, Daddy?"

"Maybe. Let's settle down first, okay?"

"Okeydokey."

As we drove into our driveway, I was surprised to see a blue Toyota parked in front of our home. An obviously peroxide blonde wearing a pink dress got out of the car. She was carrying a box. Anya and I walked towards her. The sight of her surprised me. I never expected to see her type grow in the countryside. She was one of those completely plastic girls that thrived in big cities. Everything about her was fake. Her lips, her hair, her nose, her boobs.

"Yoo Hoo," she called and raising her hand high above her head waved as if she was the heroine in a movie.

I raised a half-hearted hand.

"Well hello, Cole," she cooed, before looking down at my daughter. "And you must be Anya. What a pretty little thing you are." She looked up at me again. "I'm Tiffany."

"Hi, Tiffany."

I thought I'd bring you something I baked to welcome you."

I took one look at those fake-ass fingernails and knew this girl didn't even know where the kitchen was, let alone bake anything.

"That's nice of you," I said politely.

"We're all nice around here," she said and batted her eyelashes at me.

I blinked. I never knew women still did that. Wow!

"Well," I said, holding out my hand towards the box. "Thanks for the welcome gift."

"Tell you what. Why don't we all go in and I'll put the kettle on and we can all have a piece of this delicious apple and blueberry pie."

"Actually, it's late and it's nearly bedtime for this monkey here."

"Oh, right." Suddenly she dropped to her haunches and smiled at Anya. "I love your shoes. Gucci is the best, isn't it? And this is the most iconic design of that whole line from the season. You, young lady, have excellent taste."

"They're not real," Anya said quickly. I could hear the panic in her voice. "My dad bought them at the flea market. They're fakes. We couldn't afford the real ones."

"Let me see," Tiffany said with a frown, and lifted one wing of the butterfly on the shoe. "Hmmm." Then she stood and looked at me, and her face was contemplative. "Maybe I can invite you and your daughter to have some ice cream with me."

"Yes, why not," I said and forced a smile.

"Right then. I'll be off, but no doubt I'll see you around very soon." She turned around and sashayed over to her car. We waved as she sped off.

"You want to have ice cream with her?"

"Nope."

I laughed. "Bath time and an early night, don't you think?"

"Daddy?"

"Yeah."

"Can we ask Miss Moore to come over for dinner?"

I looked at her, surprised. "Why?" I asked, eager to hear her explanation.

"I like her. We have already gone to visit her, so it should be our turn to invite her over, right? It's only polite."

"Well, Winnie, that is a fantastic idea. Go ahead and invite her," I replied.

"Can I ask her to bring Tolstoy too?"

Now I understood why she wanted to have Miss Moore over. I grinned at her. "Sure."

Her eyes instantly lit up at my agreement. "Thank you," she cried and ran into the house.

While she had her bath I quickly checked the perimeters of the house to ensure that everything was exactly as I had left it. Then I turned off the lights and reviewed some of the surveillance clips from the day.

So far, no one had come around or stopped in some car and watched from a distance. They were still unaware of where I had moved to, but I didn't expect that to continue for too long. Paganini was not a man to just give up. His motto was if you fail, try and try again, until you find the motherfucker and make him pay.

Anya called out to me and I headed over to her bedroom. I tucked her in, read to her, and going through our ritual of telling her not to let the bed bugs bite her, I returned to my own room for a shower.

Then I called my mother's nurse for an update. I got to speak to the Hungarian woman and I was pleased to hear that my mother was settling in well. I was even happier to hear that she finished a second portion of her favorite meal. I asked to be put on speaker phone and for a few minutes, I spoke to my mother. It was a monologue of course, but I lived in hope. That she could hear me and know that I'd never stopped loving her. That I'd always be there for her, no matter what. As long as there was breath in my body, I would never let her go.

I was lying propped up in bed and closing off some of my old clients' accounts when there was a knock on my door. I didn't think. My survival instincts immediately went into overdrive. Flinging the computer aside, I jumped out of bed and rushed to open the door.

Anya standing there, desperately clutching her favorite stuffed animal close to her body. I didn't need to ask her to know that something had terrified her.

"I didn't die. I just... I had a bad dream," she whispered.

Relief washed over me. It was just a nightmare. It would have been abnormal if she didn't have nightmares. So many changes had happened to her within the last few days, and so far, she had adjusted, and I loved her for it, but she was still just a child, it was too much too soon.

"Want to sleep here with me tonight?" I asked.

She nodded.

"Come on then," I said and brought her into my bed. Soon her little body was tucked cozily in my arms, but she didn't fall asleep right away. I could hear her heart still beating erratically.

"What was your dream about?"

"I'm not sure," she whispered.

I knew it was a lie and it saddened me, but I had to accept as she grew older, she would keep even more secrets from me.

"Goodnight, sweetheart. Don't let the bed bugs bite you."

She nodded against my chest. "Goodnight, Daddy."

Chapter 34

Montana

"He's not here?" Pearl asked. She was leaning against a table edge in the Pottery room and munching on a bag of popcorn.

I heard the question alright but I ignored it because I didn't really think I had any business answering for Cole.

Pearl refused to take the hint. "Most parents are here. Everyone looks forward to these Friday events. Did you call him?"

I pulled my head out of the oven I had been so diligently cleaning and turned to her with a wry expression. "Thanks a lot," I muttered.

"Why?" She popped another handful into her mouth.

"I just hit my head."

She looked entertained. "That's not my fault."

"He should be here, though. Do you think he didn't get the message? The moms are all waiting for him."

I looked up and could see a cluster of parents gathered around the punch station. The women were all dressed in their best.

"Hmmm ... This is supposed to be a session with parents supporting the kids in their lessons yet they're all just standing around relaxing. I think this has become another weekly town gossip meeting."

Pearl laughed because it was true. "It has. It really has, but lighten up, what's your problem? The kids are okay. Everyone's having fun."

Just then, a very familiar car drove in. Despite the fact that it had only been to the school a few times, almost everyone turned to look towards it. The women ogled as Cole killed the engine and then got out almost as though they were watching a movie.

"Ooh, there you go. The main protagonist has just entered the chat," Pearl said.

I sighed again and began to wipe down the counters. "The students need to start bringing their bakes over."

She gave me a look. "For God's sake, live a little. Your almost-boyfriend is here."

"Keep your voice down," I admonished, looking around to see if my father was within earshot. Thankfully he wasn't.

"Oh, please, this place is rowdy, no one will hear, but will you take a look at him though? Those boots, the itty jeans... the tucked-in flannel. How tall is he?"

"6'4," I replied.

She turned to him. "He is so interesting to look at and so handsome. How big is he?"

"Yeah, Montana. How big is he?" Kelly asked, sliding next to me.

"You can't possibly want to keep that private," she said. "We've always shared that info with each other."

"Yeah, but—"

"Yeah, but what?" she accused. "It doesn't feel right because this one's a little bit too personal, or you just don't want me to die of jealousy."

I stopped and laughed at this, which caught the attention of Natalie.

"What happened?" Natalie asked. "Why is she laughing like that?"

"She's thinking of Mr. Swift's dick size," Pearl replied.

The laugh instantly died in my throat and I glared at Pearl. "Keep your voice down," I exclaimed.

"How big is he?" Kelly asked again. "I'm just curious because guys like him are usually a complete disappointment. They look like they're packing and all until they drop their pants and you want to choke."

"I'm confused," Natalie sipped from her drink. "Choke from being impressed. Or?"

"Choke from tears!" Kelly said dryly.

"You all, we're still at work, we need to supervise the baking."

"I'm ready with my students," Kelly said. "We're now waiting for your oven to heat up, Miss Moore."

"By the way," Natalie said. "I was at the hairdresser's yesterday and Tiffany comes up to me."

"What did that bitch want?" Kelly asked aggressively.

"Information about Anya's father, obviously. She didn't get anything from me, but she said something weird."

My ears pricked up. "Weird?"

"Yeah, weird. She told me she had gone to Cole's house to deliver some cake she bought from the bakery and she noticed that Anya was wearing an iconic, limited edition pair of Gucci shoes."

"What is so weird about that?" Pearl asked. "There are so many fakes floating around."

"That's the weird part. Apparently, Anya claimed they were fakes that her father had bought for her at a flea market, but Tiffany being the fashion victim she is, knew how to check if those types of shoes are fake. She checked them and they were the real thing. That pair costs, get this, $1200.00!"

"Whoa!" Kelly mouthed. "$1200 for a pair of kid's shoes."

"It doesn't make sense. He's an accountant, right?"

"That's right," I confirmed. Natalie's story was wild, but it kinda confirmed my belief that something was not right. The beat-up car was wrong and now the shoes were wrong.

"This is just silly. You guys are just looking for trouble. I'm sure there's an absolutely reasonable explanation," Pearl said.

"Listen, the kids will be coming soon. I should get ready," I said.

"So you're not going to answer before we leave?" Kelly asked.

"Answer what?"

"How big is Mr. Swift's cock?" Pearl reminded.

Sighing, I stopped then and looked at a lump of clay in the plastic bucket. I pulled more than two handfuls out and began to roll it. They all watched me. I looked at my creation, then added another handful. Natalie sniggered.

After I had rolled to the right length and consistency, I looked up at them.

Kelly had her mouth hanging open. "You're exaggerating, right?"

"Nope." I flattened the roll, returned it to the bucket, turned away, and couldn't help but smile.

Their little faces!

Chapter 35
Cole

This event was more or less what I had expected. It was early afternoon and we were under the canopy of a large tree. Everyone was drinking cocktails and holding onto portable fans.

The mood seemed jovial, but it was tiring to be watched by so many pairs of eyes. I made my way further into the grounds. There was only one pair of eyes I wanted on me. I looked around and did not see Montana. It had been a couple of days since our rendezvous in the car, and not a full hour had gone by that I hadn't thought about her.

I wondered if I took up space in her mind even a fraction of the amount of space she was hogging in mine.

"Dad! Dad!" I heard the sudden piercing call. For a second, my heart lurched and I felt a strange sense of loss. She was calling me Dad. She was only seven and had already outgrown the word Daddy in public.

I turned in the direction of her voice. My little poppet was wearing a tiny apron and running towards me. Her hands were covered with ... that better be mud.

"Hands to yourself," I said as she reached me.

She giggled and I was incredibly happy to see her look so happy and carefree. She had made a couple of new friends and I was pleased with her progress in school, but for the past two nights, her nightmares had recurred to the point where I had begun to suspect she was feigning them just so she could stay in bed with me because she was unsettled by the sudden move out of everything that was familiar to her.

But now she seemed free and happy.

"What are you doing?" I asked.

"Pottery," she replied. "I'm trying to make you a mug. Since we couldn't bring your favorite white and green one since we moved from New York."

"Hmmm," I said. "Remember what I told you about mentioning where we moved from?"

She slapped her hands around her mouth. "Oops," she said and smiled so foolishly and sheepishly I had to laugh at her clay-covered face.

"Hang on," I said, and taking my phone out snapped a photo of her.

"Let me see," she asked.

I showed her and she began to laugh uproariously. "I look funny," she said, between bouts of more laughter.

Everyone was looking at us. "Come on. Let's get you cleaned up," I said.

She pointed to somewhere behind me. "There's a tap in there."

"Okay, little soldier. Let's go." We began to head over to it.

"It's Miss Moore, Dad!" Anya screamed suddenly.

And so it was. Montana was standing in front of four medium-sized ovens. It looked like she was in charge of baking the raw dough and cake batter that the children were bringing in from another shed. I headed over to her counter to watch as she pulled out a batch of seriously burnt muffins and laid them on the table.

"Yikes," I couldn't help but say.

"You couldn't even pretend," she scolded under her breath, but her eyes were twinkling.

My whole body felt warm. It must be the ovens. "Is that your fault or theirs?"

"At this point, I have no fuck— " she stopped when she noticed the mud-covered girl by my side. "What's that on your face?"

She produced a tea towel which she dipped in some water and went over to wipe Anya's mouth.

"What's this, sweetie?" she asked.

My traitorous daughter pointed to me. "It's Dad's fault."

"Of course, it is," Montana agreed.

"Are you guys ganging up on me?" I asked.

She looked at me then and my heart skipped several beats. Her irises were like sunlight on a gorgeous golden-green pond.

"You haven't answered my question yet," I said.

"What question?"

"Are the burned muffins your fault or theirs?"

She looked around her. "Truthfully?"

I smiled slowly. "You're going to say it's my fault, aren't you?"

She looked deep into my eyes. "It's been your fault from the first moment I laid eyes on you, Cole Swift."

"I-," I began.

"Hello, hello, Mr. Swift," a woman's voice called. I turned. It was the woman I'd met from last time, although I could no longer remember her name.

"Hey," I said and nodded to the five other moms behind her who were advancing quickly upon us.

It looked, smelled, and felt like an ambush so I winked at Montana, snatched my little girl's mud-covered hand, and began to walk away.

"I need to find a tap for Anya to wash her hands, so I'll catch up with you guys soon?"

Without waiting for their response, I was out of there, dragging my kid with me.

Chapter 36
Montana

I had no doubt in my mind that I was going to catch all the daggers and criticism for seemingly being the only one Cole had talked to and dashed off after. And it didn't take long at all for me to feel the first stab.

"Do you need any help?" Marilyn Curtis asked, her voice sweet, but poisonous.

"I think I'm okay," I replied as I slipped down my oven mitt and grabbed the next batch that had been sent over.

"There's a lot to be done. And that last batch of muffins were burnt to cinders. Let me help," she offered, and it would have been rude to do anything else but accept her offer.

"You're right. The muffins were slightly burnt."

"They were blacker than coal," she said with a smile and came around the counter to join me.

I could smell her strong perfume and I instantly regretted being polite. I should have told the witch to fly off on her broomstick instead.

"You seem to have quite the rapport with Anya's father,"

she commented sourly, while absolutely not helping and just standing, moving a little bit closer to annoy and quiz me.

"Not especially," I replied as I shut the oven door. "But I am her class teacher, after all."

She smiled again. "Is there a way you can get him to participate more with the other parents? For instance, a bunch of us are chatting and having some refreshments over there."

"I really don't know," I told her. "You'd have to ask him."

"You're really no help at all," she said with another irritated smile before walking away.

A few minutes later, the widely-wanted hunk came over with his daughter.

"The moms hate me," I told him. "They're wondering if I'm holding you back from socializing with them."

"You're holding me back from socializing with them?" he asked, his eyes sparkling like diamonds.

"Yes, I'm being blamed for monopolizing you. So could you go hang out with them for a bit?"

"Anya, go join your friends in the pottery shed," he said, and she ran along. Then he pulled his phone out of his pocket and without looking up spoke.

"Fine. Give me your phone number and I'll go hang out with some Moms."

"What? Are you kidding?" I asked, shocked. "With all the attention on us right now."

He looked up. "Do you want me to hang out with them or not?"

"I'm not giving you my phone number in front of all these people."

He grinned. "Then I'm going to keep on standing here and … er … monopolizing you."

My heart went soft at his words. "Everyone's gonna know, though."

He put his phone away. "Just say the number out aloud. I'll remember it."

I stared at him. "You'll be able to remember my number if I say it out once?"

"Yeah, I'm good with numbers."

I called it out and he nodded. "Just to be clear. I'm doing this for you and only you."

Truly, I felt like I was melting. "Thank you," I said. "But to annoy them just a little bit more, please say that I told you to come over."

"Of course," he said and reached out then to touch me, but I shook my head with alarm.

With a sigh, he walked over to where Marilyn Curtis and the other moms were gathered together.

I watched him go, dazed by the gorgeous sass of him. I could see the women watching him and I didn't blame them at all. I was them, only that by some stroke of good fortune, I had met him first, and we had connected. It made me wonder, though, as I turned around to check on the muffins if things would have progressed as they had so far between us if we had met not at the Dead or Alive bar, but here in school.

Maybe not. Here at the school, the setting would have been too proper for us to have come together in such an exciting and incendiary way on the very first meeting, but here then, we would have had the instrument storage closet in the music room.

Wow! Where did that come from?

The thought was crazy, but I had to admit that it was a wonderful one too. I was so busy making insane plans that I was startled when I heard Pearl's voice close to my ear.

"You sent him to do that?" she asked.

I turned to see what she was talking about and my mouth hung open. He was surrounded by women and had taken his jacket off. He was wearing a tight white t-shirt and over it a freaking apron that looked tiny on him. It should have been ridiculous, but to me, he seemed even more strikingly masculine. The concentration on his face, the way he sat with his strong thighs spread apart ... His huge, wet hands were shaping and molding the clay.

"Holy fuck," Kelly gasped by my side as he dug his hand in the middle to form the pen.

"I'm sure someone just fainted a few feet away," Pearl said in an awed voice.

"That's one hell of a man you caught there, Miss Moore," Natalie said.

"Hmmm ... I'm not sure I'll be able to keep him, Nat. Seems I have a lot of competition. Even Tiffany is trying to get her claws into him."

"Fffftttt," she dismissed. "He didn't even invite her into his house. He wants you."

"I don't know, Nat. I used Kelly's techniques, but I'm not her. I'm not experienced enough to keep a man like that."

"You're totally wrong," Kelly said. "Men don't want women with a high body count. If anything, they're intimidated by such women. Men are simple creatures, far simpler than women, anyway. They just want a sweet girl who responds to them, falls in love with them, and makes them feel they're special. Take it from me, I should know what I'm talking about, I claimed the title of slut a very long time ago."

"You're not a slut," I said fiercely.

She laughed. "I've slept with more than half the single men in this town so, of course, I am, but I'm cool with that. I wear my slut crown with pride."

"You should. You have no idea how much Cole loved your blowjob technique."

Kelly laughed and I turned away from her and looked at Cole at that very moment he lifted his head and stared pointedly at me, and even though it was too far for our eyes to meet, I knew that he was seeking me out. Such a small gesture, but it made me feel absolutely divine.

And it made me want to … fuck him.

Chapter 37
Montana

https://www.youtube.com/watch?v=4DwEni2N_-A

-you sexy thing-

ME: Do you feel like having sex? Feel free to say no.

I clicked the send button before I could change my mind. I wasn't sure he would know it was my number because I had called it out to him so fast and there was so much noise around, but even before I'd closed Anya's file where I found his number, my phone pinged with an answer.

HIM: YES. My place, tonight?

ME: Sorry. Can't wait that long.

HIM: Name the place and time.

ME: Right now!

HIM: Where are you? (emoji with tongue hanging out)

ME: In the office, but meet me in the storage room. Do you remember where it is?

HIM: Ten-minute walk from here. Four minutes if I run.

ME: Don't run. We have to be discreet ... and quick.

HIM: Discreet? Hard if both of us mysteriously disappear at the same time.

ME: Hard but not impossible.

HIM: Quick check on Anya to make sure she's gainfully occupied first. See you in 6 minutes. I'll be walking quickly.

ME: Clock is ticking...

I knew I was behaving in quite an insane way, but I felt quite exhilarated by my new daring self. I locked the office and walked quickly down the corridor. The sight of him in his tight T-shirt had awakened all kinds of needs in me. I didn't want to ... actually, no, I couldn't wait until tonight.

All in all, it was a great afternoon, and I needed a special memory to go along with it.

The storage room in question was my secret getaway. Behind the cans of food, gardening machinery, spare cooking utensils, and camping equipment was a walled-off narrow space with a window facing the mountain range in the distance. During the cold winter months, their tops would be covered with snow, and I would escape here with a cup of hot cocoa every chance I got. It was a special place of relief to me where I'd never ever been bothered so I couldn't think of a better place to take him.

One of the parents saw me as I left the office building

and made my way towards the store room. I casually waved and he waved back. As long as Cole and I were not seen heading over together it should be fine.

I turned the key in the door and opened it. It was vast inside. Even with sunlight pouring in through the high windows there were many dim corners. Dust motes hung suspended in the rays of light. I had six minutes to kill. There was an old honky-tonk piano along one wall and I walked towards it. I sat on the stool and played a few tunes. Six minutes seemed like a lifetime. My feet tapped impatiently, and I kept glancing at the door until eventually, I heard a sound outside.

"Come in," I called, and the door was pushed open.

I stood and faced him. My heart was pounding so furiously in my chest I could hear it. I felt nervous and excited all at once. I smiled at him, but he didn't approach me.

"Is there a key?" he asked.

I held up the bunch of keys in my hand. "You seem even more cautious than me."

He smiled as he advanced. "There are a bunch of inquisitive mommies out there. Do we want to give them any ideas?"

"Nope," I said, dropping the keys into his upturned palm.

I watched him lock the door and turn around. "Want to do it against the piano?"

He stood in a ray of sunshine, unaware of how beautiful he looked. The dust motes danced around him. His eyes ... God, he was heavenly. I was afraid he would smell my utter fascination for him ... my desperation.

"Not here," I said urgently." Come with me."

I took his hand and led him to my secret hideaway.

I shut the door behind us, and we stood beside each other. It felt too good and too real. Even just standing beside him was making me feel things I hadn't ever felt before. I looked up at him, studying the contours of his face, his tanned skin, the sheen of his dark, gorgeous hair. His attention was momentarily caught by the gorgeous scenery of the woods and mountains beyond.

"Wow! Sunsets and sunrises must look absolutely magical through this window," he noted.

"They're breathtaking," I replied softly.

He turned then toward me and stared into my eyes wonderingly. As if he couldn't believe his eyes. As if he was almost afraid to touch me. As if I would disappear into a wisp of smoke if he did. He shook his head as if to clear away a thought.

It was so quiet I could hear the harshness of my breathing. His scent of spices and lime and a hint of something else filled the air, expansive and intoxicating.

"We have to be quick," I reminded, in a shaky voice.

Taking my chin in his hand he stroked his thumb across the soft skin of my lips, rubbing away my lip gloss. I was completely powerless under his touch. He leaned forward and kissed me, stealing my breath from me. He took his time, quietly but potently, sucking softly on my bottom lip. I was already melting when his tongue slid in. It teased mine, sucking and stroking, lush and heated, nearly driving me out of my mind.

My body pushed against him, needing his body to be glued to mine. In response, his arm snaked around me, drawing me so close, that my breasts were pressed tight against the hardness of his chest. My clit had swelled and the sensation was almost excruciatingly intense.

"Jeans," he growled as his hands reached down to grab my ass. "Why do women love wearing these horrible garments so much?"

"They're easy to take off, trust me," I said.

"If you were mine, you'd be wearing dresses and no panties because I'd want to get my cock inside you every chance I get." He walked me backwards until I felt the window ledge against my ass.

His words turned me to jelly.

"Turn around," he ordered.

I complied and his hands came around the waistband of my jeans, undid the button, and pulled them halfway down my ass. I couldn't help but writhe with excitement and anticipation. His fingers grazed my skin, and the heat of his touch caused goosebumps to break out all over me.

I loved the way he caressed my hips, the possessive way his big hands felt me up. He leaned forward to place a feathery kiss on the dip of my back.

"Hurry, Cole," I breathed.

He licked my back. The wetness of his tongue, the soft press of his lips ... I could do little more than moan. Holding onto my jeans, he yanked them down till they were touching the floor.

"Ah," the soft gasp left me when he kissed my ass. He went around the soft cheeks, and I felt my body shudder.

"You dress so tomboyish," he said. "It's a crime to hide all this beauty under your baggy clothes?"

I thought back to the night we had met. "Would you have even looked at me if I hadn't come in Kelly's sexy dress?"

"What would you have worn instead?" he asked quietly as he grasped the straps of my thong and pulled them down.

I was so restless with anticipation that I wanted to touch myself for some sort of relief, but I knew just how out of the world it felt when he did it. I shut my eyes and tried my very best to exercise patience, focusing on his questions and the masculine, smooth, quiet sound of his velvety voice.

"It was long," I whispered. "That's all you need to know. Long and decent."

He grabbed my hips and lifted them, then with his thumbs parted the cheeks of my ass. I was completely exposed to him! Both my entrances!

My eyes flew open with shock.

"I noticed you in the car when I was standing by the side of the road. Before I saw your dress."

"What?" I exclaimed, amazed, but in the next moment, he had flattened his tongue onto my pussy and licked all the way up the crack of my bottom.

Every trace of amazement immediately dissipated. "Oh," I trembled as pleasure struck my lower abdomen with an almost painful zap.

He licked me, the pressure hard and thorough.

"Fuck."

The movements of his tongue teasing that ultra-sensitive tip of my clit. My mind scattered into pieces.

"Oh ..." I gasped.

I was being eaten out right here, during school hours,

and in a storeroom. This was the school where I taught! My father was somewhere close. The kids' parents were within hearing distance. I should be ashamed of myself. This was a terrible thing to do, but oh, it felt so good.

I felt no shame. Not one tiny bit of shame.

There was something extra decadent and dirty about him taking me from behind. Without him asking, I spread my legs even wider, allowing him to get his head deeper in. All I wanted to do was to ride him, and as soon as he took my soaking wet cleft in his mouth, I lowered my knees and did as I wanted. I rode his mouth and tongue as he continued to suck hard against my sex, stroking and licking. By the time he stopped to take a breath, my legs had already begun to shake. I was going to come without any shame, without any reservations, and it was going to be right in his mouth, against his face.

"Go faster," he instructed.

Maybe it was this command or the way he had licked so deeply into my pussy, but in that moment, I lost my head. I rode him without mercy, chasing the pleasure, chasing the insanity, and being as inconsiderate as I could possibly be with his tongue and mouth.

My excuse was that he had done the exact same thing to me when I'd sucked his cock. He had held my head and thrust his dick down my throat, and I had taken it without any complaints. I'd even enjoyed every moment of it, and so far, it seemed as if my pleasure was everything to him. As his was to me when I was pleasuring him.

I marveled at the fact that we were almost strangers. It felt as though I'd known him for ages, as though we were a couple already completely in tune with each other and possessing the knowledge of how to bring the other to their knees.

It made me doubt if I'd ever find this kind of deep connection with anyone else. Neither Kelly, Pearl or Natalie had ever spoken of this level of instinctive bodily communication.

"Cole ..." I cried hoarsely. The woods and the mountains beyond had become a blur, and my legs felt so incredibly weak I had to hold on tightly to the window ledge. My entire body seemed to be stuttering like an engine, jerking, clenching hard ... I tried to control my breathing, but I couldn't. Tried to slow my speed as I rode his face, but I was already gone.

"Cole! Oh my God!" I gasped as the orgasm threw me over the edge. My hand instantly flew to my mouth because, obviously, I had to be quiet. I couldn't let anyone hear us. But even muffled my scream was loud. I felt incredibly fierce. I couldn't control my volume. I knew then that this had been a terrible idea, but there was nothing I could do.

I heard my voice resound across the room, filthy curses and moans echoing endlessly. I tried, I truly tried, but all my strength and will was worth nothing as I came hard.

My juices gushed out of me, spilling down my thighs, and running into his greedy mouth. He kissed me. I couldn't even tell if he had been the one to turn my head, or if I had searched for his lips, but the second our lips sealed together, nothing mattered.

I tasted myself on his lips. This intensity of sharing was so fucking intimate, I wanted to belong to him. In every single way, body, mind, and soul. At that moment I was completely owned. It was a level of possession and safety I'd never experienced before. My cries and whimpers disappeared into his mouth just as he had intended.

I thought he was done, but he wasn't. Not by a long shot.

He curled his arm under my waist and lifted me up until the heels of my feet left the floor. I was balancing on my toes like a ballerina.

"Fuck!" I swore breathlessly.

He smiled against my cheek. "I love how foul-mouthed you can get when the going gets rough."

I didn't know how to respond to this, partly because his long fingers had slid into the slickness of my folds, and the pad of his thumb was rubbing circles around my ultra-sensitive clit. I basked in the pleasure. He was going to leave me in a puddle of my own cream for the second time in minutes, and I was completely powerless to stop it.

His fingers found their way inside of me and began to thrust. At first, his pace was leisurely, but slowly he upped his speed alternating between rubbing my clit and finger fucking me. I was ready to come all over him again.

He was so in tune with my body that he knew just how fast to go and when to slow down. In this way, he delayed my climax and kept me at the edge. It seemed as though he would alternate this way forever. Slow then fast, bringing me to the brink and then calming me down.

I was going crazy, my mouth was begging for release. I couldn't even keep my eyes open. Nothing mattered besides what he was doing to me.

The intensity of my need for me scared me.

Obviously, it must have been minutes, but it seemed

like hours later, he allowed me to come. The orgasm spread through my body like exquisite waves, triggering nerves that tingled and jerked into life. By the time the highest point was reached, I couldn't even remember my name.

All I could do was tremble and twist as helplessly as a cut snake.

When I was able to bring myself to my senses he was kissing and nibbling my ear softly. When I turned to look into his gorgeous eyes I knew I still wanted more. That it would probably never be enough. I was addicted to him. His cock was so rock hard and I couldn't help grinding my ass against it. He still had his hand covering my entire sex, stroking lightly, soothing, inciting. He was a fucking dream.

"I need you," I panted, my hand reaching back to grab his bulge through his pants.

"I don't have any condoms on me," he said. "We should stop here."

"Do you want to stop here?" I asked.

"Hell no. I was pretending to be a gentleman."

"I don't need no gentleman. I want that beast I met in Stormy City, but this time I want to feel every inch of the beast. But this time I don't want even the thinnest layer of rubber between us."

And I wasn't lying. I wanted to feel the way I felt when he filled me up and pounded into me that night; it was unforgettable. I had dreamt about it on many nights and I couldn't go one more day, hour, or even minute without that feeling.

I needed to feel owned. I needed to feel filled with his enormous cock. My clit was quivering and pulsing with hunger and need.

I turned around then wrapped my arms around him and rubbed against him restlessly.

His hands instantly went to the buckle of his pants to undo his belt and in no time, he was sliding his pants down and pulling his huge steely-hard cock out of his briefs.

Chapter 38
Montana

W e had to leave. And quickly.
He had to find Anya and I had to return to my duties, but I didn't want to leave. I never wanted to let go. As the throes of pleasure ebbed away, I began to notice things I had not until now. First, I registered the delicious warmth of the sun shining down on us. And I started to hear sounds. They were some distance away, but the voices were approaching.

I looked up to him then.

"It's time to head back," he said.

He found my jeans and opened them up at my feet for me. It was a caring and endearing gesture. After pulling them up, I allowed him to button me up. I watched him the entire time. His eyelashes were so long and lush I wanted to touch them, but that would be too affectionate. He looked up and smiled at me, and my poor little heart skipped several beats.

"Ready?" he asked.

"Do I reek of sex?" I asked anxiously.

He grinned. "Yeah, but it suits you."

I frowned. "That was not what I wanted to hear."

"Don't sweat it, Montana. Claim it. It's nobody's business but ours."

We started to head out when I heard a knock on the door. My heart lurched. What if that was my dad? I was too jittery. I felt like a criminal, and the anxiety felt like it was corroding my bones.

But whoever was outside didn't insist. Footsteps walked away. I sighed with relief.

"Do you want to leave first?" I whispered my gaze on the door.

"No, you should go first," he replied. "Unless you want to lock the doors."

"No, I'll come back and lock them in a little while."

"You're the boss," he said.

"Okay. See you," I said and began to turn away from him, but he caught my hand and twirled me around to face him. He slid his hand around the small of my back and kissed me. Bad move because I had just begun to think clearly, but here I was again struggling to be coherent.

My phone began to ring then, and I drew back with confusion and panic. I saw that it was only Pearl.

As I dismissed the call I wondered why she was looking for me. I also noticed that thus far, I'd had two missed calls from my dad, and that was alarming to say the least. One from Kelly and two from Pearl. Now I was certain that our absence had been noticed.

I tried not to feel too panicked though. I had done nothing wrong. Nothing I wouldn't do again given the same opportunity. If they assumed we were fucking because we disappeared, so be it. After all, it was true.

With one last look at Cole and a tight, awkward smile I headed out, ready to face the worst. The second I unlocked the door and went out, I spotted a very familiar face waiting for me. Pearl was leaning against the wall and leisurely scrolling through her phone. There was no doubt she was aware of what had happened inside because she was looking at me, her head cocked and a look of wonder in her eyes.

"Really?" she asked.

I was nervous but also amused by her disbelief. "Really what?"

She looked at the door I had hastily closed behind me, then she shook her head and walked with me. We didn't say a word to each other, but just before we joined everyone else, I pulled her aside. As far as I could see there weren't any pitchforks waiting for us, and everything seemed exactly as I had left it. But I had to be sure there weren't any devastatingly unpleasant surprises awaiting me.

"Was there ... I mean, why were you waiting there?"

"You disappeared," she said simply.

I nodded. "And."

She tried to hide a smile. "Cole Swift disappeared as well."

"Okay." My heart was pounding.

"If even I noticed this, what do you think about everyone else? Especially all those hyenas who are stalking him."

Even though it felt as though I'd just returned from another world and lifetime we hadn't been gone very long.

Taking in a deep breath, I released it slowly. "Did anyone hear? Did we draw anybody's attention?"

"Why do you think I am waiting for you?" she asked.

I was confused. "What do you mean?"

She lifted her hand and tapped the back of my head. "Kelly ordered me to disappear as well, you moron. That way anyone curious could conclude that he went to the bathroom or something, while I was with you the whole time."

I felt so relieved, I nearly fainted from it, but as the true implications of what my friends had done for me dawned on me, I felt so grateful I wanted to hug Pearl tightly. And that was exactly what I did.

"You should have at least warned me beforehand to cover your tracks," she scolded. "What the hell do you think you're doing? At school, especially? Your dad could have gone to the storeroom."

I really didn't know what to say in response to this. I felt like a complete mess. I was a complete mess and it was all his fault.

"You're smiling?" She pinched me.

"Hey,"' I cried out.

"What are you smiling about?"

"I'll be right back," I said, and turned to go, but she caught my hand and stopped me. "You have got to be kidding me. You're going back for more. That's just neurotic This lot are gonna figure it out and the whole town's going to be gossiping about you and him."

"I'm not going to him. I need to use the bathroom," I explained and hurried away, only to bump into a man who was heading towards the sheds. There was a gorgeous smile on his face and he looked so good, as though he had taken a warm towel to his face and body, even though there was no warm towel in the storeroom. Insatiably, I inhaled his scent.

"Are we in trouble?" he asked.

His voice broke the spell and I realized where we were and how many eyes were probably on us. I retreated back from him. "I don't think so."

"Good." He nodded courteously, then passed me by.

The perfect stranger. I couldn't help but watch him as he walked away.

A handkerchief suddenly appearing underneath my chin startled me. "What the ...?"

"You'll need this to wipe off your drool. How absolutely neurotic of you. This is all my fault. I created a fucking monster."

I cracked up at her words and took the clean handkerchief because I would most definitely need it. I tried to stop myself, but I couldn't help casting one last long look at him before turning and heading off to the bathroom.

I cleaned myself up, but to be honest, I was almost reluctant to do it. I wanted to keep his scent on me. Everywhere I touched was a very vivid and poignant reminder that he had touched me there. The constant flashback made me feel as though he was right there with me. I was well aware I had to get myself back together, but before I could the bathroom door was pushed open, and a group of females headed in.

"Is she here? You said she was here. Montana!"

"Yeah, I'm here." I sighed. I had done something crazy. Something even Kelly would probably think twice about doing. So, of course, I had become worthy of gossip and conjecture. I hoped this little tidbit about my behavior would not get to my dad.

"Ow!" Kelly yelled as soon as she saw me. "Just look who's been buttering the biscuit in the school store room! Ha, ha, the student has become the master."

"Honestly, Montana," Natalie exclaimed, but she was giggling too.

"Keep your voices down," I said, but they ignored me.

"You should have taken your own advice," Kelly taunted. "Your moans and screams were audible throughout the entire school grounds."

At hearing this, my soul left my body. I turned to Pearl in horror. I could always trust her to tell the truth. "Is that true?"

"Stop scaring her, Kelly," Pearl scolded.

"Not true, Montana," Natalie consoled gently. "We only know because Pearl told us and she only heard because she had her ear stuck to the door of the storeroom."

Grinned with relief I tossed the handkerchief away and headed over to the sink.

"Hey! That's mine," Pearl complained.

I looked at her with surprise. "I used it to clean my Minnie. You want it back?"

She made a face and recoiled. "If it's been on your Minnie, I guess not."

I focused for the next several seconds on properly lathering up and washing my hands.

"Is he really that good?" Natalie asked.

"Look at her face and skin," Kelly said. "She's flushed and red everywhere. What exactly does that tell you?"

"Okay, anyone could walk in now, you guys. Please stop," I begged.

"We'll stop when you tell us how this secret affair is progressing. I mean, where is it headed? What are his concrete intentions towards you," Pearl asked.

"It's not heading anywhere," I told her airily. "It's just casual with us. Just a fling."

"Casual? Fling? Are you crazy? This is your first guy. You're going to be bawling and horribly sad for a very long time if you're not careful."

"I feel really bad … actually," Natalie said, "we all feel bad because we more or less pushed you into this. The last thing we want is for you to get hurt. The first cut is hard, honey. Be careful."

"I won't get hurt. I have it all under control," I assured with a confidence I wasn't feeling. I gazed at my worried friends through the reflection in the mirror as they considered my response rather than the relief, they just really seemed to become even more worried.

"Why can't I just enjoy this thing without thinking too hard?" I asked.

"Didn't your dad invite him over for dinner a few days ago?" Kelly asked.

"What's that got to do with anything?"

"It seems to me Papa thinks it's more serious than you do," Natalie observed.

"My dad has no idea I've been with him," I scoffed.

"I think you give your ole dad too little credit. Tell me, did he disappear a few times over dinner?"

I scowled. Holy Heck, Kelly was right. First, he disap-

peared into the cellar to look for a wine bottle we didn't
need, then he retired to bed early.

"Did you fuck him in Papa's house?" Kelly mocked. She
could barely contain her amusement.

"Of course not."

She shrugged. "No need to be so offended. You just did
so in school so your home is fair game."

"If you ask me, both of you seem to be immensely out of
control," Pearl said.

I didn't even argue this because she was absolutely right,
but it didn't feel good to admit to it, so I just remained
silent.

Pearl came close then and held my hand. "What do you
really want from him, babe?"

I thought about this question. He was exquisitely handsome, the chemistry was amazing, and I had big feelings for
him, but I knew almost nothing about him. What I did
know was concerning. There was something he wasn't
telling me. But even acknowledging the fact he was hiding
something from me caused me pain, which proved the girls'
point that I was already in too deep.

"I don't know yet," I replied honestly. "But I see where
you guys are coming from. I'll be more careful. I won't just
blindly fall head over heels with him until I know whether
he's gonna hang around for a bit."

Pearl smiled. "And that's why we're here. We're not just
here for these juicy details."

"Sorry, but I'm only here for the juicy details," Kelly
said.

I laughed. Sometimes closed-minded people said nasty

201

things about her, but to me, she was funny and had a heart of gold.

"You can tell us later. We should all go back. And don't worry, Montana. No one will guess," Pearl said.

"No one will know?" Kelly mocked. "She's still so flushed she looks like a fucking lobster. Anyone with half a brain will take one look at her and know she's been getting royally fucked when she should have been watching their kids."

"Their kids are all busy having a great time. No harm has come to any of them as a result of me getting, as you so charmingly put it, royally fucked." I ran a hand through my hair. "I have no regrets."

Kelly came closer. "Just give us one juicy detail to keep us going. Where did you do it?"

"Against the window."

"The one with the mountain range view?"

I nodded.

"Ooh, niiiiiceee," she approved.

"Yeah, it was nice. Very nice."

Chapter 39
Cole

Anya's nightmares hadn't stopped, despite the fact I'd allowed her to sleep in my bed till now. If anything, it even seemed to be getting worse. Last night, I soothed her with warm milk and waited by her bedside until she fell asleep, but in the end, it had still happened.

Even though we had been living quite normally, both of us could never let our guard down when we were out of the house. Perhaps the stress of it was adding to Anya's nightmares.

It made me sad because I had no idea how to fix it. I couldn't fight Paganini on my own terms yet. I was not ready for that and I wanted to take him by surprise. For the time being, I had no choice but to continue our life in this way. I also felt certain she was concealing something from me, which made me feel helpless. Maybe it was some sort of 'girl thing' and she couldn't talk to me about it. If only she could have maintained some sort of relationship with her mother.

The good news, though, was Montana was coming over, and Anya had come to like her. Who knew? Maybe she could talk to Montana.

I had decided on a simple meal of steak, baked potatoes, and caprese salad for us. For dessert, Anya wanted to bake cupcakes for Montana so I lifted her up on a stool and let her get on with making the batter.

The phone rang and seeing it was from Leila, I headed into the living room. There, I could still keep my eyes on Anya and lower my voice enough to not be heard.

"Hello, Leila."

"Hi, I have a few updates for you."

"Go ahead," I repeated, hoping that this wasn't the call I was dreading, either informing me we had to run again, or that we had to start preparing to do so.

"You remember the cars and the two guys that Tom spotted outside the filling station?"

"Yeah," I replied. "What about them?"

"Well, Tom's had a tail put on them, and they seem to just be moving with purpose. By their movement, I would guess that there are other teams we don't know about that are fanning out across the country. They stop at certain towns, towns with good elementary schools, and they ask questions. They are impressively relentless, fast, and effective. As soon as they're finished with one town they move on to the next. They don't stop."

I glanced at Anya. She was breaking eggs into her batter. "What questions are they asking?"

"What I would ask; if anyone has appeared in town, a single dad and his daughter?"

"Ah," I nodded.

"Somehow they seem to think you wouldn't go too far."

"Airport surveillance," I said shortly. "They knew I didn't fly."

"Right," she replied.

"Anyway, at the speed they're going, they're not far away from you. They could be as near as weeks away from you."

I had done one thing right. I didn't go for what an ordinary person would consider a good school. I had chosen something that was perfect for me and Anya, but that would not be the case for most people. Those investigators were not weeks away from Bison Ridge. I'd give them one year at the very least, and that was more time than I needed to put my plan into action.

"Thanks for the heads-up. Continue to keep your eyes on them. Any news yet about Arianna?"

"Paganini took her to a charity auction two nights ago. She looked okay, but she's lost some weight and ... er ... she looked high. High, like 'out of it' high."

"I see," I said thoughtfully.

"Sorry to give you the bad news."

"It is what it is," I told her. "Keep me updated."

"Sure," she agreed, and the call came to an end.

I sat for a little while, scowling and trying to process the information about Arianna. This was something I did not account for. High on what? What was he giving her? What was his plan? Why was he turning her into a junkie? To subdue her. To pimp her out. To hurt me?

Then Anya called me over. Her cupcakes were ready for the oven.

"Nice," I complimented.

She nodded solemnly. "Do you think Miss Moore will like them?"

"She will love them," I said and put the tray into the hot oven.

Chapter 40
Montana

As I drew even nearer to Duck Pond house, I felt equal amounts of excitement and nervousness. The talk with the girls in the bathroom had seemed light at first, but after several days of pondering about what I truly wanted, I realized that they were right. I didn't want a relationship based purely on sex. I wanted more, far more, but I didn't know if that was what he wanted too. The painful truth was: he didn't even bother to call me, and if we had not met again totally by accident, we would never have seen each other again ... and he was okay with that.

When the renovations first started on Duck Pond house a few months ago, people wondered who was moving in. There seemed to be an awful lot of work going on. There were stories of much digging, lorries carrying soil away even in the night, and huge trailers bringing in material that looked like reinforced steel blocks, but from what I could see it still looked very similar to what I remembered to be before all the works. Maybe there were new windows, definitely a new coat of paint and some landscaping work too.

I'd always loved this house and it seemed even more lovely and peaceful against the setting sun. I couldn't help just sitting in their driveway and wondering about how it would feel to be a part of this pretty picture. It didn't take a lot of time for me to come to the conclusion that I'd LOVE to be part of this picture.

Now I was just being foolish. Building castles in the sand. Heck, I hardly knew the guy. I admonished myself to keep a level head and to judge things as they were, as they were present to me rather than based on the wild fantasies in my mind.

I straightened and gave my appearance one last look in the rearview mirror, then pushed the car door open and got out.

I had dressed simply today. A white linen shirt, a striped pink skirt, and strappy sandals. Everyone was constantly commenting on how I always dressed like a boy, but with this outfit, there would be no question of whether I was a boy or a girl. To further emphasize the difference I opened two more buttons on my shirt to show everyone just enough that I had breasts and a worthy cleavage. For a minute, I was sure it was too much given that his daughter would be there, but in the end, I decided that she wouldn't notice. I wouldn't have at her age.

I rang the doorbell and it was opened almost instantly by the man I had been unable to stop thinking about for every single moment. After our last encounter, we'd only seen each other briefly with other people around when he came to pick Anya up. There was a bus service for the kids, but he said he wouldn't allow her to participate until she had completely adjusted to her new surroundings. I could see just how protective he was of his daughter, and it was something quite impressive. If only all dads would protect their girls like that, the world would be a better place. As for me, Anya had quickly grown to be one of my favorite students, not only because of her kind, gentle nature but also because she was incredibly affectionate.

"Am I too early?" I asked.

"Not at all." His eyes lingered on the skin between my open buttons. Then he leaned down and placed a light kiss on my cheek.

"Come in." He stepped back to allow me in.

Before either of us could say another word to each other, a bundle of joy dashed out from the garden beyond and ran straight for me.

"Miss Moore. Miss Moore," she cried joyfully.

Her unbridled excitement was infectious and I instantly got down onto my haunches and pulled her little body into a big bear hug.

She was so happy to see me it was surprising. Especially, given that we saw each other pretty much every day in school. Her father, I noted, was as surprised.

"We made you lots of things to eat," she said enthusiastically. "Dad said you'd love them."

"I will love them," I affirmed, as I was pulled over to the counter and indeed there was a very wonderful-looking spread waiting for me.

I glanced back at him. "I hope I haven't caused you too much trouble."

He waved my apology away. "Because of you, I got to

spend time with my daughter." He looked at Anya and winked. "And we both improved our skills, and you just get to share in the end result."

When he put it that way, the meal became more special and I wished I too had been part of creating the food we were about to enjoy.

Chapter 41
Cole

Anya's enthusiastic reception of Montana surprised me. For one, I hadn't ever seen her receive anyone that excitedly, and it made me wonder what was going on with her. Was it because she was lonely? Was she missing her mother so much she was trying to bond with another female?

And as the evening progressed, I watched both of them and how they interacted, and more than anything, I quickly realized that Anya was not behaving like a kid. She was behaving like a mother hen with Montana.

This was amusing and startling to me that I just stayed out of the way, watching as Anya carefully offered her loud vibes to tastes as well as refreshments and, most surprisingly, inquired about her state.

"You had an upset tummy yesterday, Miss Moore, how is your tummy today?"

Even Montana looked surprised that Anya was aware of it. "It's okay. I'm fine," she said. "I wouldn't have come over otherwise. I would have stayed home and used Tolstoy as my hot water bottle."

Anya laughed uproariously. "Why didn't you bring him?"

"He doesn't like leaving the ranch. In fact, he generally doesn't even like people."

"Doesn't he like me?"

"Oh no. He let you fall asleep with him in your arms. That means he LOVES you."

"Really?"

"Yes, really."

She turned eagerly to me. "Daddy, when can we go see Tolstoy again?"

"Why don't you ask Miss Moore," I said casually.

"You're welcome any time, Anya," Montana said with a smile.

"Did you hear that, Daddy? Miss Moore said I can go any time to Shadow Wolf Ranch."

"I heard," I said dryly. "Wine?" I asked Montana as I headed over to the fridge to grab a bottle.

"Actually. I'll stick to cranberry juice along with Anya."

"Okay." I poured her a glass and handed it to her. "Tour first or food first?" I asked.

She didn't have to think. "Food first, definitely. I skipped lunch because I knew I was coming here, so right now I am starving."

"Excellent choice because everything is ready," I said and began to carry the dishes out to the table on the patio.

As soon as the food was put on the table, Anya and I were ready to tuck in, but Montana stopped us in our tracks with her request. "Do you mind if we say grace?"

"Sure," I said. "We can say grace. Why don't you do it?"

Montana smiled and put her hands out to us. I placed my hand in hers and Anya, who learned about saying grace for the first time when we went to Shadow Wolf Ranch, put her hands in both of ours. I closed my eyes and assumed she had too.

"Bless us, oh Lord, for these gifts that we're about to receive from thy bounty through Christ, our Lord. Good bread, good meat, thank you, Lord. Let's eat. Amen."

We all dived into the meal. I watched with amusement as Montana waxed lyrical about the deliciousness of the steak.

"It's perfectly done," she declared.

"The secret is browned butter," I said.

"Whatever it is, I love it."

"What about the potatoes?" Anya asked.

I laughed. My daughter was so endearing. She had peeled the potatoes and now she wanted credit for that.

"They are especially delicious," Montanna said. "Did you make them?"

"I peeled them all," she announced proudly.

I stared at her. She was wearing the most brilliant smile on her little face. And suddenly, I realized, my daughter was never happy in New York. I'd never seen her like this. Here was where she was thriving.

We ate in silence after that, simply enjoying the meal. At some point, I looked out at the garden in front of us and I knew; Anya was right. We should have ducks. And we should have the vegetable garden that she wanted too. I could see the three of us creating it together. I felt stable. I felt hopeful, and I felt happy.

I turned to Montana. "What kind of plants, flowers, and vegetables do you recommend for us here?"

"Only Anya can answer that. Anya, last week we taught you how to grow tomatoes in the greenhouse, starting them as seedlings and taking care of them until you harvest them. Next week you will learn about even more plants. So ..." she turned to me. "I think you should let Anya pick the garden she wants herself."

"I'm cool with that," I said.

"As for flowers ... um... what are your favorite flowers?" She frowned, then smiled. "I remember now. You mentioned tulips in class."

Anya went still and looked down as if she had committed an offense, and I instantly understood why. It wasn't that she particularly liked tulips, but they were her mother's favorite flowers. It made me wonder as I watched her if this was the key to why she was so wounded and sad at night. During the day she was occupied with all kinds of new activities, but at night she was missing her mother. It hurt me immensely that I wasn't enough to fill that void, but there was nothing I could do. It was her mother who had decided to leave us.

"We can get the tulip bulbs online," Montana said, unaware of the undercurrents between my daughter and me. "I'll instruct you on how to grow them. Together we can build a layout and plant exactly what you need and love."

I nodded in agreement.

"Truthfully, I don't really enjoy growing vegetables," Montana suddenly said.

Both of our heads shot up.

"This is a secret, Anya," she told my daughter and

placed a finger against her lips. "Don't tell anyone. Promise?"

Anya gazed at her, her sadness forgotten, her eyes shining with curiosity. "You don't?"

Montana shook her head. "I don't like earthworms. When I look at them they make my skin go all funny, but over the years I have learned to appreciate what good little helpers they are to the farmer."

"Why do you participate so much in the farming activities when you don't find it fun?" I asked.

She shrugged. "My father loves it," she replied. "And when I was younger, it was the only thing we could do together. Till today, he still thinks it's something I love. To suddenly throw a tantrum and say I don't enjoy it all that much is unnecessary."

"Do you like swimming then, Miss Moore?" Anya asked.

I turned to look at her. "You want to go swimming?"

She nodded. "Elizabeth, at school says, everybody goes swimming at the lake."

Montana smiled. "Yes, we have two lakes in Bison Ridge. You can only fish in the big lake, but all the kids go to swim in the small lake. It's not too far away. If you want to go swimming in the lake, of course, we can arrange it for you. Would you prefer a swimming pool, though?" she asked.

Anya shook her head. "No, I want to go to the lake. We've always had a pool."

I listened to my daughter and tried not to frown, but this very blatant transmission of information about our past lives wasn't our agreement at all.

"You used to have a swimming pool when you lived in New York?" Montana asked, one eyebrow raised. "Wow! That's rare, isn't it? You must be rich."

"No, we're not," Anya denied vehemently. "We're not rich at all. We're just like everybody else. We're middle-class."

Shit. Anya was overdoing it. Montana glanced oddly at me, but I said nothing.

Chapter 42
Montana

"Do you think she did it on purpose?" I asked as he brought in the last of the dishes to load into the dishwasher. The sun had set, and the house had the kind of warm, homey feeling that made me want to curl up under a blanket with snacks and a movie.

Cole laughed and I nudged him to keep him from waking the child up. She had fallen asleep on the couch and Cole had gently covered her with a blanket.

"She actually enjoys loading up dishwashers," he said. "Sometimes she even likes doing the dishes herself."

I shuddered. "Ugh ... they were my absolute worst chores when I was growing up. Anything but the dishes."

"You liked to be outside, didn't you?"

"Yes," I said.

He smiled and continued to work quietly. I didn't mind the silence and didn't particularly feel the need to fill it up with idle chatter, but he began to speak unexpectedly.

"Why is your father's ranch called Shadow Wolf?"

"Well, it's a long story."

"Tell me. I'm curious."

"When my great grandaddy moved here, wolves still roamed these parts, but the locals kept killing them off. My granddaddy had spent a lot of time with Native Indians so he had a great love for wolves, but there was nothing he could do about it. Finally, there was only one large black wolf left. It was so elusive, they called it Shadow.

"One day, he was in the forest, and he found the black wolf with its foot caught in a trap. It was frightened and in terrible pain so it snarled ferociously at him. He had to put a metal shield with a hole in the bottom between him and the wolf so he could release its foot. It ran away and he never saw it again. Many years later, he found the black wolf on his porch. It was dying of a gunshot wound and it had come to say goodbye. He tried to give it milk, but it was already too late. It died in his arms. As a mark of respect, he named his ranch after it."

"Wow! That's some story. You should tell it to Anya. She loves that kind of thing. Especially stories featuring wolves and princesses."

"Princesses? There are no princesses in this story."

"No? I think I'm looking at one now."

I blushed and pretended to give my whole attention to cleaning a spot on the counter. "Right. I better put these cupcakes in the pantry. They last longer when they're kept cool." I opened the pantry door and was shocked to find it full of all kinds of pies, pastries, cakes, and bread. Every shelf was crowded with food. I went back to the kitchen.

"Your pantry looks like a bakery."

"Yeah, I know," he said wryly. "People keep bringing welcome food and I don't know what to do with it."

"People? You mean, women, mostly single women," I deduced.

"Aren't single women people? Anyway, would you like to take them all to school? Maybe the kids can eat them."

"Sure. I'll take them. No point wasting them, but don't you want to keep anything?"

"Not really."

"Not even Mrs. Dearborn's fruitcake?"

"Mrs. Dearborn's fruitcake?"

"Yeah, Mrs. Dearborn's fruitcake. Oh my God! You're giving it away and you haven't even tried it. You have to try it. It's to die for." I went back to the pantry and came back with her cake. I cut a thin slice, put it on a small plate and took it to him. "Try it."

He took a bite, his gorgeous teeth biting into the juicy fruit. His eyes widened. "Mmmmm."

"Good, huh?"

"Very good." He took another bite. "Actually, almost as good as your pussy."

My mouth dropped open with shock. "Cole!"

"What? I'm making a comparison. I'm not allowed to?"

I snatched the plate away from him. "You don't deserve this."

He started laughing softly. "You're so fucking adorable, Montana."

"Don't change the subject. We're talking about Mrs. Dearborn."

"Mrs. Dearborn. I remember her. She was wearing a

blue hat. She asked so many intrusive questions, I thought she was the town gossip."

"She is." I nibbled at the cake. "But every year, without fail, she wins the Best Fruitcake title during the Best Baker summer festival. No one knows her secret. That special, elusive thing that makes her cakes so delicious."

"Is that the Summer Festival next weekend?" he asked.

"Yes, the whole town looks forward to it every year. It's the best. You should take Anya to it. All her friends from school will be there. You will probably also get to meet a few more of the local women too."

He looked amused. "To help refill my pantry?"

"There'll be a waffle-eating contest."

He looked at me indulgently and I realized I deeply enjoyed this light and airy attitude of his. He seemed relaxed, or least, a bit less on guard than usual.

"I'm just mentioning it because I am the undefeated champion. No one's been able to beat me for the past three years."

"So you like waffles?" he asked.

My heart jumped like a wild deer. "Um ... yeah. Waffles are good. But you're the new face. You ready for some competition?"

"I won't enter the competition, but I'll be there."

"Good."

"When I was at your ranch I saw a photo of your mother. You look exactly like her," he said, changing the subject.

"Do you really think so?"

"Absolutely."

"You're just being kind. My mother was the town's beauty. She was heart-stoppingly beautiful."

"So are you," he said.

I blushed. "I still miss her."

"What happened to her?" he asked softly.

A smile came to my heart. As it always did when I thought about my mom. "She passed away from cancer," I replied. "I was still pretty young, about six, but I still remember her vividly. When she smiled, she lit up the whole world. My father was never the same after she died."

"I'm sorry, Montana."

"It was a long time ago. I will see her again. What about your mom? Where is she?"

"My mother suffers from dementia. She's in a care home."

"Oh, Cole. I'm sorry."

"Yes, it's sad. Very sad."

We were done with uploading the dishwasher. I drained my glass simply because I was getting even more nervous about the part of the night we were now approaching. The moment of truth. I needed to distract myself; otherwise, I was going to jump him.

"So ... how about the house tour?" I asked, then realized just how suggestive I sounded after the words had left my mouth. "I mean ... it's what we were supposed to do earlier. Did you forget?"

"I didn't forget," he said as he set his empty glass down and then turned to glance at his daughter.

"Don't worry. She'll be asleep for a couple of hours, at least."

I let him lead me up the stairs. He didn't bother to show me any of the rooms. Instead, he led me straight down the end of the hallway and pushed a door open. I walked in, wondering if this was his room. It wasn't. It was just a spare room with a divan bed in it. Before I could turn around, I heard the key lock turn with a click behind me.

Chapter 43

Cole

I hadn't exactly planned to seduce her this way, especially not with Anya downstairs, but the woman before me was a witch. She had cast a spell on me. I just couldn't say no. She was so damn beautiful she held the lure of a vixen in the palm of her hand. Her beauty was electric in a way that made my body throb, yet so soft it made my heart want to melt. She wore her allure lightly, in her eyes, her smile, and her flushed cheeks.

Fuck, I needed her.

I couldn't help it.

I needed to come inside her again and forget myself, even for a little while. I instantly grabbed my t-shirt and pulled it over my head.

Her eyes widened.

"Oh! Is this the tour you meant?" she asked, retreating as I approached her.

"If it's not the kind of tour you want, then why are so many of your buttons open?"

The backs of her knees hit the edge of the bed and she stopped. What I wanted more than anything was to suck on those breasts. With one finger on her chest, I pushed and she fell backwards, her arms flailing. Wasting no time, I joined her.

"Anya," she whispered hoarsely.

"Anya is sleeping. Usually, when she falls asleep like this she won't awaken for at least an hour." I stroked her nipples, watching her, feeling hot lust build in my body. It was hard to imagine how someone could be this wholesome and beautiful and at the same time be such a temptress. She truly was dangerously close to my heart, and if I let down my guard, she would open the door and enter.

She smiled, and it was so beautiful I leaned forward and kissed those sweet lips.

I had intended it to be brief, but I couldn't hold myself back. My tongue slid into her mouth, and I was gone. Ever since the storage room I had been dying to do this to her.

We saw each other at school, but it was from a distance. I could only eye her from afar, and that had tortured me.

Numerous times in the middle of the night, I had woken up with a hard-on, from dreams of being inside of her. It was impossible for me to go to sleep after that, so I'd get up and head over to rub out my cock until I was spurting hard, but what else could I offer her? I might have to leave in a moment. Worse, Paganini's men could turn up here and kidnap her to use as a bargaining chip.

In my heart, I knew she was the one for me, and one day, when things worked out the way I planned, then I would come back and claim her, but until then it could only be this; stolen moments.

"I can't promise you anything."

"I didn't ask for anything."

"I know. I just wanted to make sure you knew. I don't want to mislead you."

"Don't worry. I get it. You're hot stuff and you have a lot of choice-"

I put my finger against her lips. Sighing, I pushed her hair out of her eyes and tucked it behind her ear. I wanted to commit every bit of her features to memory.

"No, I'm not ... hot stuff. I can't think of a serious relationship right now because I have problems that I have to sort out first."

"What sort of problems?" she asked.

I let my gaze slide away as I thought of what I could say that would be as close to the truth as possible without endangering me or her.

"I don't want to go into details, but Anya's mother is not well," I replied. "She got herself entangled with the wrong crowd in New York, got involved with drugs, and now she is unstable. Anya is very attached to her, so her absence has caused significant damage. We just got away from all of that, but as it stands it's still an unresolved problem ... Anya needs time. We both need time without new distractions or obligations."

"That's what I am? A distraction or obligation?"

"Distraction? Yes, you'll always be that. I can't look at you without wanting to carry you off to my bed. But an obligation? That's not the right word. You'd be a responsibility. Sounds like a negative thing, but it's not. It's the only way I want to be with you. Just like Anya is my responsibility to love, cherish, and protect. It will be the same with you, but right now I want all of my focus to be on Anya until I've solved this problem. Until she stabilizes mentally."

"Stabilizes mentally," she repeated. "Is there something wrong with her now?"

"She's been having nightmares, but I don't want to take her to see anyone yet because that might make her start thinking there's something wrong with her when it could be a problem that will resolve itself."

Her forehead creased. "What kind of nightmares?"

"She won't exactly share what they are. She tries to brush it off, but she never used to do that before so it bothers me that she's so hesitant about sharing it with me."

"Oh," she nodded, shifting slightly underneath me to get more comfortable. I had most of my weight on my arms, but that moment had passed. I rolled to my back and stared at the ceiling.

"Okay," she said.

"Okay, what?"

"Okay. Nothing serious."

"You sure?" I asked.

She smiled, but the lights had gone out of her eyes. "I don't know how I will feel in the future, but for now I'm not ready to let go of this thing we have going on."

I smiled too, pleased to hear that for now I could still keep her, but a part of me felt sad for dimming the happiness from her face.

We remained silent, neither of us moving towards the other.

I looked at my watch. "Our one hour is nearly up," I said softly.

There was a knock on our door, and she turned to face me. "Bullseye."

I sat up and put my t-shirt back on, and Montana jumped to her feet. I watched as she headed over to the door. She unlocked the door and opened it.

"You did the tour without me?" Anya complained.

Chapter 44
Montana

"Actually, we haven't started yet," Cole told her. "But it's getting late. Maybe next time, huh?"

"Okay."

"Come and join us," he invited.

I took her by the hand and brought her back to the divan. She seemed to have the biggest smile on her face, and as she wriggled around and settled in between us, I laid back down on the divan once again.

It didn't feel strange to be with them even though I'd never really given much thought to having a family. I guess I hadn't exactly met anyone that made me even want to consider it, but with him and with Anya, I couldn't help but imagine.

Part of me was relieved that Cole was honest with me, and the dreaded discussion had gone relatively calmly. I was lost in my thoughts, but I could suddenly feel his eyes on me, watching me, and so I turned, and indeed, he was looking at me.

I knew I had so much more to say to him. Our discussion wasn't over yet, but at that moment, I didn't really want to speak. I just wanted to bask in the strangely peaceful time with this man and his child.

"Miss Moore, is your home safe?" Anya suddenly asked.

I pulled my attention away from her father and looked at her without understanding why she was asking me such a strange question. "Yes, I think it is safe."

"That's good," she said. "Dad wants to keep us safe at all times. Sometimes though, I still feel as though nowhere is safe."

I watched the little girl curiously. "Why would you feel like nowhere is safe?"

My heart's pace began to pick up. I felt anxious at what she would reveal. Maybe, I'd been waiting for the other shoe to drop because he just seemed too perfect, too good to be true. I wasn't hoping for it to drop since I was still infatuated with him, but if there was something that could bring me back to my senses, I dreaded it and wished for it.

To my surprise, Cole didn't try and stop her, instead watched her intently, as though he too was curious about what she wanted to say.

"Because there could be bad people coming. If you're in danger, you can come here. Dad said this house is really safe." She looked up at her father. "Dad, it will be okay, right? If Miss Moore feels scared, she can come over to the safe room, right? So that she can be safe?"

It would have been so easy for her words to fly over my head. They seemed like the normal chatter of children, but I was able to pick out the peculiarity in what she was saying. I turned towards her.

"There's a safe room?"

"Yeah," she began, sitting up, excited to share this with me. "It has food in it and a lot of—" Suddenly, she stopped and slapped both her hands over her mouth guiltily and looked at her father as if she just remembered she was not supposed to tell anyone about this room. She had done what her father had told her not to do, though I couldn't quite understand why the presence of this room needed to be a secret. Mischief rose in my heart. I turned to Cole, but he remained neutral and unfazed by what his daughter had revealed.

"Cole, what's the room about? Could you show me?"

Anya's head fell forward with shame, and instantly I regretted asking. It was obvious she felt bad about disappointing her father.

"It's just a safety room in case there is an emergency of some sort," her father explained. "I hope to always be with her, but until I find a nanny I can trust, if for some reason I'm not home and she is, I made a room that she could run to, to feel safe in. She may never need it, but it's just in case she ever felt worried for any reason."

This made total sense, and it was quite thoughtful and wonderful of him. I nodded, impressed at how caring he was as a father.

"That's a very good idea." Then I went a little closer to Anya and whispered to her. "I'm also here if you ever feel worried. Never hesitate to reach out to me, alright?"

The excitement and smile came back to her face and she nodded eagerly. Impulsively, she reached forward to hug me. I hugged her back and felt I had started to truly care for this affectionate and loving child.

Chapter 45
Cole

The time for Montana to leave came much too soon.

Anya was seated on the couch, wide awake and watching a new animated movie she had selected for all of us, but neither Montana nor I had any interest in watching it.

"Anya, wave goodbye to Miss Moore," I said.

Anya put her movie on hold and ran over to the front door. "Bye, Miss Moore. See you tomorrow at school."

"Good night, Anya. Thank you for this evening. It was lovely, and I especially loved the cupcakes.

Anya went back to her movie and I closed the door and headed out with Montana.

"Thank you for a great evening. I really enjoyed being with you and Anya," she said, nodding as we walked down the steps. We went over to where her old Volvo was parked. It was a charming green, though thoroughly scuffed and old. She stood against the door and it took everything in me to keep from kissing her.

"Was this your dad's?" I asked, simply because I didn't want to let her go yet.

"Yeah. When I turned sixteen, he wanted to get me something fancy, and I refused. I told him to hand this over to me while he got what he wanted, which was a newer truck. It was a whole battle, but eventually, he conceded. The main issue was that it wasn't safe, so he worked on it for months and installed an airbag at least to the steering wheel."

This immensely amused me. "So there's only one airbag? The passenger's seat has none?"

"Absolutely none."

"Do you tell your passengers that when they get into the front seat?"

"It depends on who the passenger is and how much I like or dislike them," she replied.

I laughed out loud. She made me want to try even harder to resolve my feud with Paganini so I could get back to living life the way I wanted ... with her, hopefully.

She smiled then and briefly lowered her head in thought. Then she lifted it once again, her face was pale, and those enchanting eyes of hers were sad.

"I ... I think maybe we should end things here."

My heart seemed to stop for a moment. Obviously, I knew this moment could happen, but I had not expected it right now. It had come out of the blue and was a monumental blow.

"I understand, but what brought this on? You were fine a moment ago." My voice sounded strange.

"I know, I must sound like some ditzy female, but I've never been in this kind of situation before, and I honestly thought I could go on this way ... casually, I mean, just taking the pleasure and not wanting more, but ... I realize now, I can't."

She looked at the house, her gaze soft but distant.

"You and Anya, and this is me being honest, maybe too honest, you two paint the prettiest picture ... and I want to be a part of that picture. That meal we had tonight was everything I ever wanted, but now you're walking me out. And it doesn't feel good to know that, that's what all our meals are going to be like. Me leaving.

"Even now, I cannot trust myself not to start wanting far more than you're willing to offer, let alone as I start to feel more and more for you. You've been straight with me from the very beginning; you can't offer more, and I think it's time for me to take your warning seriously. For my sake ... and for Anya's as well. She's starting to get too close to me.

"So now, while we're still on good terms, while I can still walk away without too much heartbreak, I think it's best to. It's also a good thing to give you two the time and space needed to settle down and actually get the change that you both need right now. To find solid ground."

She looked at me then, and I couldn't help but stare desperately at her. It was such an incredibly sad moment, but I knew it was what we both needed at the time. It was the right thing to do for now. She didn't know it, but there was no way I was letting her go. I would solve my problem and I would be back to claim my beauty.

"One last kiss?" I asked. "One last time?"

She smiled then, but it was too bright, almost dishonest. She was trying her very best to shield her hurt, but I could see it too clearly."

"Of course," she said, tears slightly pooling in her eyes. "No hard feelings."

"No hard feelings," I nodded. I leaned forward and sealed my lips over hers. Shutting my eyes, I savored her taste one more time. No matter how painful and bittersweet this moment was, I knew in my gut that for the sake of my daughter, and her too, this was the right decision.

The kiss was brief because she pulled away. I wished she had held on just a bit longer, but I understood why it was difficult for her.

I stepped away and swore to myself that the next time I kissed her again, she would not pull away. She would never pull away, because I was going to give her everything she wanted.

She got into her car. Then the engine started. My hands were clenched into fists.

I waited while she turned the car around, and she drove off into the distance. She never waved, she never even looked at me. It was time to leave, time for me to head back into the house and continue on with my life with Anya. My life without Montana. However, I found that I couldn't move.

My heart was mourning her exit. My heart was waiting for the blue car to return. To say it had been a monumental error. I knew she was not coming back, but I waited a few more moments so Anya did not see me the way I was.

Then I turned around and returned to the house. My chest was tight with pain, but I plastered a smile on my face so Anya would think nothing had changed even though everything had changed. The world was a grayer place than it had been just a few minutes ago.

Chapter 46
Montana

https://www.youtube.com/watch?v=6dYWe1c3OyU&
list=RDfNFzfwLM72c&index=10
-I will survive-

"You are mourning," Pearl said.

She had dragged me out to buy groceries simply because she hadn't been able to persuade me to go out with the girls the previous night. I had stayed in and eaten a whole bunch of pastries from the bakery and regretted it afterwards.

"I'm not mourning," I denied and started moving away from her, even though she was dead on the money. Of course, I was. I was never the best person to deal with difficult parents, but this week I had been like a bear with a sore head. I had actually visualized attacking one mother with a pair of scissors! I tried to hide it, but my sadness had been noticed by everyone. From my dad to the other teachers and even some of the students.

The first day after our breakup I went to school nervous about seeing Cole. It was unavoidable, and I spent the entire day bracing myself for it, convincing myself that all I had to do was avoid direct eye contact. But when the moment came and he arrived to pick up Anya, I found that I didn't even have to ignore him. I didn't know how he did it, but he behaved as though all the familiarity and intimacy we had shared had all happened in my fantasies.

He was a civil, polite stranger.

I had become Marylin or any of the other women who chased him persistently. He addressed me politely, looked me straight in the eye, and yet he didn't see me. Or at least, that was what it felt like to me. I marveled at his inhuman ability to pull such an act off. While I hurt so deeply I nearly didn't know how to contain my pain. I had to escape to my classroom. There I paced the floor for a few moments in distress and confusion. Then I sat at my desk, lay my head on my arms and sobbed.

That was when Pearl came in.

She swore at him until she was blue in the face. I thought I hated him then.

How could he simply wipe me off his mind? It was then I understood. I had been playing at the notion of separation. In my immature, inexperienced mind, we weren't really separated. We were always going to be attracted to each other and flirt. Sometimes the attraction would get so great we would sleep together. To me the break up was temporary. Perhaps it had even been a way to make him choose. Have all of me or nothing. And he was supposed to come running back and say I want it all because I can't live without you.

I wasn't been able to go back to school the next day. It was easy for my father to believe I was sick given how down and sluggish I was the day before. Pearl, Kelly and Natalie had come over outside school time to find me wallowing in the forest. They told me I was in love.

I didn't believe them.

Or rather, I didn't want to acknowledge that they were totally right. I told them I couldn't understand how we could become complete strangers in that way overnight.

Pearl wondered if that was his way of trying to cope as well. But Kelly was more uncharitable. She thought he was being an asshole and completely alienating me so that I wouldn't get any ideas of proposing a return to what we had before. The most upsetting thing was that he had acted like there was some nonsense magical connection between us. Was it simply because he wanted to get in my pants? My mind was turning dark, but maybe for once I was actually using my brain.

"Hey! Montana!" Pearl called from the bakery counter. She was holding two loaves of bread that she'd been comparing. "You running away from me won't change facts. Which one?"

I sighed. "The one on the left."

"Mine or yours?"

"Yours."

I headed off on my own and went over to the candy aisle to pick up some sweets. Before now, I wasn't a big fan of sweets, but lately, it was all I could think about. Life had become quite bitter and I was turning to sweets to make me feel better. Kelly said I was being dramatic and I should stop it before I got too fat, but what did she know? I remember quite a few times when she had turned to ice cream and alcohol to make her feel better.

"Dad, look at that!" I heard the familiar voice from a few isles away, and instantly, before I could even realize what I was doing, I had dropped the box of milk chocolates I was holding and hurried after the voice. I didn't need to speak to him; I just needed a safe glimpse from a distance.

I peeked out from the corner of the aisle, my gaze going around the store in search. It was easy to see everyone at a glance, even though the store was large. All I had to do was look for the tallest head. He was one of the tallest people in town. Before I could zero in on anyone, a sudden smack on my ass startled me.

"Ow," I complained, turning around to see Pearl looking at me with a curious expression on her face.

"What are you doing?" she asked.

"Ditching you."

"Because I was trying to talk some sense into you?"

"Yes," I replied, turning back to continue my search. "Now go away."

I saw him then, at the check-in counter. He was waiting in line. I couldn't see Anya, but I'd heard her voice so I knew she was with him. I didn't want to feel hurt, but I couldn't help it. If Anya had seen me, she would have run to me. But this was for the best. He was keeping to what we had agreed, so why did I feel this way? Furious with myself, I turned around and began to storm off.

"Montana!" Pearl called.

"I'll be waiting in the car," I said.

I waited in the car with my oversized hood over my head and buried my eyes behind her huge sunglasses. Not long after, Pearl returned. She got in, and instantly I started the car. She held her hand against mine as I turned the ignition and stopped me.

"Hey," she said softly.

"We don't need to talk," I told her. "I know I'm acting out, but I still feel he took things to the extreme. We parted amicably. This avoidance, or whatever the hell this is, is completely unnecessary and fucking aggravating. I'm allowed to feel this way."

She nodded. "You're right. You're absolutely right."

I was startled since I wasn't expecting her to agree with me, but to tell me to grow up and snap out of it. Suddenly, I felt so incredibly sad I couldn't drive, so I got out of the car and went out to the other side. Even though I was too choked to speak she understood. She scooted over and took the keys from me. I managed to hold back the tears until I got home, but the moment I was in, I ran straight to the stables, got into Lola's box, and tried my best to muffle the truly pathetic sounds coming out of my mouth. Poor Lola, she gazed at me with distressed, mournful eyes.

Why, oh why, hadn't I just held onto the scraps he was willing to offer?

Chapter 47
Cole

https://www.youtube.com/watch?v=uVXVO_vF2Io
-when you're in love with a beautiful woman-

"Dad, look," Anya shouted excitedly above the noise of all the festival-goers, "that's the stand for our school. We are raising money so Mr. Moore can bring underprivileged kids from the city slums and ghettos to come and spend a week learning survival skills."

Even from a distance, I could see Anya's gold head. My heart longed for her, but I steeled myself. My inability to control my emotions could get her killed. That was the right line of reasoning to take because it stopped the longing in its tracks. "We can visit your school stand later and make a donation. How about some candy floss, first?"

"No, Dad. The auction is now. All the teachers are lining up for it."

"What auction?"

"People have to bid to kiss the teachers. The teacher who gets the most money for the cause gets a prize. Come on, let's go bid for Miss Moore."

"No, honey. Let's just make a big donation later, okay?"

"No, Dad," she insisted. "We have to support Miss Moore. All the other kids are supporting their teachers too. I want Miss Moore to win."

"What about the candy floss?" I asked desperately.

"Later. Come on, Dad." She tugged on my hand. "Miss Moore is going up to the stage. It's her turn already. Hurry up."

I had no choice but to let her drag me to the edge of a small makeshift wooden stage. Montana was standing on it, and she looked embarrassed. Her hair was loose and the slight breeze blew strands into her face, and she impatiently pushed them away. Across the sea of faces our eyes met. She froze, then looked away, her face bright red.

"Bidding starts at twenty dollars for a kiss from the blondie", a man's voice chanted. "Do I hear a forty? Forty bid. Gentleman in the left. Now forty. Sixty? Sixty bid. Gentleman in the center. Eighty. Will ya give me one hundred dollars? One hundred dollars bid. One hundred dollars. Got ya, Sir."

"Bid for Miss Moore, Dad," Anya cried.

I looked down at her eager face and grinned. "Relax. We'll bid for her. We just won't show our hand yet."

"Would ya bid? Bid now. One hundred and eighty. Gotta get it now. One hundred and eighty. Will anybody give me two hundred? Show us your money. That two hundred, right there. Two hundred and twenty bid. Will ya give me two hundred and forty for the blondie?"

"Five hundred dollars," a voice rang out.

I turned towards the voice. He was tall and broad and wearing a cowboy hat and I saw instantly that he was in love with Montana. He was looking directly into her eyes and he had a secret smile on his face. He wanted her and he was letting everyone know that he did. To me, Montana was the most beautiful girl in the world, but because she was a virgin because of the way we were together, I'd naively assumed I did not have any competition.

But he was; my rival.

"We have five hundred. Five hundred bid. Five hundred bid. Going once. Going twice."

A red mist clouded my brain. I didn't think. I just reacted.

"Ten thousand dollars," I called.

Montana's mouth dropped open with shock. There was a gasp and every head in the crowd turned towards my voice.

"Ho, ho, there you have it. Ten thousand bid. Ten thousand bid. Any more bids? Bid Now. No more. Going once. Going twice."

I looked at the cowboy. He was looking at me with shock and rage.

"SOLD for ten thousand dollars to the gentlemen in the back."

"You won, Dad. You won," Anya screamed happily next to me. The auction fever had got to her and she was bouncing with excitement.

Everyone was staring at us as we made our way up to

the stage. I leaned down and lightly kissed Montana's blazing cheek while she stood as still as a statue. Then I turned around and walked down the two steps of the stage. "I'll wire the money tomorrow," I told the shocked face of Mr. Moore's assistant.

I noted the speculative look on her face as she nodded.

I pulled Anya along with me. "Dad, where are we going?"

"Home," I growled.

"Why?" she cried plaintively.

"I forgot something important. We'll come back later this evening," I answered, as I strode out of the festival grounds.

I was furious with myself. What the fuck was I thinking? I had one thing to do and I had allowed my dick to ruin it. I had effectively just blown my cover. I had just made myself the talk of the town and not in a good way. Everybody will now wonder about my finances and what I was really doing in Bison Ridge.

"Why didn't we stay and talk to Miss Moore?" Anya asked restlessly.

I could see she was upset, as I walked quickly with her through the kiosks and stalls, the last thing on my mind was having fun or greeting anyone.

"Dad, can we at least, please, get some Amish pies at the bakery stand?" she begged.

I stopped then and looked down at her. She was just a kid at a festival. She didn't understand or deserve to be treated this way.

"Sure, of course, we can," I agreed with a smile. "Okay, let's go over to the bakery stall."

The light came back to her eyes, and I apologized silently to her in my heart. 'Things will be fine soon, sweetheart. I'll handle this. We won't have to run much longer.'

We headed over to the stand, and she began to pick out the pastries she wanted.

"Hello, Mr. Swift," the owner, Mrs. Sherman, came up to us with a smile on her face. She had huge curls in her brown hair, a flowery apron, and a friendly boisterous presence about her.

I smiled. "Hello, Mrs. Sherman."

"Have you just gone and broken the gossip centers of the town?" she asked with a laugh.

My rash behavior had already travelled to her ear. I winced inwardly. "I was just trying to help a good cause."

"Yes, it was a very good cause. Actually, I've been hoping you would stop by."

"Oh! Why's that?"

"There were a couple of men asking about you."

My body stilled. "Who were they?"

"They said they were Police detectives, but I didn't believe them."

I frowned. "Why didn't you believe them?"

"I don't know. The moment I met you, I knew I liked you. I could trust you. They ... they both had sly eyes. Untrustworthy faces."

"What did they want to know?"

"They were asking if there were any newcomers in town. Specifically, a man with a daughter."

"What did you tell them?"

"Told them nope. No one new in town. They went away, but they didn't give up. I saw them go into the café where I saw them talk to Mrs. Garrett's daughter, Tiffany. I think you met her once. Very irresponsible girl. She's told everyone in town about Anya's designer shoes, and since they spoke to her for some time, I'm gonna assume she told them too."

Chapter 48
Cole

Fuck! Fuck! Fuck!

Paganini's men were already in town!

Something didn't add up. Finding me shouldn't have been this easy. They had to have tracked or traced me, or something. If they were already here I had very little time left.

"You should go and see the Sheriff, Mr. Swift. He's a good man, he'll help you."

"Yes, maybe I will, Mrs. Sheridan," I replied with a smile and handed my card over to her.

"Be careful, Mr. Swift. I didn't like the look of those men."

"Thank you for being so kind and thoughtful. I really appreciate it."

"Take care, son," she said and moved away to take care of another customer.

The girl helping behind the food table handed Anya her box of pastries. I thanked her and we moved away into the sunshine. There was a chair and table right outside and I pulled out a chair for Anya. After she was seated, I took a seat as well.

I lifted my face towards the warmth of the sunshine. What a beautiful life it would be if I didn't have the problem I had with Paganini. I realized I could live the rest of my life in this town. The sense of neighborliness, camaraderie towards one's fellow man, and plain goodness amongst the town folk was a marvelous thing to witness. They took these qualities for granted and did not realize how precious they were. Coming from the city, I valued them greatly.

"The cornbread is really tasty, Dad," Anya said. "Derek's mom brought a box to class, and she shared it all around. It looks like a cake, but it's actually bread. It's really cool."

I nodded and watched her. Had my daughter done something that she shouldn't have? It had to be her. She was my weakest link. I'd made my plans meticulously over a long period of time. I'd left no traces. Anya had done amazing, but at the end of the day, she was still just a child and could have made a mistake.

She broke a piece of the bread off and offered it to me.

I was running out of time, but I needed to know. Otherwise, I would be running blind. I bit into the piece. It was good bread. "I'm going to ask you a question and I want you to tell me the truth, okay, honey?"

She looked at me with a full mouth and nodded.

"Did you ... have you in any way been in contact with your mommy recently?"

She blinked, then hung her head in shame and my heart sank.

"I'm sorry. I ... I kept having bad dreams."

"What dreams?" I asked, leaning closer and trying to be as soft as possible.

"That she was dying. That I would never see her again. I ... I didn't contact her, I just ... I just ... it was her birthday and I wanted to send her a card. I made one and I ... Miss Kelly Douglas helped me to send it, but I didn't put a return address on it ..."

My mind was whirling. That was how they found us. I tried my best to keep my expression neutral so she wouldn't burst into tears or clam up.

"What address did you use for your mom?" I asked.

"She gave me one before she left. A year ago. I kept it. I don't know if she received it, I mean, we moved so she could have moved as well. I'm sorry, Daddy. I just wanted to know if she was okay."

"It's okay, sweetheart. It's okay. You did nothing wrong, but we have to get home now."

She jumped to her feet.

Quickly, I led her away from the crowds towards where the car was parked. All I had to do was get home as quickly as possible and get Montana to the safe house, and then I could be on my way to New York. I pulled my phone out of my pocket then and placed the call to Leila to make arrangements. I needed eyes on the house and on Anya, and I needed the current location of Paganini. For all I knew, he might not even currently be in the country. I picked up my phone to call Leila and my phone began to ring. To my surprise it was Leila.

"They're there. Paganini's men are already in Bison Ridge," she said urgently.

"I know. When did they arrive?"

"This morning."

"Can't be. They must be working in teams because one lot already arrived here yesterday. They were asking the locals about me."

"How did they know to go there, though? Yesterday, they suddenly stopped following the good schools lead and instead they went straight to your town. Which means the town must be crawling with them. At least two teams."

"You're sure they are Paganini's men?" I asked, more out of hope than anything else. Of course, Leila was sure. She wasn't the owner of one the top private detective agencies in New York for nothing.

"Pretty certain. Just got a message from Tom. He couldn't believe it either. They must have some new information. You haven't done anything out of the ordinary, have you?"

"No, nothing."

I hurriedly put Anya into the passenger seat and went around to the driver's door. As I did so my eyes spotted two men who had just arrived at the festival. Something about them caught my attention. My eyes connected with one of the men and a cold shiver ran down my spine. They were dressed like the locals to blend in and they had done an excellent job, they looked local, but I recognized the stone-cold look in the man's eyes. I had grown up with it. He was wearing my father's eyes. Instinctively, I tapped my side to feel the gun I had in my holster.

"Shit, they're here. At the fucking festival," I said to Leila. "Where are Tom's guys?"

"Well, if they are already at the festival, then so are Tom's men."

"Get them to stay close to Montana Moore. She's Anya's teacher. Don't let her out of their sight. I'll send you a photo."

"No need. I know who she is. I'll call Tom now."

"Keep me updated," I said and got into the car.

They didn't come towards me. They just stood watching us. As if they were not in a hurry. As if they had all the time in the world.

I turned around to look at Anya and saw her watching me. I had been too sloppy. I had not hidden my fear well enough. She was filled with alarm and on high alert. "What's going on, Daddy?"

"Nothing's going on. Put your seatbelt on, honey. Everything's going to be fine."

I drove home as fast as I could.

"Go to your safe room, honey. I need to sort a few things out, then I'll join you. We'll watch a movie together and relax, okay?"

"Daddy, come with me."

I smiled at her. "Don't be scared, honey. I'm just going to make sure all the video surveillance feeds are working, then I'll come, okay? There's no one here. Go and choose the snacks you want."

She frowned. "Hurry, Daddy.

"Of course. Go on. I want to see if you remember how to do it."

"Okay," she said and ran towards the kitchen.

I called Leila. "What's going on with Montana? Is she still there?"

"Yeah, she's here. At the Waffle Eating Competition stand. Tom's men have eyes on her."

"What about the men I saw? Where are they?"

"No sign of them. They could be heading towards you."

"Do you think they'll follow Montana Moore?" I insisted.

"I don't think so," she said. "I don't think she's the target. They may not know you have a special interest in her."

I winced with regret. "If they were already at the festival they will. I did something stupid. I think everyone knows how I feel."

"Shit!"

"I know."

"Regardless, they are heading for you."

"I've sent Anya into the panic room, and I'm about to activate all the booby traps before I join her."

"Your panic room is blast-free, right?"

"Even if they burned down the house or threw a bomb on it, she would be fine. I'm prepared for anything. Paganini is insane. He could do anything to get to me, but if I know him well, taking my daughter is his plan. Once he has her, he can get me to do anything he wants. He can keep me going for as long as he wants."

No more running. I hated running. I did it to buy myself some time so I could take him on, on my terms, but it was not to be. Paganini proved to be more resourceful and relentless than I had given him credit and I had given him plenty. But so be it. I would meet him head-on and we would see who walked out of the battlefield alive.

"Good luck," Leila wished grimly.

"I'll call you later."

Chapter 49
Montana

"That was weird," Natalie muttered.

"I know," Pearl agreed, her eyes massive in her stunned face.

"Ten freaking thousand dollars!" Kelly screamed. "What the hell was that all about?"

"He's rich, isn't he? That story Tiffany told me about his daughter's designer Gucci shoes is real. He's rich, but he's pretending to be a poor accountant driving a beat-up car. The question is why is he doing it? What's actually going on?" Natalie turned on me. "Well, do you know?"

"No, I don't. He told me and my father he's an accountant. My father even offered for him to be the school accountant, and he accepted. As for the beat-up car, I believe, he finds it interesting to soup up a car and see how well it can go."

"This is getting creepy now. To think he bid ten thousand dollars and then he pecked your cheek and walked away. What the hell is that all about?"

"Well, that sure pissed Jesse off though. His little face.

Poor guy thought he had a clear road to victory," Kelly noted with amusement.

I stared at my friends. I felt so confused I couldn't think anymore. "Look, I don't know what's going on. I think I'm just going to enter the waffle-eating competition and just forget all this bizarre stuff had ever happened. I'll sort it out in my head when I get home."

"I ... really don't think you should enter the contest," Kelly said.

I took a big gulp of the cup of alcoholic punch she was holding and spluttered with the strength of it. "God, how much vodka did you put in there?"

She grinned. "Most of the bottle."

I shook my head. "How you don't fall down drunk I'll never know. Right, I'm off to the competition."

"You shouldn't go, Montana."

I turned to her. "Why? I've been doing it for years and winning."

"It's so unladylike."

"My dad does it. He thinks he's cool?"

Pearl laughed as she adjusted her straw hat further down her head. "Cole might not think it's all that hot to see you gobbling down twenty waffles."

"Fuck Cole," I said aggressively. I felt angry with him. True, he had not led me on, but he had definitely lied to me, and he had ruined my life. I was a shadow of the person I was before I met him.

"She'll never give up that crazy contest," Pearl said.

"Your dad's not participating this year, is he?" Natalie asked

"That's not out of choice; that's because of his health."

253

"And you don't think you should look out for your health as well?" Natalie asked.

They continued yapping on about it, but my mind was determined. I could have easily skipped out on it, but we had invited all the kids and parents to the funfair. There were rides and stalls and contests and all in all, it was the best summer event in town. Everything was brightly lit and in colors; it wasn't rainy, thank God, and not too hot either. It was a perfect day, and I wasn't going to let Cole spoil it.

"What's the prize?" Natalie asked.

"A $200 grocery certificate."

"I'll give you the two hundred dollars," Natalie said.

I smiled, turning to her. "You're one to talk; your boyfriend participated last year."

"And I almost broke up with him because of such behavior. As you can see, he has turned over a new leaf and lost ten pounds. He will not be found near that sloppiness."

"Well, I'm going," I rose to my feet.

"Let her be," I heard Kelly say.

I headed over to the waffle contest stand. They would be starting shortly, and I was ready. I was determined to win it this year. I didn't even know why, since I didn't particularly need that $200 grocery certificate, but I needed a win in something after the very rough time I'd had, so I planned to throw myself into it.

"We begin in ten minutes," Mr. Vaughn, the librarian, said.

I nodded and took my place, but when I saw who slid in next to me, I was immediately irritated. I didn't know him, but over the years, I had seen him in town, of course.

He was the nephew of another one of the locals and was always causing trouble at the bar. He wasn't exactly a bum, but there was just something always messy, loud and upsetting about him.

Instantly, I lost my interest in participating, but I was already here, so I decided to just suck it up.

"Go for it, Montana," I heard a shout and looked to see the crowd slowly gathering.

Of course, it was my dad. He had brought a chair over. I was amused, knowing he was going to have a blast watching me while complaining for the next week or so that he wasn't allowed to join in.

I shot him a look, and then we were ready to begin.

"Don't choke," the man beside me said. "It'll be a shame to go out with anything down your throat other than a dick. The only thing a girl should ever choke on is a big dick."

It must have been because of the confusion I felt about my life, but I experienced the kind of black rage I'd never before felt. I closed my eyes and inhaled deeply. The show was about to start, and I had to make the decision to either give him the hardest, dirtiest slap I could and make a beeline for it or just continue on with the game and ignore him.

It was extremely difficult to choose the latter option, but for the sake of my dad and the gathering crowd, I conceded. I would totally and absolutely ignore him. The asshole was not worth one second of my time.

"Ready?" Mr. Vaughn announced on his microphone.

I got ready.

The whistle was blown, and I began wolfing down the

waffles. I loved the waffles. They were provided by Mrs. Sherman's bakery and they were incredibly delicious. I didn't look to my left or right despite the grunting ridiculous noises everyone was making. I just tried to chew mine properly so they would go down easier. I had a bottle of water in my hand to facilitate this.

I kept going, but I was sure I wasn't going to win this time around because the monster by my side was barely swallowing. It made me realize that the only reason I had succeeded in the past was that I had been playing with lightweights: older people in the town with absolutely no stamina and, of course, my dad, who I was sure now allowed me to win. Suddenly it all seemed so pointless. I didn't want to sit with this asshole next to me. I didn't care to win. The waffles tasted like mud in my mouth.

I stopped, unable to go forward. There were tears in my eyes. I was crying for Cole. He was supposed to meet me at the waffle stand and he never showed up. I felt disappointed, sad, and confused all at once. Why on earth did he bid ten thousand dollars for a kiss from me? It was all so baffling. I jumped to my feet and the idiot next to me sniggered and continued to chomp down on his pile of waffles. Looked like he was going home with the prize.

"Maybe next year, Montana?" Mr. Vaughn said consolingly. He was a kind middle-aged man and I had a soft spot for him.

"Yeah," I said. "Maybe next year."

My dad stood and came towards me, his forehead creased with worry lines. "What's wrong, Buttercup?"

I hid my hurting tears from his searching eyes. "Nothing, Dad. I'm just tired. I think I'll go straight home."

"Want me to take you home?"

"Nah, you stay and have fun. I'll give Lola a ride. She'll like that."

Chapter 50
Montana

The girls had told me not to do it, but I didn't listen.

Now I felt worse than ever. The waffles were like a big heavy mass in my stomach, my heart felt like someone had stabbed a knife into it, and my head was fucked.

"Self-pity doesn't suit you," I told myself as I walked away from the festival and turned into the shady lane, a shortcut to the carpark. As I made the right turn, I bumped into someone.

"I'm sorry," I immediately apologized, but did not look up because I was too lost in my own suffering. I would have continued on my way if a heavy, painful hand had not clamped down around my arm. To my shock, I was yanked back into one of the stalls close to the edge of the field where the festival was being held. The grip was so hard and painful that it knocked the breath out of me. That was the last straw. I lost it.

"What the hell is wrong with you?" I lashed out. It was then I realized who had manhandled me so roughly.

My heart leapt into my throat. It was that dick. The one that had been by my side during the waffle-eating contest.

"Hey! Every time I meet you, you seem ruder than ever. What is it this time? Is it because you lost?" he taunted.

"Let go of me," I spat, glaring at him, trying to twist my arm, but it wouldn't budge from his grip. Now he was truly beginning to piss me off.

"What is your problem?" he asked.

"I said, let go of me."

He laughed. "What, you think you're too pretty to stop for a moment to have a conversation with me like a normal human being? What are you? Some sort of princess?"

"One last warning. Let go of me," I enunciated clearly, slowly, so that even his two brain cells would understand I meant business.

I heard laughter from behind and realized then that his friends were outside the stall watching and acting as backup. He leaned forward then to whisper closer to me, and his breath nearly made my already upset stomach heave even more. It reeked of rotting meat and vomit. I was more disgusted and upset than I could explain. I swear I was about to puke on his cheap shoes.

"Aye, you really need something down your throat to get you to relax. I'm offering up my cock to do the deal. What do you say? We could go over to my truck-"

Before I could stop myself, my hand swung out and struck his pale, ginger-bearded face. It was sloppy, but I was so mad that I felt the sting vibrate all the way up to my shoul-

259

der. My palm had left a bright red imprint on his cheek and I was sure he saw stars, and I wasn't about to apologize for giving him something he richly deserved. I saw the other men go silent, and I realized that I had made a very bad move. These men were nothing like him. They had cold, dangerous eyes. I was clearly involved in something much bigger than a low-life trouble-maker trying to keep his dick happy.

The men began to advance on me. Oh my God! What the hell had I got into? I was ready to run; but before I could, they fanned out around me. Three men against one. One of them reached out and I swerved out of his way. The other tried and I took a step back. Soon I would be against the wall.

Shit, I was in so much trouble.

Terrified, but knowing that I was no helpless female. I had fighting skills. I just had never taken three men on at the same time. I knew I should focus on getting away any way I could ... I started to bounce on the balls of my feet like a bouncer. It was a useless gesture, but I was just doing it to confuse them. Unfortunately, it didn't work. One of them lunged forward suddenly and caught me. I was dragged over like a weightless doll. My heart was beating so fast I could feel it like a palpitation. One thing was clear. This was going to turn into a mess.

It was so fucking embarrassing. I was the best in my self-defense class. My teacher would have been mortified to see what a poor effort I had put into this fight. I kicked my leg out as hard as I could and connected with someone's soft groin. Balls. I got him in the balls. Well-aimed kick, Montana. Fantastic. He howled with agony and dropped to his knees.

"You bitch!" he yelled as he grasped his groin and curled up on the floor.

A hand came swinging towards my face. I instantly dodged, and he missed. He stumbled, showing the force with which he had lunged at me.

"Fuck you," I spat.

"Fucking wild cat," a man snarled, as he grabbed me from behind.

But a fist came out of nowhere, and a blow landed on his face. It sent him reeling to the ground and pulled a gasp out of me. The man who had lunged at me earlier tried to stand so he could resume his attack, but before he could find his footing, another man appeared from behind and kicked his legs. He screamed with pain and crashed to the ground.

In the distance, I heard a shout.

Two other men appeared. They had guns. I was in shock. I didn't know how to react. I just stared as they made short work of downing the two remaining men.

I stared down at the three men who had collapsed on the ground and were unable to get up.

"What the fuck?" I didn't know what was happening. Then I saw the man who had landed the blow flexing his fist. He looked at me with furious eyes.

"Who are you? What's going on?" I gasped.

He grabbed my hand. "Get the fuck out of here right now?"

"Okay, okay," I said, but my limbs were frozen.

"Go!" he yelled. "Go find your dad and leave! Right now! Go to the ranch where you will be safe."

I was finally able to move my frozen limbs.

"Quickly," he urged.

I ran.

Chapter 51
Cole

Ow things had escalated so suddenly, I had no idea.

"Is she safe?" I barked.

"Yeah, for now," Leila said.

"For now? Fuck that. Keep your guys on Montana and her father. Don't take your eyes off them for an instant until I tell you otherwise."

"What about Anya?" she asked.

"I've got her. Focus on Montana right now; she might be more in danger. Anya is as safe as she can be."

"Okay, We can send more men to guard the ranch."

"Good. Assign as many as you can find to guard Montana and her father. Bring in extra reinforcements if you need to. I don't care how much it costs, keep her safe."

"Gotcha."

"Let me know if anything goes amiss."

"Alright," she replied.

I ended the call. I turned on the security cameras on the monitor and kept my eyes on it as I searched for things I wanted. Two more guns, one silent, my special shoes, and of course, two portable devices - my hard drive and USB stock.

Then I headed towards the panic room. I opened the door and Anya was standing in the middle of it. She looked terrified. I left the duffel bag on the floor and headed over to her. Crouching down before her, the first thing I did was give her a hug. It was a very, very long hug, and I tried to give her the strength and assurance that she would need. Truthfully, I didn't know if I would ever see her again, but I ensured to push that thought out of my mind. As I pulled away and looked into her eyes, I loved her so much it physically hurt, and so even when I tried to speak thereafter, there was a very visible strain in my throat.

"Oh, Daddy, what's happening?" Tears streamed down her cheeks.

I rushed to hug her. "Oh honey, don't cry. Everything is fine."

"It's all my fault, isn't it?" she sobbed.

"No, it's not. They would have found us anyway. It would have been a few days more, but they would have found us."

"I ... I only sent the card out because I was scared she would die."

"I know. It's not your fault. It's okay, honey. It's okay."

"I thought she was dying. She was sleeping on a big black bed. I've been dreaming about her. She's not well, Daddy. Something is wrong ..." her voice trailed off.

"Your nightmares were about your mom?"

She nodded. "I'm sorry, Daddy. I just ... I wanted to make sure she was okay."

I paused and took a deep breath. It wasn't the child's

fault but mine, because I never should have run. I should have gone for the nuclear option, but I was afraid of the blowback on Anya and my mother if anything went wrong. But now that I had protected them both, it was time to fight. The jackal had come to the lion's den and the lion must respond.

So be it.

"Listen to me," I said.

She sniffed. "I'm listening."

"You know I have to leave you for a while, right?"

She began to shake her head and cry pitifully. "No, Daddy. Don't leave me. Don't go."

"Listen to me, Anya. I have to go. I have to save your mommy. Do you understand me? You have to be brave and stay here until I come back, okay."

She stared at me. "You're going to save Mommy?"

"Yes." I smiled. "You think you can be brave until I come back?"

She nodded.

"Good girl." I switched on the video feed of the surveillance cameras and all the little screens came alive. Their bluish light fell upon her little face. I pointed at them. "Now, I want you to watch the videos. Can you do that?"

She nodded.

"Keep your eyes on it, and if you see anyone lurking around the house, whether good or bad, ring me using that phone over there, but don't ever open the door. Never. No matter what, don't open the door to anyone until I come back in twenty-four hours. If I am going to be later than that I will call you. If I don't call you and I don't come back in twenty-four hours, you call Sheriff Johnson. His number is here." I pointed to the notes I had made for her. "Do you understand me?"

She nodded, but I wasn't convinced. Her life depended on this, but I didn't know how to properly convey the importance to her. Shock tactics were needed.

"Anya?"

"Yes?"

"If you open this door your mother could die."

Her face turned pale and her eyes opened wide. I felt bad, but I didn't know how else to get her to recognize how important it was for her not to open the door.

"I understand, Daddy." Her voice was soft, but finally, she understood. She must not open the door under any circumstances.

"Good girl. There's one more thing for you to remember. This room can survive a bomb blast, so I don't want you to be frightened if you see men with guns, okay? You're totally and completely safe here. Unless you do one thing. What is that?"

It took a few seconds, but eventually, she replied.

"Unless I open the door."

"Exactly." I smiled at her. "Don't open the door for absolutely anyone except me. Promise?"

She nodded solemnly. "Promise."

I pulled out the USB. "See this? It contains very important information. I will be back very soon, but I could be delayed. So, if you don't see me in twenty-four hours, I want you to use that phone," I pointed to the phone, "and call 911 or Sheriff Johnson immediately. And when they come, you must give them this USB drive. Can you remember that?"

She nodded again, her eyes full of fear.

"Daddy, why can't you take me with you?"

"Because I am going to a place where children are not allowed."

She thought for a couple of seconds. "Can I wait for you in the car?"

I hid a smile. "No, it's not safe. Come on, chin up. I'm leaving you in the safest place on earth to go look for your Mommy, okay? Do you want me to look for her and make sure she is safe?"

"Yes."

"Good. I'll be back soon, sweetheart," I reassured, my stomach twisting. It wasn't exactly a lie, but there was a small but very real possibility that it wouldn't end up being the truth."

Tears were streaming down her cheeks.

"Are you going to be brave?"

She nodded.

"You do want me to find your mommy, right?

She nodded again, this time more vigorously. "I'll be brave, Daddy."

"Good girl." I smiled encouragingly at her.

"Bye-bye, Daddy."

"Bye, honey," I rose to my feet. If I hung around any longer, I didn't think I would be able to leave. I turned around then to check the camera feeds once again. They were working fine. Then I checked that everything she could possibly need was in place, and then I kissed my daughter and opened the blast door. Anya was standing in the middle of the room looking as if she was about to burst into tears. I waved at her. She waved back tearfully.

I watched the door lock before I left. Just as I was strolling through the living room, however, the hairs on the back of my neck stood. Just then my phone began to ring, but I didn't really need to pick up to understand what was going on.

They were here.

The last place I wanted to deal with them was inside the house. First, I sent Anya a text.

ME: The video feed is going to go down for a few minutes for maintenance. So don't worry if the screens go blank.

ANYA: Okay, Daddy.

As soon as I got her message, I remotely switched off the video feeds. No need for Anya to see what was going to happen next. Then I grabbed my duffel bag and rather than exit the house, I sprinted upstairs. They followed and one of them spoke, quite confident and leisurely I might add.

"This cat and mouse game you're playing," he said. "You know how this is going to end, right?"

I disappeared into the secret panel door and waited for them to come up the stairs. When I heard their footsteps just outside my hiding place, I hit the remote and triggered the first booby trap. It hit one of them. The one that escaped screamed like a girl with shock and fear. I popped out and fired one shot. My gun had a silencer and it barely made a sound. The axe booby trap had got the bigger guy squarely in his head and cleaved cleanly through his brain. I recognized him, Looney Lenny. I had shot the other in his shoulder. I did not recognize him. He was dark-haired and in his thirties. He staggered backwards, shocked and in so much pain he couldn't help but grunt like a stuck pig.

"You just killed one of the Don's best men, you're a dead man walking," he shouted as he stumbled and fell on his back.

I stood over him.

"You won't get away with this, you fucking monster," he cursed.

"Monster?" I asked. "If I was such a monster, then why I am of a mind to send you to the hospital now? Unlike your … partner, you still have a fighting chance … but that will depend on how you respond to my questions."

He continued to groan, the blood seeping out of his shoulder onto my new floors. It was going to be a bitch to clean.

"What is it? What do you want to know?" he muttered. He was becoming pale with blood loss.

I smiled darkly. "Where's that old fool?"

He shut his eyes at the pain and he relayed the information to me. "His house. He's at his main house, okay?"

It was just as I expected. "Thanks," I said.

He was looking at me with wide eyes. All the earlier adrenaline-rush-bravado was gone. I stared down at him and considered sparing him, but then, I changed my mind and pointed the gun straight at his head.

"No … no, no, no," he pleaded.

But it was too late. My heart had turned to stone. I pulled the trigger. "Back to hell, where you belong."

Chapter 52
Montana

I paced the kitchen floor restlessly. What the hell was happening in our little town? Something bad. And it was connected to Cole. I could feel it with every fiber of my soul.

"What's going on, Montana? How did you end up in a fight at the festival? It's all everyone's going to be talking about for the next month or two. Or maybe even forever."

"Dad, that's not it." I groaned and continued to pace.

The phone rang and my dad ambled off to answer it. He returned a few minutes later. The adrenaline was rushing through my veins and I was still pacing the floor like a caged tiger.

"Your aunt called," he said. "She wanted to know if you're all right. Apparently, Jeb's son had to be sent to the hospital in Stormy City. Damn kid says you kicked him in the nuts. He's demanding compensation. This could have gone very, very badly for you, Montana. How the hell did things get to this? Can you please tell me what's going on?"

I stopped then and stared at him, too much in a bad mood and confused state of mind to feel apologetic.

"What happened? He attacked me. That's what happened! He made a sexual threat, and then he grabbed my hand till it hurt and wouldn't let me go. What did you want me to do? Give in to him?"

Dad looked shocked then red-faced with fury. "What about all those other men?"

"I have no idea where they came from, but they were with him. If those other men had not arrived and beat the living shit out of the first lot, who knows what would have happened."

"We have to report this to Sheriff Johnson," my father said angrily. "How dare Jeb's son attack *my* daughter. Who the hell does he think he is?"

"You go ahead and report him, I need to go see if Cole and Anya are all right."

"Don't you dare leave this house. There's something dangerous going on and you're not going to get involved."

I spotted my car keys on the table and grabbed them. "I won't be long."

"Montana Moore, I forbid you to leave this house!"

"I'll phone you as soon as I get to his house," I called and made for the back door.

"No, stay here, please, Montana," he insisted desperately. "Please, for my peace of mind."

"Dad, I have to go and make sure they are fine. I'll be fine and I promise to call you as soon as I get there."

I ran out of the door to my car. I would just check on them as best as I could, even if it's from a distance. I just needed to be sure that all was well, and I didn't think I

Georgia Carre

would truly be able to rest otherwise. It took me a bit of time because of the traffic from the festival which caused me to cuss and swear, but eventually, I arrived at Duck's Pond. I parked on the side of the road, not exactly willing to announce my presence yet. However, after a few more minutes of being there, my frustration and worry got the better of me. I needed an explanation for several things, and I knew he held the answers so I refused to cower like a coward.

Getting out of the car, I locked it behind me and marched over to the house.

His car wasn't parked in its usual place, which implied that they weren't home. I wondered where they could have possibly gone. I headed up their porch toward the front door and wondered what to do. Should I go back and return at another time or call him and wait here until he got back?

The latter option was obviously a bit over the top, but I didn't know if I would ever find the guts to return, or to ask him anything if I left now. Plus, I was so hyped up I would be driving my father up the wall if I returned to the ranch without knowing what was happening. I decided to wait on the porch.

It was at that point that I realized that the lock to the door was broken. The wood had been splintered, broken open by force, and the door was slightly parted. I was instantly on guard. Fear filled my heart as I wondered if they had been robbed, or maybe those men who had come for me had come after them too.

Slowly, I pushed open the door. The whole house was silent, and not in a good way. I went through the kitchen and grabbed a knife before creeping up the stairs. I went into the hallway and came upon an unbelievable sight.

Two dead men were lying in a pool of their own dark red blood. And one of the men had an axe in his face! I couldn't help the scream of terror that rushed out of my mouth. Unable to process the grisly scene in front of me, I immediately turned around and ran down the stairs. The house seemed even more eerily quiet. I prayed with all of my heart and soul that Cole and Anya were safe. As I ran I pulled my phone out of my pocket. I had to call Cole to know he was safe. Then I would call 911.

My hands were trembling so much I could barely find his contact, but eventually, the call went through and began to ring, but before he could answer, a huge, heavy fist socked the side of my head.

The pain was excruciating.

It felt as though I had been struck by a hammer. It was so painful I collapsed to the ground with a cry of agony. There were men around me. Everything was blur and my ears were ringing with the blow, but I could see their shoes. What had happened? Who were these people? They didn't even give me a minute to recover. I was roughly pulled up and forced to face the blazing, reddened eyes of a dark, bearded, bald man. He seemed so furious and terrifying. He yelled into my face, but I could barely hear what he was saying. He grabbed me by my arms and pushed me along. We were heading down the stairs into the basement. Immediately, I guessed there was nothing here except Anya's safe room, and I understood what was happening.

Were Anya and Cole hiding in their secret room? My heart started to pound and I felt sick to my stomach when I realized what was about to happen. These men were going to use my life to bargain for theirs. What a prize fool I'd been! I didn't listen to those men who came to save me and told me in no uncertain terms to go to the ranch and stay there. I had no business coming here. I should never have come. Why didn't I just call Sherriff Johnson as my father had suggested? I was full of bitter regret.

I glanced around at the men. There were three of them. They were tight-lipped and stern. The bargain was obvious. Open the door, or else I would be killed. I had no clue if they would really do it, but one look at them and they looked like they meant business. I had barged in where I was told not to go, so I wasn't going to force Cole and Anya to suffer because I was an impatient little shit.

I began to fight and struggle, but the man's grip on me was like iron.

With a vicious shove, I was thrown against a metal door. It was so thick my body made a dull thud when I collided with it. My entire body hurt like crazy. The man then banged against the door. He grabbed me by my shirt and pushed my face against what looked like a camera.

"See who I have here," he growled. "You don't want to see her dead, do you? If you don't, then open the door right now, and we'll talk. We just want to talk. The longer this takes the more hurt she gets."

One of the other men banged the door with the edge of his gun, and I swallowed, and started to shake my head to tell whoever was on the other side of the camera, since Cole's car was not in the front my guess was it was Anya, not to open the door. I didn't speak lest I pushed them too far over the edge, and they killed me immediately, but I was almost certain they were not going to kill me while I was useful to them. Once the door was open and they got what they wanted though ...

There was no movement.

The man who was holding me up sighed. "Go on," he said to the guy who was tapping his gun against the door.

The man lifted his gun and pointed it straight at my head. My heart stopped beating. I was so terrified I couldn't even scream. He cocked his gun, and I knew it was the end. There was no point in fighting, they were going to do what they were going to do, but at least, I could save sweet little Anya. I closed my eyes and called out to God.

"I know you can see this," he said to the camera. "I'm going to count to three, and if you don't open up by then, she's dead."

"One ..." he began, and despite how brave I wanted to be, I couldn't stop the tears that ran down my face.

"Two-"

"Don't open the door!" I yelled and squeezed my eyes shut. This was because I was sure they were going to hit me again or perhaps they were going to put the bullet in my head. I didn't care.

"Don't open it," I screamed again, trembling, and the blow came behind. I fell to the floor in a daze. I couldn't even see properly. Suddenly, I felt a blast of cool air.

The door was open. She had opened the door.

A commotion followed and I heard a scream. My mind registered it as Anya's voice. With that, I was shocked back to my senses. When I managed to pull myself up, I felt her small, warm hands on mine, trying to see if I was alright.

"I'm sorry," she apologized, her face soaked with tears. "I couldn't allow them to hurt you."

"Oh, sweetheart," I cried and hugged her. I whispered in her ear. "Where's your dad?"

Before she could respond, she screamed and flew into the air. I watched in horror as she landed on her back on the ground. One of the men had kicked her so hard she was almost six feet away from me. She was screaming in pain.

I was so furious, but I couldn't lash out. Her father was not around, and so from now on, she was in my care. I needed to protect her, if necessary, with my life. It was my fault. I came here when I shouldn't have.

I heard one of the men speak on his phone. "We got the girl and the teacher."

I wiped my tears away, pushed away my pain, and sharpened my focus. I was going to find a way for both of us to get out of this frightening trap, no matter what. And if both of us couldn't survive it, then I would make sure at the very least that she did.

Chapter 53
Cole

"He just wanted you to come over for a friendly chat, but now that you've killed his men, you have to pay for that, *bello*?"

I received the call when I was midway back to the city. It was Anya's phone, but it wasn't her. For the first few seconds, I couldn't understand it. The room was blast-proof. How could they have her? Was my phone hacked so that it seemed as if the call was coming from her phone? I was confused until I heard her crying in the background. They had her. Somehow, they must have tricked her into opening the door. The line went dead. My knuckles on the steering wheel were bone white as I pressed down on the gas pedal and flew even faster back to the city.

My phone rang again. It was Paganini.

"You heard?" Paganini's voice was gloating, "Vinny and his men have your daughter."

I didn't respond.

He sighed. "I actually just wanted to talk to you. You left my finances in a mess. Imagine coming to depend on someone for such a vital aspect of your operations and then you find all of a sudden they have disappeared. That would be deeply upsetting, don't you think?"

I still didn't respond.

"By the way, the little teacher fell into Vinny's net too. You know, the one you were willing to part with ten thousand dollars for a kiss.

My heart was pounding. Who could he possibly be referring to?

"She was supposed to be a part of this, but thanks to the Madonna and her son, the teacher was at the wrong place at the wrong time. She was the reason your daughter opened the door for us."

I swallowed hard as the pieces slotted into place. I understood now what had happened, and I wanted to slam my fist into something. What had Montana been doing there? Why had she gone to the house? My fault. I should have explained everything to her, instead of keeping her in the dark after I had exposed her to danger. Of course, Anya would have seen her in distress after Paganini's men had started to torture her and been unable to stop herself from rescuing her teacher.

I didn't know what to do, but I remained calm and waited for him to say all that he needed to without interruption.

"Just as we have your wife, we'll be keeping your daughter and teacher as well for your cooperation. You'll get them all back, rest assured, but after you perform. From reports, you're on your way to see me? That's wonderful because I have a whole backlog of work for you and a transfer that is especially urgent, so get here as fast as you can. I will make sure Vinny doesn't lose his head, that temper of his is bad, and hurt the child or the woman because I know I won't get your cooperation if I do. Also, you have killed two of my men today, so it is only fair that you find a way to compensate for that too?"

I didn't respond, but he went on.

"Perhaps you can let us have the teacher, a looker for sure. But from what I hear, a real wild cat. Maybe the men will have a bit of fun with her, or maybe I will. I like wild cats in my bed. In case, she's disposable ... everything is up to you. See you soon then. Hurry because I have a plane to catch tonight. Goodbye."

He laughed then, a sick sound, and ended the call without me having said a single word.

I felt sick. I actually felt dizzy with fury. There was a red mist over my eyes. I couldn't see the road in front of me, let alone focus on driving. I pulled over to the side of the road and got out of the car. I couldn't believe what had happened. This was exactly what I had worked so hard to avoid. Somehow, I had even managed to pull Montana into my mess. I hated myself for it. My hands clenched and unclenched as I paced the ground next to my car.

"It's going to be fine. It's going to be fine. I can do this. I know I can," I mumbled to myself. I took deep breaths. I exhaled them slowly.

I got back in the car, leaned my head against the steering wheel and tried to sort out my thoughts. This couldn't go on any longer. I couldn't continue to be at the beck and call of this man, but he had the two people I cared about the most.

My heart hurt. I wanted to turn the car around and go

back to the house and fight them. I knew all the secret booby traps in the house. I felt as if I could take them on, but even if I did, the head of the snake would still be alive. Paganini would never stop coming after me. No matter how many of his men I killed or how far I ran, he would always find me. Going back could do more harm than good.

I decided that it was best to comply for the moment. I had a plan. It was slightly more dangerous to carry out now because he had my loved ones in his grasp, but it was not impossible. I would just have to be extra careful. No time to wallow. I restarted the car and put it back on the road. I sped faster towards the city. I was resolved to fix this problem once and for all. I put a call to Leila.

"They have Anya and Montana," I said.

"What?" she replied. "You told me the room was blast-proof. They couldn't get in. What happened?"

"They got Montana. They must have threatened to kill her. Anya opened the door for them."

"But Montana was supposed to be at the ranch. Our men told her to go there and stay there."

"Well, she didn't listen."

"What do you want us to do?"

"Nothing. For the moment. There is nothing you can do," I told her. I was so frustrated I was barely able to get the words out.

"All right."

"I'll call you when I need you. Hang on, there is something you can do. Go and see Montana's father. Make sure you explain to him the nature of the kidnap. Convince him not to involve the police because it will severely jeopardize their chances of survival."

"Got it."

I ended the call and saw that I had a voice message from an unknown phone. I played the message

Anya's voice came on,

"Dad," she said, and I could still hear the tremble in her voice. "I hope you're okay. We're … " she paused. "We're alright. I hope Mommy is okay too. Please take care of yourself. And I'm sorry I disobeyed you."

That apology broke my heart. Every time she apologized to me, it broke my heart. She had more empathy and understanding than she should be expected to have for her age. The way she extended it completely and willingly to me made me even more determined to do what needed to be done.

It was clear to me beyond the shadow of a doubt that my old plan was too kind. It gave the benefit of the doubt to Paganini. He would lose his money, but he would keep his life. I saw now that the only way I was ever going to be free of him was if I took his life.

There was no other way.

Chapter 54
Montana

"I never saw a wild thing feel sorry for itself."

I remained silent because now, more than ever before, I understood that Anya's well-being was in my hands. The best method might be to cooperate with them, but I kept my eyes shut and tried to recover my mental clarity so that I could seize any opportunity to escape that came by. For the moment complete submission was the only thing that was going to work in our favor.

They kept us around the dining table. I opened my eyes to look at Anya and I couldn't believe it was only a short time ago we had sat at this very table with light hearts and peace. Now we were basically hostages to gruesome men. Our lives were on the line, and there were dead bodies in the house with us. It was incredibly terrifying, but this was not the time to indulge in my emotions, so I took a deep breath and focused. The men seemed especially angry because of their dead companions. I soon learned from their conversations that it was a man named Luca.

Because we were a clueless child and a troublesome female, they didn't censor themselves as they spoke angrily to each other. I figured out from their conversations they must be Mafia or something and they wanted this man Luca to do something for them. As their conversation went on I suddenly realized that Luca was Cole!

Luca was Cole?

I turned to look at Anya in astonishment. If Luca was Cole, then Anya must be the girl they called Bianca.

"Bianca," I whispered.

Immediately the child turned her head.

Yes, that was her name.

"Shut the fuck up," one of the men snarled.

I looked away quickly.

Jesus! Everything was a lie. All of it. But finally, it all made sense. The designer shoes, the stupid beat-up car, his effortless sophistication, the high specification panic room that must have easily cost hundreds of thousands of dollars to build.

Cole, or rather Luca, was running away from these people, but they wanted him back. They needed him back for some reason. He was valuable to them. They had gone to all this trouble to come looking for him in a tiny town like Bison Ridge. I remembered Cole, well Luca, telling me he was good with numbers. The way he instantly remembered my number, without even repeating it back to me, even though I had called it out only once in a crowded, noisy schoolyard.

One of the men made a sudden noise and my eyes swung over to him.

We were seated now, and not dead ... yet.

But that was probably only because they were waiting for instructions.

Anya had been forced to record the voice note to her father, and they were no doubt going to use that to manipulate him. Maybe they planned to kill him after he gave them whatever they wanted from him, especially since he killed two of their guys. I was sure this was going to be the case, and so it dawned on me more than ever that keeping Anya safe and escaping could be the only thing that could save us all.

I looked at the little girl, and she lowered her head. She was surprisingly calm, and I wondered if it was because of her history with her dad, which I could see could have been a cakewalk. She was used to dangerous situations like this, or was it because she couldn't process the extent of the danger we were in? Regardless, I gazed at her until she finally noticed I was looking at her, and then when she lifted her head, I managed to work up an encouraging smile for her.

She seemed confused by it, but she returned a tremulous smile. From the pain I could feel on the bruises on my face, I imagined that there was no way I could appear comforting to her.

"At least I don't have a gun pointed to my head any m-" I whispered. But before I had even finished my sentence another blow was struck across my face.

Anya gasped and began to cry.

"I said, shut the fuck up," a man's voice bellowed close to my ear.

"Do we need her?" one of the other men asked. "Isn't it just the kid?"

"Boss said we should keep both until he gives us the signal."

My blood turned to ice at their words. I was left in wonder at how casually they talked about my death right before me and right in front of Anya. She cried even harder because she heard every word. I tried to calm her down.

"I'm fine, sweetheart," I mouthed, terrified that the men would attack me again.

"Shut up," one of them shouted to Anya, but she couldn't. She cried even harder from terror.

One of the men started to approach her then, and I yelled. "Don't touch her. She'll be fine. She'll stop."

He ignored me, and then he hit her across the cheek. It wasn't too hard, but the sting was enough to make her go crazy.

"Jesus. What the fuck? What you go do that for, Tony? She's just a kid," the youngest of them spoke up.

"Ah fuck! This is just a fucking mess," the bearded man said. He sounded totally fed up.

"If she keeps going like this, we can't continue on here," the man who had hit me said. "It's bound to draw attention."

"Let's get out of here then," came the response from the younger one.

"It's not as though the boss has ordered us to remain here. He's going to tell us to go back to the city anyway, so we might as well just start to leave now. This town gives me the fucking creeps. All these busybodies every-fucking-where."

"I think Tony's right. We should get out. I don't like this place. Too quiet. And these people ... they're not normal."

"Alright, let's go," the bearded man said.

My heart clenched harder in fear. Was this a good thing or a bad thing? At least here, I still held a measure of hope, though small, that someone would come by, my Dad would send the Sheriff, and we would be found. If we left now with no one knowing there was something wrong, especially my dad, it could take even longer to find us, and by then it might be too late.

But I had no choice. I rose to my feet. My hands were tied behind my back, so I couldn't do anything but walk.

"The kid isn't shutting up," the man who had hit her complained, glaring at Anya who was still wailing with fear and pain.

"Gag the little shit," the bearded man responded cruelly.

My heart sank. It was going to get even more traumatic for her. I had been hoping that somehow her fright from this experience could be managed, especially with my presence, but if they gagged her now, this trauma would leave even more scars.

They gagged her with a cloth and duct tape, and there was nothing either of us could do but follow the men out. They led us out of the house and talked amongst them-selves, and then to my surprise, they took me to my car. They only had one car in the driveway, and two of the men got in there.

"Go with her and the girl," the bearded man commanded.

The ties around my wrists were cut and I was pushed so roughly into the driver's seat I nearly banged my head onto the steering wheel.

"Wait," the man who had hit Anya said. He was sitting in the passenger seat next to me. Outside, the younger man was dragging Anya along with him, and I looked anxiously to see what he would do. To my immense relief, he opened the back door and threw her in.

The way they manhandled her infuriated me, but there was nothing I could do.

I caught her terrified gaze in the mirror. "Wear your seatbelt, honey."

She didn't move.

I nodded at her while staring at her, willing her to obey my instructions.

For a few tense seconds, it looked like she wasn't going to listen to me, probably sapped of energy, but then she complied. She strapped her seatbelt on.

Something about her being in the car, and my car for that matter, made me realize that I might have new options that I didn't before. When the man got into the back next to her and shut the door, I was able to calm down enough to start the car. It was my car, old but familiar, and I had driven it for years. My ties were gone. I had more options. It felt like an out-of-body experience pulling it out and onto the road. I checked the rearview mirror and could see that there were two men in an SUV behind, and they were closely following us.

Their car could easily outrun my old and rickety one, so there was no hope in trying to do a Hollywood-style car chase. Besides, the man beside me ensured that would never happen. He held his gun pointed directly at me, with his hand on the trigger.

"Any funny business and you will be dead in a second," he said. "Don't test me."

"I wasn't planning to."

"Where's the GPS in this fucking car?"

"It's an old car. It doesn't have GPS."

"Leave the town altogether," he said. "You know the way, right?"

"Yes. We can take the shortcut."

He relaxed slightly in his seat, and I did as I was told. I looked behind at Anya, and she met my gaze. She had calmed down now, but her eyes were swollen and puffy, and I wanted nothing more than to pull her into my arms for a hug.

It took me a little while to build up the courage, but I was eventually able to ask, "She's not going to cry or scream any longer. Can you please take her gag off? It makes her terrified."

The guy ignored me, but I was stupid enough to ask again.

"If you say one more word, I am going to shoot you dead."

I got the message then, loud and clear, and kept my mouth shut.

I focused on driving and followed the very familiar roads that I had taken countless times in the last few days to exit the town. Every time I had left, it had never felt final, just a temporary exit, but now I couldn't help but wonder if this would be the last time I would be leaving my beautiful town. I told myself not to be so dramatic.

Especially, when a plan was forming in my head. A plan to escape.

There could be a chance of that right outside the exit of the town. Next to the road was a stretch of woods that led to a bunker my grandfather had built a long time ago. At the time, I couldn't have imagined how or why it would ever come in handy, but now that I was at the crossroads with only minutes to spare to make the decision of whether I was going to go out of line once again and risk our lives, I understood why.

It was a bunker that he had made for the students. Anyone who got lost or ill while out in the woods could hide out for a couple of days and recover or wait for someone from the school to rescue them.

It was well hidden so that it wouldn't be raided by random campers for its canned food and other supplies, but it was visible enough to anyone who knew what they were looking for. That was where I had in mind to take Anya. However, in order to do that, first and foremost, I had to find a way to get rid of the men in the car and the others at our heels. The disadvantage was they had guns, and so I had to find a way to stop so near the woods that Anya and I would have a quick head start the moment we slipped into it. Once in the woods, I knew them so well that we would finally have a fighting chance of losing them and then hiding in the bunker until the danger was past.

Chapter 55
Cole

It took forever to reach the city, or at least, that was what it felt like, but when I checked the time, I realized that I had driven so fast it had taken me just over half the time it usually took. I must have truly been flying through the roads, focused and furious. I probably triggered some traffic speed camera, but thankfully the cops hadn't stopped. But now that I was inside the metropolitan area, I was forced to reduce my speed in order.

I arrived at Paganini's address. The place was filled with guards, but I wasn't stopped at the door. I could feel the anger, though, especially from a few familiar faces. They were disciplined enough not to outrightly confront me for killing one of their own, or perhaps they were waiting for whatever Paganini had planned for me.

I was quickly and thoroughly frisked before being ushered towards an elevator. We travelled two floors down into the ground. It was probably his safe space like the one I had built for Anya, but whatever it was, it ensured that no one could find it unless they were looking for it. I stared straight ahead and focused on my sole goal of being here, which was to find a way to save my daughter and Montana, finish off Paganini, and escape with my life.

Travelling into the depths of his lair, full of dangerous psychopaths, it seemed an almost impossible goal to achieve.

Since I had defaulted and gone rogue, they gave me a second search when the doors of the elevator swished open. Once, I was considered a trusted part of their organization and so my searches had been kept to a minimum, but it was no longer the case.

I had expected it so I hadn't bothered bringing any guns.

"What is this?" One of the men asked as they tapped on the flat, hard surface inside of my jacket.

"A hard drive," I replied, and he gave me a look. He was new, so he didn't know.

"I need it to do the work I'm here to do."

He smiled and then leaned forward to whisper to me. "Work hard and fast little rabbit. Otherwise, it will be the Don's sharp knives for you. He makes his victims suffer for days. Cut by cut, until they bleed out completely."

I towered over him both in height and stature and so in that moment, all I could do was be amused because this was what Paganini had reduced me to. I'd been prepared to wait and bide my time, but I knew now that if I kept getting provoked in this way, I just might burn down the place with me in it.

I willed myself to control my temper and not let myself be goaded as I headed to my audience with Paganini.

I met him in his office surrounded by his goons. For the first few minutes, he deliberately kept me standing as he answered a phone call, his eyes were full of disdain and mockery, which made him just as insufferable as he was annoying. Eventually, he ended the call and turned to me.

"The prodigal son returns." He grinned at me, flashing his yellowish teeth. "You really took two of my men out?"

"They came uninvited."

He came closer to me and inhaled deeply. "I can smell your fear." He moved away from me and looked into my eyes. "I have your daughter and your woman so don't play games with me, Luca. I could so easily crush both their necks but don't worry, I'm a nice guy."

I swallowed hard, but I said nothing.

He smiled, and to someone who did not know him, they would call it a kind smile. "We need transfers made. Many multiples have been delayed since you left. You understand what this means, right?" he asked. "You understand how much damage this has caused me, right?"

I said nothing.

"You are a traitor and I should kill you, but I won't. I have too much regard for your father to take away his only son. And now that you are back, it would be mean-hearted of me not to forgive you. I forgive you, Luca. I have known you since you were a child. You are almost like my own son.

He smiled again, but the smile never reached his dead eyes.

"All I ask is that you teach one of my men to do the things that you do so that I can let you go and live your life the way you want to live. This way I am not dependent on you and you are free. Today or tomorrow you will pick a few brilliant men from my team, and over the next few weeks or months, you will teach them how to wire the money across the world in a safe and untraceable manner. And all that time I will keep your daughter and your woman safe from harm. Is this understood?"

"Yes," I replied.

His eyes narrowed at me. "Follow Gianni. He will take you back to your old office. I believe you have much work to do."

Just then his phone began to ring, and he waved me out of his office.

I was led then through a door to the computer room I had spent so many days in I could probably draw every single feature of it in my sleep. I had promised myself when I left this place the last time that I would never return here again, but here I was.

"Get to work," Gianni said and closed the door.

Chapter 56
Montana

My plan was extremely risky. We could all die, even Anya, but I didn't see any other way out. Going on probabilities alone, Anya was probably in the best position to come out of my plan alive, but what were her chances if I didn't carry out my plan? What happened to her after they had got what they wanted from Luca? It was hard to think of him as Luca, but that was his name. Luca wouldn't have run from them and built that room for Anya if he thought they would spare her.

As for me I definitely had a very low survival chance. I was nothing to them. I had no value at all. For sure, they were not going to keep me alive, and if the bearded guy's reactions were anything to go by, he would have no qualms about raping me and disposing of my body somewhere no one would ever find it.

I looked in the rearview mirror at Bianca and confirmed that she had her seatbelt on. She did. I stared at myself in the mirror, and it took a while, but eventually, I made the decision. I was precious as well. I loved Cole and Anya, I realized now, deeply, and so I had to make the brave choice for both myself and them. Sure, we might fail, but if I remained docile, we were all guaranteed to fail.

I stepped on the gas pedal and the car began to pick up speed.

"Why the speed?" the man next to me asked as he looked at my rising speedometer.

"We're out of town now," I said casually. "What's the point of going slow? Or should I slow down? You'd prefer we crawl?"

He stared at me, ticked at the insult. "You sure do have a mouth on you, don't you? Let's see how well you'll be able to talk when my dick is in your mouth."

I turned away without showing any reaction. This was the second threat of the same manner within the space of a few hours. What was it with idiots wanting to clog my throat with their cocks? I went faster and faster down the road. I could tell he was becoming nervous by how he sat up and stared ahead. The seconds were drawing closer, and all I could do was count them down in my mind. Nearly there. All I needed to do was swerve to go off into the bushes, but my arms felt like they wouldn't work. Suddenly, he began to panic.

"Hey, slow down," he said.

Of course, I didn't listen.

The guy at the back was leaning forward. "What the fuck?"

The phone of the guy next to me started ringing. I knew it was the guys in the SUV behind that were panic-calling. They wanted to know what the hell was going on.

"Slow the fuck down!" the guy next to me yelled furiously. He was sitting up straight. Desperately, he pointed his gun at me, and that was the moment I swerved. The car plunged off the road into the bushes and he was thrown back against the door. There was no going back now. We raced through bushes, foliage, and rocks towards the woods. I was being bounced around like a rubber ball, but I tightened my hold on the steering wheel and stomped my foot on the gas pedal even harder. The car hurtled and crashed through the undergrowth at greater and greater speed.

I went straight for the biggest tree ahead.

This was going to hurt like hell, but I had my airbag and seatbelt … and he didn't.

"Hold on, sweetheart!" I shouted to Anya, and then we crashed.

My airbag burst open as I heard the guy next to me yell, his voice so full of terror that it rang in my ears, just before he slammed into the windscreen and became completely silent. The guy sitting at the back flew over his head through the windscreen, shattering it. Anya was screaming with horror.

The car was twisted around the tree and my neck felt as though it was broken, but the guy next to me was clearly dead and the other guy was lying a few feet away on the ground. There was no movement at all from him.

"Are you okay?" I asked Anya.

She was awake, sluggish, and terrified, but she was safe. The belt had kept her in place.

Immediately, I located the gun that was on the floor of the car and kicked the car door open. I tried the back door but was unable to pull it open. I pulled her out through the window just as I began to hear shouts.

I knew that the other men were behind us.

I had to get us out of there and to the bunker. I would've loved to hold her in my arms and comfort her, but it would slow us down too much.

"We have to go, Anya," I pleaded with her.

She started to move, but she could only move slowly.

"Please, Anya. Hurry," I cried.

"Okay," she said, and we ran for our lives.

We ran in the woods for at least ten minutes straight, and with each passing moment, it felt like my legs were going to give away with pain. I realized I must have hurt myself in the accident. My heart was pounding hard and I was out of breath, but still, I couldn't stop. This was the vital moment, and everything depended on this.

Our very lives depended on it, and so no matter how much pain I was in, we couldn't stop. Anya eventually stumbled on a rock and fell. I nearly fell myself, and so I had to stop for a moment to catch my breath.

I looked ahead then and saw the stream I was searching for was only a few yards away.

"Just over there, sweetheart," I told her. "We'll be safe as soon as we get over to that side. They won't be able to find their way then."

This, however, I soon found to be untrue when I heard the men coming behind us.

I was shocked. I had taken too many turns. They shouldn't have been able to follow us unless ... suddenly I looked at the little girl and quickly began to search her person. It didn't take long to find it. I retrieved the device from the pocket of her jacket. Incredibly upset, I ran in the opposite direction from where we were going and flung it into some bushes.

"I thought we had a head start, sweetie, but we don't," I told her. "We need to hurry even more now, so get up please, Anya."

After taking a few more deep breaths, she rose to her feet, locked her hand in mine, and once again, we were on our way, scurrying through the dense, dark woods.

Chapter 57
Cole

https://www.youtube.com/watch?v=zZ1UxkjhELU

"What the fuck do you mean?" Paganini shouted.

I was instantly intrigued. Although he was a heartless monster, he took great pride in using civilized language. He never outrightly cursed, but when he did, you knew that there was a huge problem afoot.

I walked to the door and put my ear to it, but he had stopped shouting. I picked up the water glass on the desk and pretended I was going to the water cooler down the hallway for some water. They didn't notice. They were in his office trembling before him. As I refilled my glass, I was able to put two and two together.

Montana and Anya had escaped!

At first, I couldn't believe it. It was too good to be true. How was that even possible? There were at least four men guarding them. I started to think it was a mistake. Maybe I'd misheard or misunderstood. But from the way Paganini and his men were behaving the unbelievable had happened. Somehow Montana had managed to escape with my daughter. I wanted to shout with joy.

I went over to my desk and made my decision. I was going to finish the job he had hired me for. With a few strokes, I began to retrieve all the money that I had transferred to untraceable accounts all over the world.

It was the skill that had brought me to Paganini's notice. Almost half a billion dollars had been hidden from the government and ferreted away, thanks to me. I glanced through the window. Paganini was having a tantrum. I instructed the AI to initiate the process of transferring all the money, every cent of it into tens of thousands of charities all over the world. The AI asked me to confirm the order. I clicked yes. The AI began to work its magic. The money disappeared from his account at the speed of light.

Finally, when his account showed zero balance, the process stopped.

Now came the final leg of the process. I installed the malware from the hard drive, and it served to destroy all the information on the established routes. There was no going back. Now, either I lived or he did.

First, I undid the laces of my right shoe, then I rose to my feet and headed over to his office after announcing that I had done what was needed, I waited for the next bit of interaction.

"You'll be living here from now on," he said. "You and your daughter. You'll get everything you need here, so focus on serving me the best way that I need, and maybe in a few years, you'll be allowed once again to venture out on your own."

This man, I understood now, was sick in the head.

"Where's my daughter right now?" I asked.

He showed no reaction. "She's safe. We'll have her delivered to you before the end of the day."

"And the woman with her?" I asked.

"The teacher?" He came around the table then, amused. "My, but you are greedy, aren't you?"

"Where is she?"

"You'll have to work a bit harder for her. I'll tell you exactly what I need done. Do it and you can have her."

I stared at him and pretended to be worried and resentful.

"That is a fair and merciful trade, isn't it?" he asked with a smile.

"My daughter's safety is the most important thing, but I'll do whatever you want done. As long as I can have her back."

"Good. I must say it's been very easy, actually a delight, working with you, Luca. Your father raised you well," he said. He looked at two of his men. "You two go ahead and get the car ready." The two men filed out before him.

He had started to walk out of the room, when I called out, "Don Paganini."

He turned, one supercilious arrogant eyebrow raised.

"I wanted to thank you for sparing my daughter and the woman. I know you could have so easily killed them. As a mark of my gratitude and an early birthday present, I have instituted a new program for you. You will be able to launder dirty money faster than ever. It will also save you millions of dollars every year. Let me show you on the computer. It will only take a minute and I think you'll be very pleased."

He looked impressed. "You remembered that my birthday is in a week. All right. Show me this wonderful program of yours."

"Just a moment," I said and lowered myself to the ground.

Under the guise of re-tying my laces, I retrieved the special folding blade from the heel of my shoes. I went forward and threw an arm around him just as he neared the desk.

"Tommaso," I called, and he turned to me, his expression showing surprise that I'd used his first name. Almost no one dared, but in his eyes were something else too: pure sexual excitement.

Smoothly, I slipped the knife into the inside of his elbow and slashed him all the way down to his wrist. His skin and flesh opened up like an ugly flower. The blade was so sharp and the movement so quick he didn't even feel the pain until I had released him and stepped away.

Only then did he see the blood gushing out of him like I'd turned on a faucet. He was horrified. He looked up at me with amazement, as if I had betrayed him. Then his eyes filled of panic. A that moment he still believe something could be done to safe him. Then he stumbled and fell back into the chair. One hand flailed uselessly in the air.

"Don't worry," I said softly. "You will be dead before you feel any pain."

His eyes bulged with fear. He opened and closed his mouth like a goldfish. He didn't even try to call for help. He knew now he was done for. He died with his eyes open and staring, but without making another sound.

I stood just behind the office door and waited. In minutes his men had noticed something was wrong. They began to shout and run around frantically looking for him. They burst into the office, and with one leg forward at the right moment, I tripped the first guy. With the element of surprise on my side, I rammed my fist into the throat of the one behind him and retrieved his gun. With a single, well-placed bullet through the head, he was gone. Then I turned around to do the same to the other.

The silencers were very helpful since I didn't want to draw any attention.

I knew my way around, but I only had a few minutes to get to the surveillance room, so I hurried over to it. There was a guard there who was, fortunately for him, napping on duty, consequently his death was painless and even quicker. I looked at the video feed. There were only a few men dotted around the building. I saw Arianna lying on a bed on the second floor. Now that I knew where she was, I plugged in my hard drive into the system. Almost instantly every screen became white noise. I waited for the malware to wipe off every retrievable footage.

Once the red light started flashing, I pulled the drive out, pocketed it, and walked out.

I needed a new start after this, and this meant that if the authorities or whoever took over the family from Paganini came over, there would be no trace whatsoever that I'd even been here. No need for revenge.

Quickly, I made my way to the second floor.

I saw no one until I reached the hallway. One of Paganini's men who was guarding the floor saw me. His eyes widened with shock, but before he could reach for his gun, I had already broken his neck.

She was in the second room on the left. The door was locked so I went back to the still body of the guard and found his keys. Hastily, I opened the door and went in. She was so still she looked dead, but she wasn't. She was asleep and so high on drugs she couldn't open her eyes properly. I could hardly believe this emaciated waif was Anya's mother and had once been my wife. She woke up and babbled some gibberish.

"I knew you'd come for me," she mumbled. She had lost a lot of weight and I carried her easily into the elevator. I went down to the garage and stuffed her incoherent body into one of the SUVs. As ever, the keys were in the box by the garage doors.

As I started the engine more of his guards seemed to realize what had happened. About three of them ran out just as I reversed, and I couldn't help but smile as I stepped on the gas pedal. Their shots rang out, but it was useless. I ran down two of them and was back out on the street.

I was out. I was free from Paganini!

I'd called the cops while I was with Arianna, and I could hear the sirens in the distance. I avoided the routes they would approach from, and in no time, I was in the clear.

Chapter 58
Cole

After handing Arianna off to Leila to check into a drug rehab center, I took a helicopter back to Bison Ridge. I told the pilot to land on Montana's father's ranch. He ran out to meet me. He was out of his mind with worry. He couldn't reach Montana, and after checking my house to find the bloody, violent mess that it was left in, he was able to piece together that his daughter was in terrible danger.

But the second he saw me running towards him he grabbed me and nearly knocked the lights out of me. I didn't have any time to explain but told him that my daughter too was with Montana and that rather than attack each other, we needed to find a way to save them both. He calmed down then and managed to take a seat.

"There's been no word from them," I told him. "But I think they have escaped. There was talk about an accident right at the entrance to Bison Ridge. I saw the commotion on my way here, but the police didn't seem to have found anything."

Her father looked down, and it was as though something had occurred to him. "There was an accident at the entrance to the town?"

"Yes," he said, and then he hurriedly got his phone. "I'll make a call to the sheriff and get all the information."

He waited. "What kind of car is it?" he asked.

"An old Volvo?" He looked at me with wild eyes. "That's Montana's car!"

"Yes, it is!"

"What?" he said into the phone. Then he looked at me and repeated what he'd heard from the person on the phone. "She crashed straight into a tree, and so far, two bodies have been found. A man who was crushed to death on the windscreen and another who was flung out of the back seat. He flew through the crushed windscreen and landed a few feet."

He ended the call. "She did it on purpose. There's a bunker in that area of the woods. It's a bit far away, but she would have been able to make it on foot. To get to it, you have to go through an underground cave that is extremely well-hidden. Maybe that's where she went with your daughter."

There was no further need to speculate. Instantly, we got into his car. We did not speak, both of us were out of mind with worry. I had my weapon in hand however, he didn't have one. He looked at it suspiciously as he got ready, then asked, "Will we need that?"

"I don't know, but it's always better to be safe than sorry," I replied. "The men tried to take her. If they are not already dead, they will be loitering around trying to find her, so we have to be careful."

"Alright," he said, and we drove faster.

Soon, we arrived at the location, and after confirming that the girls weren't there, we began the hike toward the bunker. It took him a little while to find it, but just as we did, we waited in the corner and began to call out to them.

It was a very small building, almost completely hidden away from sight. Unless you were actively looking for it, it would be very difficult to stumble into. But there it was, and eventually, we heard a little creak. I felt her before I even saw her, and my heart nearly stopped. I put my hand out to stop her father, but he was so happy to see his daughter that he rushed for the house. He had hardly taken a few steps before a shot rang out of nowhere.

Montana screamed, and so did my little girl, but I managed to stay calm as the men showed themselves. I watched as they headed to the house while Montana hurried back inside, and slowly and quietly, I followed. The first man went down without ever seeing me coming, and by the time the second one turned around and drew out his gun, I sent a second bullet straight to his head.

Both girls were huddling in fear. I wanted nothing more than to go to them, but I couldn't. I needed to get Montana's father to a hospital and there was no reception here, but I knew the sheriff was on his way, as we had agreed. After checking him, I tore off my shirt and handed it over to Montana, and then she hurried over to stay by her father's side.

"It's a clean wound," I told her, but realized I was so choked up with emotion and nervous tension I could barely speak. Eventually, I took a moment to calm myself down because this wasn't over yet. Her father needed to be okay;

otherwise, this would be a monumental disaster. His face was pale and his breathing was shallow.

"He'll be fine. I'll go get help. Just press down on the wound, don't move him." Montana nodded in response. Her face was full of bruises, her hair plastered to her forehead in sweat, and there were cuts on her hands, but otherwise, she was all right.

"Dad!" Anya screamed.

"Be brave and wait for me," I said because I couldn't focus on her right now. I needed all of the strength I had to get help in time. I started the trek back and halfway through I saw the sheriff and the paramedics we had sent for. Together we raced back to the bunker. Montana's father was still alive, but he was losing consciousness fast; the medics worked quickly. In record time he was lifted and sent to the ambulance. Montana got in with him, but I didn't.

"I'll be behind you all," I told her, and they hurried away.

I turned then to look at my daughter, and in that moment, it was as though the world had stopped. I collapsed down to the ground, and she hurried towards me, sobbing uncontrollably. I caught her in an embrace, pulling her into my arms, and we stayed that way for the longest time. I could see that she was only superficially injured but I gave her body a thorough check up. Seeing that she wasn't hurt or harmed, I held her tightly to me.

I was unable to let go for ages.

Eventually, my strength began to come back once again, and I felt my heart beating in my chest. It was a strange feeling because for the past several hours, it had felt as though it had completely stopped. I pulled away and looked into her eyes then, and all I could do was apologize.

"I'm so sorry, sweetheart. I am so sorry," I said.

"What about Mommy?" she asked.

"She's going to be okay," I said with a smile.

"Really?"

"Yes. Soon you might be able to visit her."

My daughter's face broke into a big grin. "Daddy. She's never going to come live with us again, is she?"

"No, honey. Your Mommy and I are not meant to be together."

She thought for a while. "What about Miss Moore? Are you meant to be together?"

"Would you like that? Would you like Miss Moore to come live with us?"

She nodded. "Yeah, she's nice. And brave. She was very brave today, Daddy. Mommy's scared of creepy crawlies and snakes and rats. Miss Moore is scared of nothing."

I laughed, and suddenly out of the blue, I remembered something Anya had told me about her nightmares. In them, her mother was lying on a black bed and she was very still. That was indeed how I found Arianna. She was lying on a black bed and she was so still and pale she could have been dead. I wondered if somehow, on some psychic, subconscious level Arianna had connected with her mother and seen and felt the danger she was in.

I hugged my daughter once again and swore to myself that I would never, ever, put her or anyone else in danger ever again.

Chapter 59
Montana

https://www.youtube.com/watch?v=O2lxEVnhoxo
-Felicita-

A fter my mother died, I hated hospitals in a way that I didn't think I could put into words.

Every chance I got to avoid them, I took it, but here I was in one of them again as I sat by my father's bedside.

Thankfully, he wasn't dying.

They had brought him in just in time, and as Cole had said, it was a clean shot through his shoulder, so more or less a flesh wound. God, I had been so frightened when I saw him fall to the ground after they shot him. I wanted to kill those men. If Cole, I should stop thinking of him as Cole ... if Luca hadn't done it, I would have.

My father was going to be fine, but I didn't know if I would be.

There was still so much to process. In so many ways, the last few hours felt like a surreal nightmare, and as I watched my father sleeping, I couldn't help but wonder if I had dreamed it all. I was still waiting for someone to pinch me awake … until I looked down at the cuts and bruises all over my body. Then I couldn't deny that all of it was real. Even the dead body with the axe in its face, totaling my beloved old Volvo, running through the woods like hunted animals while those monsters came after us, and watching my father fall, thinking he was dying or dead …

I felt so much love for my father that my heart hurt. I squeezed his hand, but softly. I didn't want to wake him up.

Right now, everyone that mattered was okay, but I was very aware of how badly it could all have ended. I was so exhausted and so unhappy about my own situation, but I couldn't sleep. There was one person I needed to speak to. I knew he was waiting outside. He'd refused to leave, even after the doctor had discharged Anya, oh well, Bianca, he still couldn't go home. She was in the next room resting while he was outside waiting.

I rose to my feet, pressed a kiss on my father's head, and walked out quietly.

Luca was sitting on a plastic chair with his eyes closed and his arms folded across his chest, as though in need of comfort. I wanted to go over to hug him. Even more than me, he had taken the biggest emotional tumble, but he was physically okay, and for that, I was incredibly relieved. But still, I needed an explanation, and I hoped he would finally give it to me.

I needed him to tell me the truth himself. I needed it so desperately I felt actual dread that he might try to lie to me again. Slowly, I headed over and took a seat by his side. His eyes came open then. He hadn't been sleeping like I'd thought, but it took me a while to work up what I wanted to say.

"Who are you exactly?" I asked.

He smiled, but it was a sad smile. It made me want to reach out and touch his suffering face.

"I'm just a guy who is good with numbers and because of that, I got caught in a trap set by the Mafia boss my father worked for. I was forced to clean his dirty money for him or risk losing my unborn child."

"That's why you moved to our town?" I asked. "To get away?"

"Yeah," he replied. "For Anya's sake."

"Her name is not Anya, is it?"

He shook his head in a defeated gesture. "No, her name is Bianca, Bianca Rossi ... and I'm Luca Rossi."

"Why did you have to suddenly run?"

"The deal the Don and I had was connected to my father's stay in prison, and because his term was coming to an end, he decided to play dirty. He deliberately charmed Bianca's mother with lies and drugs and enticed her away from Bianca and me even though he never wanted her. I accepted her decision to leave and I didn't even blame her because ours was a loveless marriage and she didn't understand what she had done. But I knew, as he did, that she would want to come back to us once his lies unraveled, and she realized he didn't love her at all.

"And once she did try to come back, he could pretend that I, and not he was the one at fault. I had tried to take what was his, which by his code of honor was a mark of intolerable disrespect towards him. I knew he would then tell me I could keep my head and my family if I continued to work for him. The slippery snake wanted to tie me up for a life. I decided to run while I made my plans to bring his organization down. But I am too valuable to him. So he came after me.

"This time, he didn't want me to work for him anymore. He just wanted me to teach his men everything I did for him and then he would have got rid of me and Bianca ... and you. Do you understand now why I had to run, lie, fight back ... and kill"

I stared at him in shock, but finally, I understood. "I would have done the same," I whispered fiercely.

He swallowed hard with emotion. I thought he was going to cry, but he clenched his jaw and just gazed at me wretchedly.

"So, he's dead now?" I asked.

"Yes," he replied. "I killed him. And his henchmen are scattered away, useless without their boss."

I went quiet while I digested his statement, but before I could speak again, he did.

"This ... this risk to you was why I couldn't open up. Why I needed to let you go. I couldn't get you involved until my situation was resolved. I knew they were eventually coming for me, and it was somewhat manageable with just me and Bianca, but if you were involved, then things could have become even more uncontrollable and tragic. I couldn't stand the thought of you getting hurt, so I had to let you go. Even now it kills me to see the bruises on your face. That's my fault. That's-"

"It's not your fault," I said, interrupting him. "If I had

stayed at the ranch the way I was told to Bianca would never have come out of the panic room and you would have done what you were supposed to," I said.

He shook his head. "No, Montana. You came because I didn't make the situation clear to you. I would have done the same thing in your shoes."

I nodded and rose to my feet, then, needing to leave, needing to process, but then he caught my hand and looked into my eyes.

"Thank you for protecting Bianca the way you did. Everything turned out well because of you. I was already taken with you, but your loyalty today just proved I was right all along."

"Right about what?" I asked. My heart was racing so hard in my chest I could hardly swallow.

"Just how special you are, just how gorgeous, and smart, and wonderful. And just how fucking in love with you I am. The past few weeks, knowing I couldn't go further, was pure torture. If you'll give me another chance, I'll go to the very ends of the earth for you. I know you probably want to think about what I said, but today I realized how easily everything could change, how precious life is, and ... I didn't want to let another minute go past without telling you this."

I was too hyped up on adrenaline, anxiety, pain meds to make any decisions, but I looked out the window at the starry night and knew he was right. He had just reminded me once again of just how fragile life was, and I knew that like him, I didn't want to wait for even one more minute to accept him into my life.

I turned away from the sky full of stars and looked at

him. His eyes were full of pain and uncertainty. That was because of me. I could turn those pools of misery into beautiful twinkling stars with one sentence.

"I'm in love with you too," I whispered.

For a second, the disbelief was so great, he could do nothing and I thought maybe he had not heard me. Then he jumped to his feet, pulled me to mine, and clamping his large hands around my waist, began to twirl me around. Round and round we went until I was laughing uncontrollably, just as he was, and then a nurse came running.

"Shh..." she scolded sternly. "Stop that. Patients are sleeping."

"Sorry," he said and put me down.

"Sorry," I echoed, and she went away shaking her head, and tutting.

I saw then that his eyes were beautiful and twinkling. He leaned forward and kissed me. I didn't want the nurse to come back and scold us again so I wanted to control myself, but it was impossible. Tears of happiness flowed down my cheeks.

I'd thought I'd never taste him again, never feel the warmth and fire and excitement of his smile, his laugh, his touch. But now that I knew the truth about him, and most of the dots were connected, it made me realize the picture I'd been too afraid to dream about was possible.

"I love you, Luca. I love you, I love you," I said with all of my heart.

"I don't even know if what I feel for you can be covered by a four-letter word like love. I love you so much that my heart feels as if it could burst. Now I understand what you meant when you said, you wake up every morning and give thanks for the gift of another day. Finally, for the first time in my life, I know why someone would wake up in the morning and give thanks for another day in heaven."

I smiled with happiness. "I can see now that we'll be fine. We'll be just fine." Luca, little Bianca, and me.

Chapter 60
Luca

https://www.youtube.com/watch?v=oiAzMRKFX3c&list=
RDoiAzMRKFX3c&start_radio=1
-wind beneath my wings-

My dad was dead. Without Paganini's protection, he didn't even last a week. I went to my mother's apartment and Greta, the nurse, opened the door.

"Mr. Rossi," she greeted warmly. "Come in, come in."

"Is my mother awake?"

"Yes, she has just had her lunch and is listening to music in her room. Let me take you to her."

"It's okay. I know my way around."

I walked down the hallway and knocked gently on the door before I opened it and went in. My mother was sitting by the window looking out. Her favorite piano music was tinkling softly in the background. A tiny bird was busy at the bird feeder. It looked peaceful. I was about to break it.

I sat next to her. "Hello, Mama."

She blinked but didn't turn to look at me.

I took her hand. "It's me, Mama. I'm back, and soon I will be bringing Bianca to see you."

Slowly, her hand gripped mine and tears pooled in her eyes and spilled down her face.

Without breaking her clasp on my hand, I moved so I was kneeling in front of her. "Mama, can you hear me?"

Her eyes moved over my face, slowly, but purposefully.

"Mama?" I called again.

But she transferred her gaze far away. She stared at the sky blankly. Disappointment crushed me. For a second there, I was sure she could see me. I was so sure there had been emotion there. She had missed me. Nobody could convince me that for those few seconds, my mother was not trapped in this unresponsive body and looking at me from inside.

I sighed. "I love you, Mama."

I moved back to the chair next to her. For a while, I just sat quietly with her. I thought about how best to tell her, and finally, I just came out with it. By now she had probably forgotten he even existed.

"Dad's dead," I said.

The stiffening of her body was unmistakable. Instantly, I regretted telling her. Why did she need to know? All I had done was distressed her further. It didn't matter to her either way and I should have just left it alone.

"He can never hurt you," I whispered to try and console her.

Her mouth opened.

"It's okay, Mama," I comforted desperately.

She turned towards me, her eyes urgent. "Are you sure?"

I was so amazed I could only stare at her, speechless.

She took my wrist in a claw like grasp and shook it. "Are you sure?"

I nodded in shock. I couldn't believe the change in her.

"Have you seen the body?"

I shook my head. What the fuck was going on? "Yes. At the morgue."

She smiled then. A triumphant curve of her lips. It was bursting with irresistible, immeasurable, uncontainable joy. The smile of someone who finally wrestles victory from the jaws of her adversary after years of determination, effort, hardship, and terrible sacrifice. And suddenly I knew.

My God! It was the most unbelievable, crazy, insane thing, but there was absolutely nothing wrong with her. All these years she had been pretending to have dementia.

I marveled at her tenacity. For years and years, she had sat in a care home because that was the only way she knew to keep him away. She had waited until I left for College and then she had devised this method to get her away from him.

She reached out and touched my face, her fingers traced my cheekbones, my jaw, my throat. Almost as if she was blind and she was seeing with her fingers. "I'm sorry, Luca. I'm sorry. I cried many tears, but there was no other way."

"But you threw away so many years."

"It was worth it."

I shook my head in wonder. "You never once dropped

your act. It was so perfect. You even fooled all those famous specialists I took you to."

"Hah," she scoffed. "They were the easiest to fool. My grandmother always used to say, the more educated a man becomes, the more arrogant and foolish he becomes. They were looking for symptoms and I gave them a whole list of it."

"How did you know what they were looking for?"

"I read the books they wrote," she said simply.

I looked at her sadly. "You allowed yourself to be poisoned for years with drugs you didn't need."

Her eyes danced with merriment. "No, I didn't. It was not so easy in the place your father sent me to because I had a harder time getting them to put my medication into my palm. They wanted to drop it straight into my mouth, but the one you upgraded me to was a high-trust home so it was much easier. Here, let me show you what I did."

She reached out to a bottle of tablets, shook three into her palm, and then popped them into her mouth. She made a swallowing movement, then she opened her lips and showed me her empty mouth.

"Did I swallow them?"

I frowned. "It sure looked like it."

She reached into her lap and produced the three tablets.

"I learned the trick from a sleight-of-hand card trick guy on YouTube. The important thing is to make some other movement with your other hand to distract."

I stared at my mother in admiration and astonishment. Her ruse had been so elaborate, so meticulously planned and so flawlessly executed. I never once suspected.

"Oh, Mama, all these years, you suffered alone."

"No, I didn't. I made friends with a night cleaner called Mabel. She was very kind to me. She was the only one who knew I was not ill. She kept me sane. She smuggled forbidden food in for me. Greasy chips, hotdogs, fried chicken. The midnight feasts we used to have."

She smiled at the memory.

"Then you moved me here, and I understand why you did it, but I had to leave her behind, the only person who knew my secret, and it hurt me. I've missed her. I've missed her so much. I'd like to see her again. I don't know if she still works at the Care Home. She was old you see, and about to retire. Can you arrange for her to come here, Luca, my wonderful son?"

"Of course, Mama. I will find Mabel for you and bring her here."

"Thank you. Thank you for everything you have done. You will never know the pain I suffered to sit like a statue and never respond to you or the little one. I died a little every time she hugged me and I didn't hug her back. But I always knew, live by the sword, die by the sword. One day he would die and I would be free."

"Mama, why were you so terrified of him?"

Her eyes clouded over. "Because he killed your sister."

"What?" I barked in shock. "I had a sister?"

"You never met her. Her name was Rosella. You were only three months old when he murdered her. She was only a year old. He smothered her with a pillow. The doctors thought it was cot death. I did not see him do it, but I knew he did. An hour before he went into her room, she was alive and healthy."

"Why?" I whispered in horror.

Her voice became hard. "He was obsessively particular about the way a bed must be made. The night before your sister had colic and she had cried all night. I was tired and I got careless. I did not make the bed exactly in the way he wanted. There must have been creases, or the ends were not perfectly folded over, I don't know what I did wrong, but he was so furious his whole face changed. He looked evil. It was as if he was possessed by a demon. I'd never seen anything like it in my life before. I was terrified. When he turned away from me, I couldn't move. My limbs wouldn't move. By the time I could, it was too late. He had already killed her.

"In his mind, Rosella had kept me awake, had distracted me from my duties, so she had to be removed. And that would also serve as my punishment. He destroyed every trace of her, her clothes, her toys, any photos with her in them, her birth certificate, even the lock of hair I had kept hidden away. He threatened to kill you too if I told anyone or I tried to escape. He told me in that cold, quiet voice of his that there was nowhere on earth I could run to hide from him. He would always find me and kill you as he had done with our firstborn."

"Christ, Mama! We could have gone to the police."

"I had no proof, there were too many crooked policemen and he knew them all. I couldn't take the risk. I love you, Luca. There is nothing I will not suffer to keep you safe."

Tears of pity filled my eyes and ran down my cheeks. I never understood. I never knew. Her sacrifice was immense, unbelievable. I enveloped her inside my arms and held her thin body close to me.

"It's okay, Mama. He will never be able to hurt you or me, ever again. He's gone back to hell."

She stroked my hair. "Shhh … my darling boy. Don't cry, I am so proud of you. I couldn't have dreamed of a better son than you. You make everything I've gone through worth it. I would do it all again for you. Don't cry, darling. It's over and you have come out of it with a pure heart."

"I killed nine men, Mama."

She froze inside my arms. Then, very slowly, she pushed me away from her so she could look into my eyes. Her eyes were shining with love.

"Those were not men you killed. They look human, but don't be fooled. They are a species apart. They shouldn't even be allowed to live amongst us humans. Your father was like them, an evil monster. Many times, I wanted to kill him, but I was not brave enough. I was afraid I would be caught and you would go into foster care. You didn't do anything wrong. You did the world a favor. I'm so, so, so proud of you, Luca. Well done, my beautiful son. When you stand before your maker, you will see, that he will not condemn you."

"I hope so, Mama. Like you, I did it to protect my child."

She nodded. "Yes, there is nothing I would not have done for you too. When are you bringing Bianca to see me?"

"I will bring her tomorrow. I will also bring a woman I want you to meet."

"Ah, is that horrible woman, Arianna gone?"

"Yes. She is gone."

"Good. I hated her. Are you in love?"

I smiled. "Yes. I'm in love."

She smiled back. "Then I will love her too."

"When is your father's funeral?"

"Next week. But you don't have to go."

"I must go," she said instantly. "For years I prayed for the day I could see his dead body inside a coffin, and now God has answered my prayer. I'd love to see him, finally, cold and deceased." Her eyes were twinkling.

I stared at her with fascination because I realized I'd never seen my mother so happy. This was the first time in my life I was seeing her truly happy.

* * *

After I left my mother I went to her old care home. It was evening and I sat on the stone wall outside and waited. Eventually, I saw her coming. Mabel was the quintessential black mama. She was a force to be reckoned with. She must have been in her seventies perhaps. I remembered my father telling my mother, 'We are Italians. We don't befriend blacks.' I smiled. This was my mother giving my father the finger.

"Mrs. Mabel Jackson?" I called.

She stopped and frowned at me. "Is Hanna all right?"

I smiled and nodded. "She's fine."

She put her hand to her heart. "Oh, that's good to know."

"How did you know who I was?"

"Your photo was always by her bedside. You didn't know, did you, that fine woman kissed it every night before she went to sleep."

I shook my head. "No, I didn't know."

"I suppose your father is dead."

"Yes."

She snorted. "Good riddance."

"Would you like to go visit my mother?"

She grinned. "Thought you'd never ask, child."

"Thanks for taking care of my mother, Mabel."

"No need for thanks. She is my friend."

I held out a USB stick to her. "This is for you."

She looked at it suspiciously. "What's that?"

"Half a million dollars in bitcoin."

"What?"

"Take it and keep it safe. Tomorrow, I'll send someone over to your house who will teach you how to turn it into half a million American dollars."

She pushed her head forward and stared at me. "Are you joking, young man?"

"No. It's yours. You did a kind thing and I wanted to show my appreciation."

She hooted with sudden laughter. "Who'd have thought? Hanna's son giving me a half million dollars for a bit of fried chicken and some hot dogs. Ha, ha, ha."

Her laughter was infectious. "Yeah," I said and laughed with her.

"I never knew my fried chicken and chips was that good," she gasped, her whole body jiggling with uncontrollable laughter.

Epilogue

Montana

https://www.youtube.com/watch?v=GC5E8ie2pdM&list=
PLBuCS1pc_KoaqEXC2q1hNrEwf8WC2MZSf&
index=29
-simply the best-

I really shouldn't have been doing this. It was completely out of tradition, but so far, everything in our relationship had been out of tradition. This, I reckoned, shouldn't be that big of a deal. In fact, it was only the presence of the girls that was making it a big deal, and I decided then to rectify that before he came over.

"Hey guys," I said boldly. "I need a little bit of privacy now."

"Of course," Kelly said and started to leave, but as I expected Natalie and Pearl gave me a look.

"The bride is not supposed to see the groom before her wedding," Pearl said.

"Who made that rule?" I asked.

"People smarter than you," Natalie retorted.

"I'm nervous, and I need to see him."

Kelly laughed. "I'll go and tell him. No reasoning with this one. She's been hungry for this man from the moment she met him. Why should we expect any different now?"

"It's not that, it's not what you thi-"

"Don't bother," both women said and exited the room laughing.

I was left in silence. I turned around then to look at my dress hanging from a hook on the wall. The moment I saw it I knew it was the one, just like I had known from the moment I laid eyes on Luca that he was the one. At that time, I thought it was for one night, but oh how wrong I was, I was too anxious. Everything and everywhere was unfamiliar, and I knew only one person could calm me down. I needed to see Luca now, before the wedding, even if it was against tradition.

There was a soft knock, and he came in. He didn't have his jacket on yet, but he looked amazing. I was completely struck. I mean, he'd been breathtakingly handsome from the moment I'd seen him, but this was another level. A different level, and it made me wonder what I'd even been nervous about.

"Are you alright?" he asked worriedly. "I thought you didn't want me to see you before the wedding."

"Yeah ... I just..." I stared at him, mesmerized.

"What is it?" he asked. "You aren't having second thoughts, are you?"

"Absolutely not." I smiled. "It's just ... before I put on the dress, I thought we could ..." I shifted my weight from one foot to the other. Thankfully, he didn't need much to understand.

"Really?"

"I'm so restless. I don't know if it is these stupid stockings or the corset, or ... I just ... I just know... I just need to take the edge off."

He smiled then.

"You'll ask me to marry you later, and I'll say yes, but I'm the one who is nervous now because I'm asking you for something, and I don't know if you'll say yes."

"Why don't you ask me officially and find out?" he asked.

I sucked in my breath. Would I really be able to say the words out loud, but as I looked at the gorgeous man standing before me who I loved with all my heart and soul, I found the words were quite easy to say.

"Luca Rossi, will you fuck me, Montana Moore, before our wedding ceremony?"

He laughed and I could feel the heat surge into my face.

Then he locked the door and turned to face me. On one condition, though." He brought out his phone. "We're going to record this."

"Absolutely not."

He gave me a look as he began to unbuckle his belt, and I absolutely melted.

"We're going to keep it in a vault of some sort afterward. Don't worry," he assured. "I know a little something or the other about hiding files. It'll be safe forever for me to revisit every single year for the next seventy years."

I nodded. Yes, for the next seventy years. Even when we were old and gray.

I lost my breath when he pulled out his gorgeous cock.

Instantly, I dropped to my knees, glad that I hadn't put on the dress yet because I definitely wouldn't have been able to do this in that pristine thing. Without wasting any time, I pulled his sweet head into my mouth and began to suck.

"Oh," he threw his head back. "Fuck."

I always loved the way he reacted to me. Our fire for each other burned hotter than ever after the death of Paganini.

Even so for many months afterwards we'd had to watch our backs, still nervous and cautious about the impending threat from both the ongoing police investigation and Paganini's scattered goons. But nothing came to bite us. With time we let it. With its head, the snake was dead.

All we knew was peace, love and contentment. Sometimes it felt as though I was living in a dream and if I pinched myself, I would wake up, but no matter what I never woke up.

"I think you're more anxious than you expected because we're having the ceremony far from home," Luca said as I took him even deeper. "You're still quite unfamiliar with New York."

That's not strictly true. I loved New York too. Not to live in, but to visit at the weekends. Luca had got himself a helicopter, and we decided to live in Bison Ridge, but spend our weekends in New York. It made perfect sense. This way he could travel for work and I could teach at the school.

But I didn't want to speak. All that could be done later.

I sucked harder, my cheeks hollowing to take as much of him as I could without messing my makeup, but that, I had to accept would be an impossible feat if I wanted to enjoy this moment as much as I wanted to.

Aware of the very limited time left, I added both of my hands and worked his length from root to tip in tandem with my mouth. In no time he came long and hard. I took all of him needing that familiar taste down my throat and in my belly. I loved how he tasted; the intimacy of how it made me feel. Like he owned me in ways that I couldn't quite explain or comprehend.

He pulled me up and looked around, and I wondered what happened to his threat of recording this.

"Where's your phone?" I asked.

He smiled. "No need," he said. "I've stored every second of your award-winning performance in my heart."

It was corny, but still it made me melt.

"We shouldn't be doing this, but it looks like you're ready to go again so ..." I began to slide my thong down my thighs as I got ready to make a mental videotape of this moment. For my own personal viewing for when I was old and gray. So I could marvel at the insane things we got up too in your youth.

I felt every inch of him as he plunged into me until all the nerves were fucked out of my body and all I felt was giddy and an uncontrollable excitement.

My heart raced, as I felt his hands part me open, and his cock was sliding in hard and deep. He held my hips and thrust into me with one smooth push until he hit the very end. My eyes lifted to the ceiling as an indescribable bliss came over me.

Then he began to move.

"Fuck, I love you," I swore.

He turned me around and kissed me the way he knew I loved it best: long, slow, and deep.

"I love you more."

That's all Folks!

:

Unless... you want to linger a little longer in Bison Ridge, then check out :)

Heat of the Moment

Coming Soon...

THE GUARDIAN

Prologue

Zola

"I still can't believe you're actually here."

My father chuckled and it made me realize how much I loved hearing him laugh in his low comforting way that he only did when conversing with me. Whenever we were together hearing him laugh wasn't rare, but the problem was we were rarely ever together.

"How long are you going to torture me about not being around enough?" he asked.

"Forever," I said as I stirred the cake batter.

"Trust me, it will get better. I will reduce my workload," he consoled.

"By then I won't be here anymore," I said.

He went silent. I lifted my eyes to watch him and as I expected the smile slowly disappeared from his face.

I set the spatula down. "Don't feel too bad," I told him. "I just really want us to take advantage of the time we have together now before it becomes more difficult. Soon I'm going to be graduating high school and then I'll be off to college. After that, I'll probably be too occupied trying to find a job and with life in general. Or am I wrong?"

He slid the lined baking pan over to me. He had this look in his eyes that was at the same time amused and guilty. It tugged at my heart but I couldn't show him that.

"I'll do better, Zola," he said calmly. "But please don't do that passive aggressive thing with me. It intimidates the hell out of me."

"That's all you have to worry about? Me being passive aggressive."

He stopped and stared at me. "I supposed it could be worse. You could be doing drugs or getting pregnant."

I couldn't meet his gaze. "Are you turning red?" he asked innocently.

I burst out laughing. "Yes. Why do you have to be so awkward all the time?"

"What is awkward?" he asked. "Because I mentioned getting pregnant? You can't possibly know how that works at your age."

I was horrified. "Please stop."

But he was on a roll and refused to stop. "Oh wait! You know how that works?"

"Dad, I will walk out of here this instant."

"Why are you so shy?" he asked and stared directly into my eyes.

I squirmed internally.

"Oh, my God. I really have been absent, haven't I? You seem to know more than you should."

I set the bowl I had been about to empty into the pan down on the counter and started to walk away. Before I could go too far though he caught me by the arm and drew me toward him for a hug. I relished every single moment of it. Though of course the last thing I was going to do was show it.

"Let me go," I groaned.

But he only squeezed me tighter, and growled playfully, "Never,"

"Ugh," I complained but couldn't help smiling.

"I better hold on tight before I'm truly not able to anymore," he said and planted a sloppy, noisy kiss on my cheek, as if I was still a child. "You're already sounding way too mature for me. I can't even make up my mind if it's a good thing or if it's my fault you had to grow up so fast and be an adult."

I didn't bother sparing his feelings. "It's a hundred percent your fault. The cake's gonna burn," I said, pulling away.

"Impossible," he refuted. "We haven't put it in yet."

"Well, we should. It's almost midnight and if we don't do it now it's not going to be ready for my birthday. At midnight."

"Calm down and be a kid," he said. "You're too fixated on time and results."

"Look who's talking," I teased.

I hurried over to the marble counter, transferred the batter into the round baking pan, dropped the pan on the hard surface a few times to let the air bubbles out, and slid it into the oven.

"Done," said shooting him a smile, but was disappointed to see his cell phone had once again made its appearance.

I was determined not to say a word in protest as he scrolled through his messages. Instead, I focused my attention on making sure the oven temperature was right. But when I turned around and saw him occupied with texting rapidly onto his device and a huge frown across his forehead, I knew I had to say something or he would be lost to me again.

"Dad," I called but he did not hear me as a call came through. He took it and began to bark out orders in rapid Italian to one of his staff.

My heart fell as I tried to convince myself there was no need to be worried. After all, he had promised me he had cleared the entire night for the both of us. And so far whenever he had said that, especially on my birthdays, he always came through.

I returned to the counter and grabbed a napkin to wipe my hands with before turning on the iPad so I could review the instructions on how we were going to make the cream frosting.

The housekeeper had gotten all the ingredients I needed so I headed to the refrigerator to get them. Just as I was trying to grab a pack of strawberries to add to the pile I had gathered in my arms my father came over to help me.

"Here let me," he said softly, but his voice was different now. It was no longer playful, but full of tension.

I let him, but I didn't have the courage to look at him. I already knew what was coming. Silently, he helped set the ingredients down on the counter, but his mind was elsewhere. I could feel my throat begin to clog up. Eventually, I couldn't stand it anymore. I knew I had to let him go.

"When will you be back?" I asked.

"One-hour tops," he said, and the relief in his voice was palpable.

"One hour?"

"Yes," he replied with a grateful smile. "This is an emergency otherwise you know I wouldn't leave on your birthday. I just need to go pick someone up and bring him here."

"You're bringing someone here?" I asked, surprised

"Yeah," he replied. "He's just a kid who needs a helping hand. He needs to remain with us for a short time while I handle his case."

I didn't know how to feel or respond. It made a bit more sense as to why Dad was suddenly bringing someone from his office to our home, but the absence of any details left me feeling muddled.

"Don't start icing the cake without me," he said as his eyes turned toward the oven. "It should be perfectly ready and cooled by the time I return."

"The cake and I will be waiting right here for you," I assured

"I always keep my promises, don't I?" he said and strolled out of the room.

I stood in the middle of the kitchen and listened as his footsteps echoed in the foyer. I heard the sound of his keys, then the front door shut.

I was then surrounded by a pervasive silence. It was nothing new. It had come to live in this house ever since my mom had passed away four years ago. She left me with a father who didn't realize how much he was trying to distract himself from dealing with her loss by filling his time up with an endless amount of work and pursuing noble causes. As he was doing tonight.

I couldn't stop him or make him understand how much I wished he would spend a bit more time with me. I didn't know how to intrude in his life and neither did I want to. So, I chose to trust instead that someday, hopefully soon, his workload would reduce, and I would have him home again the way he always was when we were a family of three.

With a sigh, I headed over to the living room to lie down on the couch.

I tried to keep myself entertained by scrolling through Instagram, but eventually I fell asleep. I awakened to the sound of the door lock clicking open. I could hear voices, but I couldn't quite make out the words.

Then my father called out my name, but I was still somewhat half-asleep plus I was now in a sour mood so I didn't respond.

But I could never stay angry with my dad for any length of time so by the third time he called I felt remorseful enough to lift my hand and wave it.

"Here," I called drowsily.

He came over to the living room and cocked his head at the sight of me sprawled on the couch.

"You got tired?" he asked, and I spied a bit of guilt in his voice.

"I lost interest," I replied.

"Go easy on me," he murmured and turned to the unwanted guest he'd brought with him. "Come over Dante and meet my daughter."

I immediately shot up, horrified that he would think to introduce me in such a state.

"Dad!" I muttered, shaking my head and straightening the oversize t-shirt I was wearing.

"Dante, this is Zola," he introduced.

I lifted my gaze. I didn't know what I'd been expecting but this was not it. My father had said a kid, but the young man standing before me was no one's idea of a kid.

For one he was tall and broad. His hair was jet black, the ends curling around his collar, his features were so perfect he looked as if he had been chiselled in stone, and he had the most piercing blue eyes I'd ever seen. He was... beautiful. There was no other way to describe him. He had jammed both his hands into his pockets which made him look at once rebellious and cool. Saying nothing he stared straight at me, with no shyness or awkwardness while I could feel my face begin to heat and flush. I immediately looked away and turned blankly to face my dad.

My father smiled.

I wondered if he knew why I was suddenly so struck. It was hard to not acknowledge and be swayed by how magnetically attractive the young man was. None of the boys in my high school could compare.

He was going to be staying with us!

"He'll be with us temporarily till a few issues with his case are sorted. So don't be startled if you see him lurking around, okay," father said.

"Till his case is sorted?" I was even more curious about him now. I was certain he must be the victim, not the accused. My father would never bring someone dangerous into our house to stay with me, kid or no kid.

Coming Soon...

"So, Zola, ready to ice the cake?" my father asked, but I had completely lost interest and it was already way past midnight.

I got to my feet and shook my head. "No, I'm going to bed."

"Zola," my father called.

"It's okay, Dad. It's just a cake. Not the end of the world if I don't have one." I felt guilty at the unhappiness in his tone since I was aware that even though he had been called away, he had been looking forward to icing my cake together, but the presence of the silent young man had confused me. I headed up to my room.

I locked the door, got into my bed and pulled the covers over my head.

My wish was to sleep, not to entertain any useless thoughts, but an hour and half later I found myself still wide awake. I kicked the covers away and thought of what I could do instead of tossing and turning in bed.

Since it was already technically my birthday, I didn't want to entertain any sulking. I looked toward the shelf that was stacked with books, but I couldn't bear to read anything new due to the potential for disappointment, which I didn't want to deal with. I got out of bed and headed over to grab my favorite story '*As You Wish*'.

But my hand stilled as it reached for the spine of the book. No. Not that now. I felt restless. I no longer wanted to stay in my room. It was a hot night and I opened a window and looked at the night sky. I thought about the young man, the way his eyes had moved hungrily over my body and then I thought about my mom. I imagined she was wishing me a happy birthday. Tears slightly filled my eyes but I didn't let them fall.

A swim. A swim was what I needed.

I changed into my swimsuit, grabbed a towel and headed out to the kitchen. The pool in our backyard glistened underneath the starlit sky.

I dived into the cool water.

Oooo... bliss.

Dante

I heard the splash and was immediately on alert. I switched off the light, sprinted to the window, parted the blinds with my fingers, and looked out.

I could see a pool, which wasn't surprising given the size and grandeur of Mr. Leone's home. I could see the lights from the gazebo illuminating the water.

His daughter was in it, doing laps. She was a beautiful girl with a very sexy mouth, but I was too messed up to even think about girls. I was about to turn away when she began to lift herself out of the water. Water dripped from her body. And suddenly, I couldn't look away from her. I was frozen with desire to have her. She stood and began to hurry toward the gazebo. Without warning I felt that rush of sensation in my gut, the old instinct that had always served me well.

Something bad was about to happen.

Even as the thought formed in my head she slipped on the wet tiles. It happened so fast. One moment I was lusting for her, next moment her arms were flailing as she had landed on her back. I saw her hand lift to her head and realized she must have hit her head. She grabbed onto the edge of the pool and twisted her body to try and get up, but her arms became limp and she fell into the water with a splash

I ran from my room hoping to find my way down into the unfamiliar home. Most of the lights were off and navigating through the dark was a nightmare. It felt like a lifetime passed before I rushed through the back door.

The water's surface had soft ripples on top but was eerily still. A dark shadow was slowly sinking. I instantly plunged into the cold water. I grabbed her body and pulled her out of the water. The moment I emerged out of the water I began to yell out to her father.

"Mr. Leone!"

"Mr. Leone!"

Up until that moment in my life, I had been attacked with every sort of weapon imaginable, but I couldn't recall ever feeling as afraid as I did when I held her in my arms and looked down at her pale, lifeless face.

Chapter One

Zola

Ten Years Later

"And?" Nina asked.

I reached for my wine glass, a small smile playing at the corners of my lips as I took a sip of the exquisite Garblèt Suè Barolo and savored the fruity notes and aromas of raspberry and menthol. I had to admit my colleagues from the Literary Agency I worked for were right. It was perfect for the one time a year we were allowed to splurge on the company account. led me down the path of sharing an old story with them.

"She's enjoying this," Stella accused.

"Actually, there's nothing more to say," I replied with a smile. "The story ends there."

"What do you mean by, it ends there? Did you drown?" Steven, an intern demanded.

The table erupted in laughter.

"Clearly, she did," Samantha, our in-house legal counsel, said as she smacked Steven on the shoulder. "God you're dumb."

He turned beetroot-red. "That's not what I meant. I mean, she could have drowned and been resuscitated."

I set my glass down and decided to bring the story to some sort of satisfactory end.

"Well, I was resuscitated. They called the ambulance and I was rushed to the hospital. I was unconscious from a concussion, and I was a bit ill for a little while, but I was fine in the end."

"And what about the gorgeous boy?" Nina asked.

"I never saw him again."

Enjoyed the sample?
Then pre-order here
The Guardian

About the Author

If you wish to leave a review for this book
please do so here:
Sweet Poison

Please click on this link to receive news of my latest releases
and great giveaways.
Georgia's Newsletter

and remember
I **LOVE** hearing from readers so by all means come and say
hello here:

Also by Georgia Carre

Owned

42 Days

Besotted

Seduce Me

Love's Sacrifice

Masquerade

Pretty Wicked (novella)

Disfigured Love

Hypnotized

Crystal Jake 1,2&3

Sexy Beast

Wounded Beast

Beautiful Beast

Dirty Aristocrat

You Don't Own Me 1 & 2

You Don't Know Me

Blind Reader Wanted

Redemption

The Heir

Blackmailed By The Beast

Submitting To The Billionaire

The Bad Boy Wants Me

Nanny & The Beast

His Frozen Heart

The Man In The Mirror

A Kiss Stolen

Can't Let Her Go

Highest Bidder

Saving Della Ray

Nice Day For A White Wedding

With This Ring

With This Secret

Saint & Sinner

Bodyguard Beast

Beauty & The Beast

The Other Side of Midnight

The Russian Billionaire

CEO's Revenge

Mine To Possess

Heat Of The Moment

Boss From Hell

Made in United States
Orlando, FL
18 June 2024

48009142R00217